continued...

Murder Uncorked

"All the sparkle, complexity, and romance of a fine champagne. This mystery is one you'll want to read right through with a bottle of good wine and some of the author's tasty canapés at your side. I loved it and look forward to more installments."
—Nancy Fairbanks

"A superb amateur sleuth tale starring an upbeat heroine and a fabulous prime suspect." —*Midwest Book Review*

"A perfect blend of murder and page-turning fiction!"
—Holly Jacobs

"The first in a series that has great potential...The Napa Valley is a lush setting, and foodies will drink in the wine lore and will savor the recipes for tasty tidbits."
—*The Mystery Reader*

"Edgy and suspenseful...Sleek, smart characters add realism to a mystery made more colorful by the fabulous Napa Valley setting." —*Romantic Times*

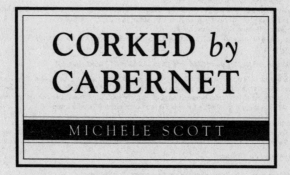

CORKED *by* CABERNET

MICHELE SCOTT

BERKLEY PRIME CRIME, NEW YORK

THE BERKLEY PUBLISHING GROUP
Published by the Penguin Group
Penguin Group (USA) Inc.
375 Hudson Street, New York, New York 10014, USA

Penguin Group (Canada), 90 Eglinton Avenue East, Suite 700, Toronto, Ontario M4P 2Y3, Canada
(a division of Pearson Penguin Canada Inc.)
Penguin Books Ltd., 80 Strand, London WC2R 0RL, England
Penguin Group Ireland, 25 St. Stephen's Green, Dublin 2, Ireland (a division of Penguin Books Ltd.)
Penguin Group (Australia), 250 Camberwell Road, Camberwell, Victoria 3124, Australia
(a division of Pearson Australia Group Pty. Ltd.)
Penguin Books India Pvt. Ltd., 11 Community Centre, Panchsheel Park, New Delhi—110 017, India
Penguin Group (NZ), 67 Apollo Drive, Rosedale, North Shore 0632, New Zealand
(a division of Pearson New Zealand Ltd.)
Penguin Books (South Africa) (Pty.) Ltd., 24 Sturdee Avenue, Rosebank, Johannesburg 2196,
South Africa

Penguin Books Ltd., Registered Offices: 80 Strand, London WC2R 0RL, England

This is a work of fiction. Names, characters, places, and incidents either are the product of the author's imagination or are used fictitiously, and any resemblance to actual persons, living or dead, business establishments, events, or locales is entirely coincidental. The publisher does not have any control over and does not assume any responsibility for author or third-party websites or their content.

PUBLISHER'S NOTE: The recipes contained in this book are to be followed exactly as written. The publisher is not responsible for your specific health or allergy needs that may require medical supervision. The publisher is not responsible for any adverse reactions to the recipes contained in this book.

CORKED BY CABERNET

A Berkley Prime Crime Book / published by arrangement with the author

PRINTING HISTORY
Berkley Prime Crime mass-market edition / February 2009

Copyright © 2009 by Michele Scott.
Cover illustration by Robert Crawford.
Cover design by Rita Frangie.
Interior text design by Kristin del Rosario.

ISBN: 978-0-425-22644-5

BERKLEY® PRIME CRIME
Berkley Prime Crime Books are published by The Berkley Publishing Group,
a division of Penguin Group (USA) Inc.,
375 Hudson Street, New York, New York 10014.
BERKLEY® PRIME CRIME and the PRIME CRIME logo are trademarks of Penguin Group (USA) Inc.

PRINTED IN THE UNITED STATES OF AMERICA

10 9 8 7 6 5 4 3 2 1

To Jessica Park,
who is a dear friend and without whom I think
I may have either wound up
totally insane or—yeah—
totally insane.
Here's to you, J.P., and the dream.

ACKNOWLEDGMENTS

They say it takes a village to raise a child. I'm here to say that it takes a village and then some to support a writer. There are so many people who help me do what I do as a writer. During the writing of this book, life kept getting in the way and I am grateful to have had the support I've had during this process. I want to thank my dream editor, Sandy Harding, for her encouragement, support, and belief in me. Thanks to Connie Hagey for giving my daughter riding lessons while I typed away at the picnic table at Willow Glen Equestrian Center. Also, Scott Willeford, who is a dear friend and who has helped me a ton with the police procedural stuff, letting me know what I can and can't get away with. Kudos to Bob Gelman of Grape Connections, who helps me tons with the wine pairings. Thanks to my friends Lisa Lakey and Siobhan Debenedetto for reminding me that it's okay to let loose once in a while, and for all the times you picked up my kids and helped out. A huge thanks to my friend Kristi Inzunza for going to bat with my nemesis. Who knew I had one? And to her husband, Joey, for having no clue what the word meant and we're still laughing about it. As always, the Cozy Chicks get their deserved due! You chicks are the *bomb* (okay, I suppose that I have been hanging with teenagers for far too long when the bomb is part of my vocab). And to my new gal pals—horsewomen and writers! Check us out at www.equestrianink.blogspot.com. To my

mom and dad for their never-ending support and guidance—
thanks for always being a soft place to fall, Mom. To my in-
laws, Sue and Jack, who allowed me to write away while on
our visit. I'm sorry I had my nose in the laptop all the time.
Thank you for feeding me, letting me have your chair, Mom,
and not caring if I wore my pajamas all day. Sue donated the
chicken-fried steak recipe and biscuits. Try it! You won't be
disappointed. I want to shout out to my sister-in-law Cathy,
who took us on the best and most humorous tour of New York
City. You rock, Cathy! To my son Alex, who reminds me that
good things do come to those who wait. I will never forget
NYC with you, kid. One of the best times of my life, even under the circumstances. You are a GIFT. By the way, Alex, do
you think Nanny has been there? Just remember—"Silence! I
will kill you." To my son Anthony, who is so sure in his heart
that Mom will be a bestseller he makes my heart ache with
pride and love. Thank you to my daughter, Kaitlin, who no
matter what kind of day it's been brings a smile to my face and
makes me feel like I am a goddess. And to my husband, John,
who stands by me in all of this insanity that a writer endures
and never doubts me or my dream. Last but most definitely not
least—to every single solitary reader who picks up one of my
books. At the end of the day, it is you whom I write for. It is my
prayer that you somehow connect, feel, laugh, and relate to
Nikki and the gang. Keep the e-mails coming and I'll keep answering because you are what makes a writer keep wanting to
create.

One

NIKKI Sands dropped the box in her arms onto the kitchen counter, not believing what she'd just heard. "What did you say?" She turned to her friend Simon Malveaux. Ollie the Rhodesian ridgeback, who was sleeping smack dab in the middle of the kitchen floor, lifted his head. He looked up at Nikki, obviously sensing that she didn't sound thrilled.

"I know, isn't it exciting? I'm kind of thinking a lot of curry dishes on the menu. You know, even lean toward more vegan meals—gotta keep things green. And there is this wonderful New Age musician, amazing with the flute, lives up the road in St. Helena. I thought he'd be great for entertainment. It'll be wonderful," he rambled. The realization that maybe Nikki wasn't thinking along the same lines made him stop. Placing a hand on his jutted-out hip, he frowned. "I know that look, Snow White. Why are you looking at me like that?" He waved a hand in the air. "All pissy-like, like I'm bugging you."

"You are bugging me. I can't do this right now. In case you hadn't noticed, I have several events to prepare for. We're already into March and in only a few months harvest and crush will be on us. Plus, can't you see what I'm doing? I am a little busy." She opened the box and started unloading a set of plates—all white and traditional, a stark contrast to the eclectic kitchen done in a Spanish style that matched the ranch house. The walls were painted a turquoise and enhanced by the rustic-colored Spanish tiles that paved the floor. This room was a feel-good room where Nikki could cook and entertain—two things she looked forward to doing in this home—her new home.

Ollie stood up and walked out of the kitchen, heading to the sofa where Nikki had given up trying to make the dog understand that he was a dog and not another human. Ollie had decidedly made the couch *one* of his beds.

"I can see, you're busy making your new *love nest*, but Derek said that you'd help us." Simon smiled his pretty-boy smile and ran his hand nervously through his platinum-dyed buzz cut.

"He did not. He wouldn't do that to me. He knows I'm behind and swamped."

"Yeah, he did. He said so," he replied, punctuating his words with a loud cluck of the tongue.

She unwrapped one of the plates and opened Derek's cupboards. Oh jeez, she was going to have to rearrange everything in the kitchen. The man had been a bachelor far too long. Nikki couldn't believe she was standing in Derek Malveaux's kitchen moving in her things—because yes, they were doing it, "shacking up," as her aunt Cara had put it to her over the phone when she'd told her. She preferred "living together." It didn't sound seedy that way.

Since their trip to Australia they'd spent almost every waking hour together. Slowly but surely her *stuff* gravitated to his house. It seemed to make sense to both of them to do the right thing and shack up. Well, live together. It was a financially and logistically sound idea. Even though she only moved from the Malveaux Boutique Hotel on the property.

Simon, Derek's brother, also lived on the vineyard with his partner, Marco. They were two of her good friends, but could definitely be royal pains when they wanted. This latest antic they were pulling on her was bee-lining them smack dab onto that pain-in-the-ass list again.

She sighed, not believing that Derek would do such a thing. This was only Simon trying to manipulate her. "Let me get this straight. Your guru, the Guru Sansibaba"—God, that was the most ridiculous name she'd ever heard—"his family, his people, and some of his followers are planning to come here for a weeklong workshop?" She shook her head. "And the Malveaux Spa and Winery is hosting them?"

"No, now it's not like that. We're not *hosting* them. It's big money, and it'll be good promo for us. Think of it like that. It's the Baba himself and his crew, which apparently does include his wife and three grown children, but we aren't talking about hordes of people. See, Marco and I just joined the Source Enlightened Elite group, otherwise known as S.E.E. Get it—as in see the light. Isn't that clever?"

"The what group?" She took a couple of empty jelly jars out of the cupboard. Interesting. She doubted Derek ever did any canning. Recycles.

"It's the *it* group for enlightened souls, and we made it in." Simon clapped his hands together.

"Uh-huh, why don't you *enlighten* me, and explain what your joining this group means exactly in regards to this workshop thing? And what did this cost you guys? An exclusive club is never free."

He sighed and she could tell by the way he fidgeted around, moving like a kid needing to pee, that he was considering telling her a lie. "It was a little expensive. But we had to go through an application process. It's not like just *anyone* can get in. It's like the Harvard of enlightenment teachings."

She frowned. "Harvard? A *little* expensive? Like how little?"

"A hundred thousand dollars," he muttered and lowered his head.

"A hundred thousand dollars! You better have a ticket straight to heaven for that kind of cash. Does your brother know about this?"

"No." He shrunk back. "I don't have to tell Derek how or where I spend my money. And don't you say anything. I only told you because I trust you."

Ooh, he knew how to get to her. "Tell me, Simon, what do you get for that kind of money? I hope you get a contract stating that it'll be God himself, not Saint Peter, who'll be opening the pearly white gates for you. And you get an automatic 'Go on through' pass."

He rolled his eyes. "Please. We don't follow any one religion. We believe all faiths have validity to them. But I'm so glad you asked about the money, because after I tell you, you'll see how great all of this is going to be. For the big hundred thou, we get to be with only a handful of other people in our group. We get all of the guru's books, CDs, and DVDs for free, plus we get to be seated in the first front rows at all of his celebration seminars. That means we get to be seated first *and* we get our photo taken with him at each event."

"Ooh, a picture. Impressive."

"Come on," he whined. "You haven't even heard the best part."

"Do tell."

"Well, three times a year we get to go on vacation with

him to some exciting locale and learn from the master himself."

"Oh yeah, I can see how that would be the best part."

He smiled as if he were the cat who swallowed the canary.

She stared at him. "Come on, Simon! You're kidding. My God! When are you going to see that this guy is simply a master in making money?"

"You are so not hip or fun anymore. Now you're like Suzy homemaker and I can see it, you're gonna be a buzz kill from now on. You'll be all brownies in the afternoons with a glass of milk, and watching soap operas. Your ass'll get wide and, gawd, just no fun. Domesticated. That's what you're becoming."

"Sounds like me. Actually sounds kind of good. I like brownies." Except for the expanding backside. That didn't sound too appealing. "Soap operas, I don't know about. Reruns of *Will & Grace*? Maybe."

"Oh I loved that show. I wish they'd never taken it off TV. See what happens when you settle down? Next thing you'll be like Debra Messing, baby and all and blah, blah, blah..." He lifted himself up onto the counter and sat on the edge.

Nikki stomped her feet. "Shut up!" Simon went wide-eyed. "Look, I'm only trying to help you see that this guru Sansibaba nut knows how to market and sell his product, which he labels 'enlightenment.' That's crazy. Enlightenment comes from within."

"I know that. But he's not what you think. And you know what? It doesn't matter what you think. The plan for S.E.E. was to go to Bali, but then a typhoon hit and so the winery is what we've come up with. You be a good girl and play nice. You don't have a choice anyway. Since Marco and I are the newest members, we thought it would be good to start off by giving back. You know, paying it forward from the get-go. Everyone will be here next week, and you are going to help me and Marco see that it runs smoothly. Just ask the boss man himself. He said it would be no *problema*."

Excuse me? Nikki found herself speechless. Simon never took that tone with her. He could be bitchy—yes. He was always that way and she played right along—it was just Simon. But downright bossy? That was new. "Good, I'm glad we're in agreement." He glanced at his watch. "Gotta run. I have a manicure scheduled. I'll be back at six for a little powwow. I can see the wheels churning, Snow White." He jumped off the counter. "I know you. You're already getting on board, aren't you? That's what I love about you You're a regular Pollyanna. Good karma coming your way. Before long you'll have the domesticated gig down and it'll be everything you ever dreamed because you are a good person. See you later, love." He blew a kiss at her, scrambling to get out the front door.

She watched him, unable to grasp the entire reality of what he'd just told her. Next week? Next week this freak show and his cronies were coming to Malveaux Estate? She shook her head and picked a plate up off the counter. Without another thought, she threw it against the wall and watched it shatter into pieces while yelling out, "Simon!" Ollie let out a loud yelp as if he'd been kicked. It wasn't the dog who was going to get a swift kick in the rear. But Simon was another story.

Derek had gone into the city to personally take care of a larger account that they'd recently had problems with, making him incommunicado all day. He'd called on his drive home, but his cell died right after he said something about being on his way home. Nikki's irritation had reached a high note after hanging up the phone. By the time Derek got home, she had worked herself into a tizzy.

"Did you tell Simon that I'd help him out with this guru

thing he and Marco have going?" Nikki asked as she set aside the onion she'd been chopping. "Because if you did that, well, first of all, what are you thinking letting those two have that, that, guru guy and his entourage here? We can't have that. Think of all the work. I mean one week, plus I understand this guy is gaining in popularity. We don't need a bunch of tourists coming in here all at once. We can't handle that. We don't have the staff right now."

Derek had barely closed the door, wine bottle in hand, which he set down on the table. As irritated as she was at him, she couldn't help noticing his golden looks. Her stomach sank. Don't pay attention to those blue eyes, wavy blond hair, and that six-pack she knew was under the suit. Don't even think about it. He had some questions to answer first. Ollie had finally gotten off the couch when he'd heard Derek's voice and was now stuck to his side. The dog was smart enough to understand Nikki's state of mind.

Derek walked over to her and placed his hands on her shoulders. "Hi to you, too, and I don't think I'll ask how your day was. Should I? I hope you had nothing to do with this." He glanced down at Ollie, who cocked his head to the side.

"I'm serious. What's the deal?" She picked the onion back up, but while slicing through it, the knife nicked her thumb. "Dammit!" She pulled the knife back and blood trickled down her hand. Ollie hightailed it back to the couch.

Derek rushed over and looked at her thumb. He quickly grabbed a paper towel from the rack and ran it under cool water, then began dabbing at the injury.

"It's only a little cut. I wasn't paying attention." She tried to yank her hand away from his. She knew she shouldn't jump to conclusions about him telling Simon that she'd handle the details of the event. But she had and she was kind of grumpy from moving boxes all day, her back now hurting.

He brought her hand to his lips and kissed her thumb, then turned it over and kissed her palm. "Better?"

She looked at him and realized how horrendous she'd just behaved. Man oh man; he was sure easy on the eyes— all blond and rugged-like, and blue-eyed, and sweet and sensitive. Maybe it was time to lose the attitude. "A little. But one right here would make me feel even better." She pointed to her cheek.

"Ah, now c'mon, I think I can do better than *that*." He kissed her hard and long on her lips. "Better now?" She nodded. He walked over to one of the cabinets above the sink, and got a Band-Aid to wrap around her thumb. "I know it seems strange to keep my medicine cabinet in the kitchen but this is where you'll find all of the antacids, pain relievers, and vitamins you might need."

"I already discovered that."

"You've been snooping."

"Snooping in what is also my house is sort of impossible. You did say that it was my house, too, now. Even when I said that it was still your house..." She lowered her voice, mimicking him. " 'No, Nik, my house is going to be your house. Our house. You know the saying, *mi casa es su casa.*' " She winked at him, imitating him. "Ring a bell?" She couldn't believe how comfortable their relationship had become. Joking with him like this less than even a year ago wouldn't have happened.

He laughed. "Do I sound like that?"

"Exactly."

He put the Band-Aid on her thumb and opened the wine, handing her a glass. "Now would you like to get back to the interrogation? By the way, what are you making for dinner? It smells delicious. Garlic, onions, hmmm. Girl, with you around, something tells me I won't starve."

"Ah, a little something, something, like portabella mushroom drizzled with a balsamic sauce, a classic Caesar, and braised pork loin with pearl onions and grapes." She smiled proudly, leaning back against the counter.

"A little something, something, huh? Yeah. I think I can get used to having you here. Go ahead and call it your house, too. I think I do remember that *mi casa es su casa* part."

"Good. So, do you also recall telling Simon that I would help him and Marco out with this event their guru wants to have here? Or should I assume what I have been all day and know that Simon was trying to undermine me?"

He sighed and set his wine down. "Yes," he said slowly. "I did do that. Simon wasn't trying to work you."

"Well, do you want to tell me what's going on?"

"Come on; let's go sit down in the family room. I don't want you chopping off your hand, much less my head, in case you get mad at me."

"Are you thinking I might?"

"You might." He smiled sheepishly and grabbed their wineglasses, taking them into the ranch-style family room, replete with leather sofas, a cow hide rug, and wooden floors. "Look, sweetie. First, here's to you. To us. Our house. *La casa.*"

Please. Oh yeah, he so knew he was busted. He never called her sweetie. Neither of them was into mushy name-calling. She sat down on the couch and smiled back at him. "Okay, sweetie. Here's to us."

"To us." He clinked his glass with hers. "I see you got some more things moved in today. I told you to wait until the weekend and we can get it all in here."

"No you don't. I'm not falling for that. Don't try to change the subject. Lay it on me. What did you tell your brother dear?"

He sighed and set his glass down on the coffee table. "Okay, I did tell him that you would help."

"What? Do you realize how many orders are going out right now? Plus, I have three major restaurants breathing down my neck because they're all sold out of the Cab, and with our change in distributor last month, things are screwed up. Oh, and that charity event I promised to take care of. You know, the one you said would be good for Malveaux to be a part of? Now I'm going to have to play cruise director for a group of lost souls! Lovely. People who have enough money to buy their bliss at seminars that teach them how to breathe and chant."

He held up a hand. "Wait. I think *you* need to breathe. Hear me out. I know this is short notice, and trust me, I wasn't exactly keen on it either, but then I got a call from Alan's people."

"Alan?"

"Yes. Believe it or not, the Guru Sansibaba is really named Alan Sansi."

She closed her eyes. "Why do I have this sick feeling in my stomach that I'm not going to like this at all?"

"Here's the deal. You know how much I sank into building the spa and hotel?"

"Yes." Nikki did know exactly what Derek had put into it, and how he'd also absorbed the cost of the gourmet restaurant on the vineyard after the famous chef, Georges Debussey, who'd partnered with Derek, met an early demise. It hadn't been a cheap endeavor when Derek committed to building a world-class spa and boutique hotel on the vineyard. On top of all the promotion in glossy magazines, he'd shelled out a pretty penny to make everything top notch.

"The company is not recouping the costs as quickly as I'd like. We'll be fine, but I can't take money from the winery and funnel it into that end of the business right now because of the major promotion with the Hahndorfs in Australia and the Salvatores in Italy."

Derek had also taken on international enterprise by importing wines into the United States and giving them the Malveaux label.

"Okay, what are you saying?" Nikki asked.

"This Alan Sansi is becoming pretty big, what with law of attraction being so popular these days along with holistic medicines and aromatherapy." He sighed. "Alan gave me a call after talking to Simon and he explained why he needed a retreat in such a hurry."

"Yeah, next week." She crossed her legs and leaned back into the couch.

"I know, I know you're busy. I'm going to get you some backup. In return for holding the event here, Alan mentioned that he would be interested in licensing his name on our spa products. Right now he has one of the major cosmetic companies after him to do this, but he claims that big commercial business doesn't interest him."

"What does he think we are?"

"I know, but you know that we're totally organic and green here, and he likes that about us. He's willing to put money into the spa and into the products. It might not be a bad idea if I'm going to continue to grow the place. He's also interested in promoting our wines because they're organic. You know red wine is good for the heart."

"So is less stress—something I need. And I thought you didn't want huge crowds at the spa and hotel. I thought they were supposed to be a rare luxury. A treat. Now you're talking about promoting to the masses?"

"Nikki, I'm a businessman, and yes, the spa and hotel will stay a top-of-the-line luxury. They have to. As you said, we can't accommodate a lot of tourists here. I have no intention of expanding. Twenty-five rooms are what we have, and we can only treat a handful of guests at a time at the spa. But everything we do here is costly, and to maintain that kind of expense, I need cash flow. The spa products with

Alan Sansi's name on them could do that for us. Besides, we actually don't have any rooms booked that week because it's our downtime. We could use this."

She took a sip of her wine, and setting it back down, she rubbed her sore thumb, seeing his point. She didn't want the hotel and spa to tank. They meant a lot to him, and her as well. "What about the wine? You say this guy is interested in promoting it, too. What are you thinking? How would you go about that?"

He shrugged. "I'm not sure. I've got Simon and Marco working up a campaign now for me to present to him. But I think this guy is going to go big like Dr. Weil or Wayne Dyer. Before long we'll probably see him on *Oprah*. It could be a nice boost for us. I've been going over our demographics and we have expensive wines that are selling well, but our ten- to twenty-dollar wines aren't. We've spent a lot of money advertising to luxury and wealth and now we need to look at a mass advertisement scale. You know, the mom who goes to yoga in the morning. The family man who likes to barbeque on the weekend for his wife and kids. Couples who get together and talk about the day-to-day stuff over a glass of wine and dinner."

"You mean normal people." She laughed, because she was normal. Okay, a little crazy normal—but normal as in driving an economy car, buying most of her clothes at Target, clipping coupons, and becoming anxious when the checking account dipped below five hundred dollars. She'd had enough bounced check charges during her acting days that keeping money in the bank meant she'd go without a meal or two if need be. That was why Derek's wealthy world was so different and, yes, exciting. Thankfully, he wasn't a pompous egomaniac.

"Yes. Normal." He punched her lightly on the shoulder. "Like us."

"Us. Yes, and *us* is going to help Simon and Marco."

Derek cringed. Not because he didn't want to help, but because he was about to get in more trouble. "Um, babe . . . ?" *Yep. Another endearment.* "You're going to hate me, so I'm going to say it quickly and get the pain out of the way."

"What are you talking about?"

"I've got to fly out to New York on Thursday, so I'll be here when everyone first arrives, but after that . . ." Derek wrinkled up his nose. "Don't look at me like that with those baby blues. You're killing me. I don't have a choice here."

"New York!" Nikki shouted.

"I know. Look, I planned to take you, but this came up. You remember meeting old man Vicente a few months ago? The Italian winemaker and owner of the Salvatore Winery?"

Nikki knew her face was turning red because the heat spanned all the way to her ears. She remembered old man Vicente from the Salvatore Winery. The man had more money and power than Caesar had, and he ruled in the same fashion. *And* he'd had the gall to smack her on the butt when they'd all gone out for dinner after a business meeting. She'd about cold clocked the old fart (who had to be somewhere in his eighties) when Simon convinced her to chalk it up to the antics of an old Italian Romeo. "Please don't patronize me. How could I forget Vicente? So, what's the New York thing about?"

"The deal isn't sealed with him. He's balking at some of the prices."

She frowned. "You think you have to go and deal directly with him in New York?"

"He likes the Big Apple, and it's halfway. And he has some family there. He didn't want to come to California and I can't take the time to go to Italy right now." He shrugged. "Pretty much, if we want the deal, I have to meet with him. I'm sorry. I wanted to take you. I'll be home Monday night, so it's not like I'll be gone the entire time this group is here. Only a few days."

"A few days?" she whined. The sound of her voice even annoyed herself. She sighed, knowing that ever since Derek had walked through the door, she'd kind of sounded like a brat. She hadn't always been his girlfriend. She'd started out as an assistant and manager of the winery, and a couple of years ago she wouldn't have balked if he'd told her he needed her to manage this large affair by herself. Well, she might have a little on the inside simply because she hadn't exactly started out as best friends with her gay pals. But things had changed, and no matter what type of personal relationship she had with her lover/boss—lover (she liked that description much better)—she still had a job to do for the company. "Okay, I give, what do you need me to do?"

He kissed her cheek. "Thank you. I won't leave you hanging. In fact, I begged off the charity event with Alyssa and she said she could handle it."

"You planned all along for me to say yes, didn't you?"

"I was hoping."

"Stinker."

"I'm getting off easy. With Alyssa taking care of the charity deal, I'll take care of the distribution issues myself. I've read all of your notes about the problem, and since we've gone over it, I don't see why I can't give them a call and try to use my finesse to work things out." He winked at her.

"Bad. You are bad."

"To the bone, baby."

"And cheesy, too."

"Like a slice of Felipe's extra cheese." He smiled.

They finished their wine and he detailed what he needed for the Alan Sansi event. It wasn't going to be easy, but she'd do it, and she'd do it to the best of her ability. "You do realize that Simon isn't likely to be much of a help?" she asked.

He nodded. "I know, but Marco is the best. He'll dive in."

"Yeah, I'm sure he will. Thank God he's there for Simon."

"And thank God you're here for me," he said.

"Oh, no, there you go with the cheese ball crap again."

He took her face in his hands and shook his head. "I know it sounds like a line from a soap opera, but I mean it, Nik. I wake up every day and the first thing I think is how grateful I am for you."

She swallowed hard, and then smiled. "You are a lucky son of a gun, aren't you?"

He laughed and kissed her, and she kissed him back, thinking she was damn grateful *and* lucky she had him, too.

Pork Loin with Pearl Onions and Grapes
with Tablas Creek Vineyard Côtes de Tablas

What is Nikki about to get herself into? All she wanted to do was get moved in with the love of her life and get all domesticated, as Simon put it. And she had a decent start there with that pork loin meal she was preparing for her honey. But Nikki is a sucker for those baby blues of Derek's, and when he said the word, she didn't need much more convincing.

When you want to impress your other half, put this meal together with some sliced tomatoes on the side and rice pilaf. This is one of those dishes that are so tasty and unforgettable that it will likely become a requested meal in your household.

A great wine to drink with the pork loin is the Côtes de Tablas by Tablas Creek Vineyard. It has a wonderful blend of 43% Grenache, 24% Mourved, 18% Syrah, and 15% Counoise. It's similar to a French Rhone. It's not too fruity and has a nice peppery spice flavor on the palate.

SERVES 4.

3 lb boneless pork loin
salt and pepper
1 cup balsamic vinegar
2 tbsp honey
2 cloves garlic, chopped
1 tsp red pepper flakes
10 fresh thyme sprigs plus 1 tsp chopped fresh thyme leaves
¼ cup red wine
3 tbsp warm clarified butter (recipe follows)
1 lb small pearl onions
1 lb red seedless grapes (about 3 cups)

FOR CLARIFIED BUTTER

unsalted butter, cut into 1-inch pieces

Prepare the pork loin by trimming off any excess fat except for about an ⅛-inch layer on the outside. Salt and pepper pork on both sides. Combine vinegar, honey, garlic, red pepper flakes, and thyme in a small bowl. Marinate pork in ingredients for 4 hours up to overnight.

TO CLARIFY BUTTER

In a heavy saucepan melt butter over low heat. Remove pan from heat and let butter stand 3 minutes. Skim froth and strain butter through a sieve lined with a double thickness of rinsed and squeezed cheesecloth into a bowl, leaving milky solids in bottom of pan. Pour clarified butter into a jar or crock and chill, covered. Butter keeps, covered and chilled, indefinitely. When clarified, butter loses about ¼ its original volume.

When ready to cook pork, drain marinade and add ¼ cup red wine into a small saucepan and boil over moderate heat, stirring occasionally, until reduced to about ½ cup, about 5 minutes. Pour glaze through a fine sieve into a small bowl, discarding thyme, and reserve. In another small bowl stir together 2 tbsp reserved glaze and 2 tbsp clarified butter.

In a saucepan of boiling salted water, blanch onions 3 minutes. Drain onions and peel.

Heat a flameproof roasting pan, 15 by 10 by 2 inches, in oven 10 minutes at 350°. In the heated pan, toss onions with remaining tbsp clarified butter, and salt and pepper to taste and roast in upper third of oven, stirring occasionally, about 15 minutes. Take onions out.

While onions are roasting, prepare pork loin. Brush pork loin with about ⅓ glaze-butter mixture.

Roast pork loin for 15 minutes at 350°. Add grapes and onions to the roasting pan. Arrange pork loin over onions and grapes, and roast 15 minutes. Turn pork loin over and baste with about half of remaining glaze-butter mixture. Roast pork loin, basting with remaining glaze-butter mixture, 10 minutes more.

Transfer to a platter. Arrange grapes and onions around pork loin.

To pan, add reserved glaze and on stovetop boil over high heat 5 minutes, or until thickened and reduced to about ½ cup. Season sauce with salt and pepper and drizzle over pork loin.

Two

ONE week later, Nikki thought she'd turned into Linda Blair from *The Exorcist*.

Surely her head was doing three-sixties at two hundred miles an hour and she felt like puking up anything she tried to eat. This all started after she and Simon had had it out earlier over the fact that she'd placed calla lilies and tuberose in each guest's room.

"No, no, no. We talked about this, Snow White, and I told you that I wanted freesia and gardenias." He did that hand-on-hip-jutted-out thing he does so well.

Simon buzzed around her like one of those giant flies that never stopped long enough to be swatted (and he was grating on her nerves in the same manner) while she placed candles in all the votives inside the front lobby of the hotel. Everything about the hotel had a Tuscan feel to it, from the butter and dusky peach colors to the oversized chairs and sofas in gold and rust, to the pavers on the floor and the

arches leading in and out to the gardens, café, spa, and restaurant. Plus there were the candles—lots and lots of candles, which Nikki typically found beautiful, especially in
the evening when they were lit. But right now with Simon
the fly on speed, rambling on, and several more details to
contend with, she did not find the bazillion candles quite so
charming.

She stopped long enough to give him a piece of her mind.
"I'm not sure that you're super clear on this, but here's the
thing. Have you ever done gardenias in an arrangement?"
He didn't respond. "I didn't think so, because guess what?
That is exactly what the florist asked me. After she chewed
me out because *apparently* someone sent back the rose arrangements we ordered for the café yesterday." Now it was
her turn to do the hand-on-hip thing.

He frowned. "I had to. The roses didn't smell strong
enough. They're roses, and I'm sorry but when you walk
into a room with a couple dozen roses, I would think that
their scent would be permeating the air so strong that bees
would be buzzing around."

"More like flies. A big one," she muttered.

"What?"

"Nothing. Now, come on, drama queen. You said that
you'd work with me on this and gardenias brown at human
touch. The only way we can do them is in a potted plant."

"*Oh puhleeze*. Isn't that what a florist does? Make arrangements? Gardenia or not? I would think an *expert* could
have handled it." Nikki growled at Simon's words. "Oh no,
no you don't. Don't go all she-cat on me."

She shook a finger at him. "You know, you told Marco,
your brother, and me that you'd support me with this thing
you dumped into my lap. Instead, you've given me nothing
but grief by sending back the flowers, complaining about
the menus, *and* demanding a rush shipment on that essential
oil from Maui. An expense, by the way, your brother is go-

ing to probably shoot you for." She grabbed Simon's shoulders. "I need you to stop the nonsense."

"I'm sorry," Simon whined.

"Simon!" One of the housekeepers walked past with a stack of towels in her arms and turned at Nikki's raised voice. "You have no idea how hard this has been, do you?"

"Yes I do. I'm working, too." He rolled his eyes while wiggling his shoulders up and down, like a seesaw. A sure sign he was getting nervous with this conversation and she was gaining the upper hand.

"Here's the deal. I need you to stop bitching and do what I tell you if you want your guru and his pals to be happy. Or else, I'm walking and this will all be on your shoulders."

"Well, okay, fine. Whatever you want." He stormed off with a wave of his hand in the air and a dramatic sigh, as if she were the difficult one.

An hour later, he sidled up to her with a hot carne asada burrito from Roberto's in town. "Your favorite," he said with a chagrin smile crossing his face.

"Peace offering or ass kiss?"

"A little of both. I'm not ashamed to admit that maybe I could be a little more grateful."

She took the burrito. "I accept. Call the florist and apologize."

"I brought you a Diet Coke, too. Could you call them? You're so good with people."

"Call the florist," Nikki ordered.

He jutted out his lower lip. "Okay."

She tried to eat the burrito, which was usually her absolute favorite, but there was no way. Her stomach was tied up in knots because she knew guests would be arriving in less than an hour and the numerous problems hadn't ceased. The wrong wine had been pulled from the warehouse for the guests' arrival. The towel delivery service claimed the spa wasn't scheduled for that day. And instead of oyster mushrooms being delivered from their distributor, shiitakes had arrived and the chef was having a fit over being stuck with the apparently unsuitable mushrooms.

Derek popped in to check on things. He'd been wrapping up the business with the unhappy clients and needed to get his things packed to leave that evening. He put his arms around her waist. "How's it going?"

She frowned. "A little bit stressful, but I'm handling it."

"You always do." He looked around. No one was in the lobby, so he kissed her. Everyone who worked at Malveaux knew they were an item, but they still needed to keep things professional while at work. Not always easy. "You look beautiful today. I'm sorry that I won't be here to help you out more."

After his kiss and compliment, she had no complaints. "You're forgiven."

He kissed her again.

They were interrupted by someone clearing their throat. Pulling away from each other, Nikki felt her cheeks blush. She immediately put on her best Vanna White smile and an "Oh yes, Napa Valley truly is heaven on earth attitude."

She wished she were still kissing Derek as a squatty middle-aged woman who looked like she'd sucked on a few lemons in her life stared at them. "I'm Rose Pearlman. My husband..." She turned around. "Rube! Ruben! Oh God. Where is he? I told him to leave the bags in the rental car and that someone would get them." She gave Derek a once-over. "Do you think you could do that? Go see if my husband is out front with the bags. Or are you too busy with your girlfriend here?" She clucked her tongue and shook her head. "I wonder what your boss would say if he knew what you two were up to."

He smiled. "Yeah, I suppose that could be a problem. I'm sorry about that, Mrs. Pearlman. I'll go check on your husband."

"Thank you."

Nikki was holding back her laughter. If the lady only knew.

She turned back toward Nikki with a narrowing of her eyes. "You do wash your sheets and towels with lavender essential oils, right? And they are organic? That's what your website said."

"Yes we do. Absolutely," Nikki replied.

"Uh-huh, well, I called two days ago, and I requested that my husband and my sheets and towels be washed in *rosewater*. Ruben doesn't care for lavender."

Nikki didn't skip a beat. "I remember your request, Mrs. Pearlman." In reality, she had no recollection of the woman's call. "I'm certain you'll be pleased to know that the staff has taken care of it."

"Wait a minute, I don't mind lavender at all. I like all scents. Come on, Rosie," a gray-haired gentleman with one honker of a nose and nice blue eyes—obviously the Mr. to the Mrs.—said as he smacked his wife on her rear.

Derek came back inside with two suitcases in hand.

"That's not all my bags," Mrs. Pearlman said.

Derek nodded. "Yes, ma'am, I'm aware. I need to get a roller for the bags."

"Rose, quit giving these kids a hard time."

Kids? Nikki liked the sound of that. At thirty-seven, she hardly thought of herself as a kid any longer.

Rose's eyes bugged out. "Ruben. Go sit down. Weren't you going to check out the place?"

"I was waiting for you, dear. Look, they have appetizers set out already. This is wonderful. I tell you, when Alan Sansi puts something together, it's always first class."

Nikki cringed. Alan Sansi had not put a damn thing together. She still had yet to meet the wonderful guru.

Ruben walked over to the console where the appetizers

were. Alyssa, who worked at Malveaux, walked in on cue with a tray of champagne flutes and handed one to Mr. Pearlman.

He took a second one and came over to Mrs. Pearlman. "Drink this and don't be such a pain. Can't you see that these people are doing all they can to make this a nice stay? Jeesh, we *are* here for further enlightenment."

"I don't need any more enlightenment other than a good glass of plum wine, some pickled herring, and *All My Children*. Did you know they don't have TVs in the rooms? I'm going to miss my shows. And please, Rube, you know that I don't drink champagne." She shoved it back into his hand.

Yep, that green puke was right at the bottom of Nikki's esophagus, just like in *The Exorcist*. Nikki could feel her neck beginning to turn and her head pound. Not good. "Well, Mrs. Pearlman, we don't have any plum wine, but I can have someone bring you a very nice glass of Chardonnay." Get the lady tanked. Maybe she'd pass out. Nikki needed to get someone to redo her room. How to have sheets and towels laundered in *rosewater* and the room made up in, what, ten minutes?

"No plum wine? That's what I like. What kind of winery is this?"

Derek placed a hand on the woman's shoulder. She flinched and looked up at him as if this was the first time she actually saw him. Nikki could see the woman's features soften. *Yeah, sister. I know the feeling.*

"Ms. Sands is right, we do a wonderful Chardonnay here and it'll be on the house. Why don't you give it a try, and if you don't like it, we'll find something else that will suit you."

"Fine. I suppose that'll have to do if that's all you have. *Chardonnay!*" She threw her hands up in the air.

"You two must be hungry. I know that you flew in all the way from New York. My guess is that the food on your flight left something to be desired," Nikki said.

"You're not kidding," Mr. Pearlman replied.

"Why don't you head on through those arches to our outdoor café and I'll have lunch sent over on the house. Our chef is preparing some excellent specials for today. My personal favorite is the sautéed chicken breasts in a walnut cilantro cream sauce. It's excellent with a bottle of our best Chardonnay." Nikki glanced at Derek, who gave her a slight nod of approval.

Mrs. Pearlman wrinkled up her nose. "I'd really like to get settled into our room first." She twirled her tennis bracelet around her wrist.

"We'll take care of your bags and have you squared away in no time. In fact, since you're the first guests to arrive, you're receiving a complimentary couple's massage treatment," Derek jumped in.

"Oh, I like the sound of that." Mr. Pearlman smiled. "Come on, Rose, live a little. Let's check out the eats, and the wine, and then a massage. I love this place already."

His wife sighed and stared at him for a few seconds before agreeing. "Fine. I suppose I could eat. And I could use a massage."

Mr. Pearlman looked back at Nikki and winked. His wife walked on ahead. "Food will get her every time," he said in a near whisper.

"Ruben!"

"Coming, dear."

Nikki and Derek looked at each other. "Wow!" they said in unison and started laughing. "I hope she doesn't tell the boss about us," Nikki said.

Derek pulled her to him again. "Let her. I hope the guy fires me."

"I better get cracking. She wants the linens washed in rosewater."

"Of course she does." Derek glanced at his watch. "I hate to leave, but I need to head back over to my office. I expect Alan Sansi to arrive shortly. We have a meeting set up in an hour."

"You want me to bring him over to you?"

"That's okay. Simon and Marco have eagerly volunteered."

"Of course. They must be primping. I haven't seen either of them in a while."

"I'm sure you'll see them soon." He kissed her cheek. "Better take care of queenie."

She watched him walk out of the lobby and sighed. Life was pretty good. Then she glanced down at her notes, full of unfinished business for the day. She picked up the phone and called Housekeeping, asking them to redo sheets and towels in room twenty-two. Marie from Housekeeping complained that the room was finished and ready for the new guests. "Just do it!" Nikki hated being demanding, but she had no time to explain. She slammed the phone down and started reading off her notes.

"Breathe. Just breathe."

Nikki looked up from her papers to see a balding gentleman standing opposite her. A pleasant smile (that struck Nikki as a permanent feature of his face) and the kindest-looking, almost turquoise-colored eyes reminded Nikki of what Santa Claus might look like sans the hair and beard, and with fewer pounds. She blinked several times. The smile was still there. Was there a glow around this guy? Behind him stood an entourage of people, but she couldn't take her focus off him. "Excuse me?" she finally mustered.

He reached out a hand. "Alan Sansi, and you are Ms. Sands. Simon and Marco have told me wonderful things about you. It's so nice to finally meet you. But you really must take some time to breathe." He elongated the word, and then took a deep breath in himself for several beats and let it out. "Try it with me. No one or nothing is worth being stressed over. Life happens as it should. But you have to keep breathing for it to happen, and if you allow the stress to get to you—which is all a façade anyway, because there really is no stress—you will die. That is a fact. It is all in your hands and it is all your own creation." He took another long breath. "See, four beats in, four held, and four on the exhale."

The luster wore off as Nikki realized she was in the presence of Mr. New Age shyster himself. "Mr. Sansi. Nice to meet you, too."

"Sansibaba." Simon and Marco appeared from off the outside patio. Simon's arms spread wide as if he were ready to take a curtain bow. He wore one of his designer T-shirts in his favorite color of lavender and a pair of yoga pants. Marco followed behind, always willing to let Simon be the center of attention. Marco was the opposite of Simon's golden boy, blond image. He was dark, Italian, and the kind of man who was simply so gorgeous that it really should have been a crime. He also had more fashion sense than the yogin next to him, dressed tastefully in a pair of black jeans and white button-down. Nikki had coined them "the boys of summer" one summer a couple years ago and that was now the only way she could think of them—two boys, having way too much fun for their own good. This Alan Sansi character was another one of their indulgences, as far as she was concerned.

"Hello, Simon and Marco. You can call me Alan, remember?"

Was Simon blushing? "You two have perfect timing," Nikki said, wondering if the boys hadn't been lurking around the corner.

"Everything is already in perfect alignment. There is nothing out of balance," Alan commented, folding his arms across his chest.

Oh boy.

"Of course you're right." Simon clapped his hands.

"We're all right. All right?"

The group behind Alan Sansi started laughing almost on cue when he laughed.

Was this a sitcom Nikki was watching? She cleared her throat. "I have everyone's rooms set. If you would step forward or have a representative of the group give me the names, I can direct you to your rooms. I have an itinerary that I worked on with Hayden."

"Of course, I couldn't do anything that I do without my Hayden." He turned and motioned for a young woman in a light pink knit suit—very Chanel, very springy. Nikki wanted it. She was surprised at the woman's appearance. She wasn't sure what she'd expected, but Hayden Sansi was Alan's daughter. Again, the family appearance didn't fit the original image she'd had in her mind. What had she expected? A group in Birkenstocks and white robes, maybe some dreadlocks? A little Bob Marley playing in the background? Patchouli flowing through their auras or chakras, or whatever they were called? Not this, though. This was a total surprise. Here was Alan Sansi, polo shirted out, and his daughter, looking as if she'd just walked out of a store on Rodeo Drive with her light brown hair stylishly cut into a layered bob, and her makeup looking as if it had been applied by a professional.

"Nice to meet you." Hayden shook Nikki's hand.

Strong, confident handshake.

"I appreciate you having my father and the S.E.E. members here at Malveaux."

"Certainly."

"While you two work out the schedule and arrangements, we'll take Alan and everyone for a tour of the grounds and over to meet with Derek," Simon said.

"Can I get some wine first?" A striking young woman with long brown hair and dark brown eyes approached the counter.

"Sierra," Alan said with a hint of warning in his voice.

"What, Daddy?"

Daddy? The other daughter—Sierra Sansi. Nikki knew there was a son as well, but she didn't spot him. There was only one other woman with the crew, and Nikki was banking that it was Mrs. Sansi.

"I think it will be time for a glass of wine when we have our meals. Timing is everything." Alan looked at his daughter and smiled.

"I thought it was everything happens at the perfect time," she said with a hint of sarcasm. "And *now* is the perfect time for me to have a glass of wine. We are in Napa Valley, for God's sake. If I want a glass of wine, why should you care? I'm perfect. You're perfect. We're all perfect, remember?"

Whoa, ho, ho. What was this? A little family dysfunction going on with the guru and his grown kid? Might be interesting.

The pretty, middle-aged woman who looked like her daughters—but a bit rounder and with shorter hair—placed a hand on Sierra's shoulder. "Of course you're perfect, as your dad says, but it will be a long day and you'll need to be available to the attendees. And isn't it true, Ms. Sands..." the woman began as she reached her hand out elegantly. "Sorry, I'm Mrs. Sansi. Call me Lulu." Nikki nodded and Mrs. Sansi continued, "We do have a lovely train ride trip planned for this evening, isn't that right? The dinner train, I believe." Lulu Sansi had a style all her own, with a page boy haircut and a poet blouse that flowed over a long flowered skirt that almost reached the ground, where pretty white sandals with a faux yellow daisy in between each big toe adorned her feet. She wore a half dozen gold and silver bangles on her wrist.

"We do. The Napa Valley Wine Train. I'm sure we'll see a beautiful sunset and I promise there will be plenty of wine and fantastic food."

Sierra frowned but reluctantly agreed to hold off on drinking any wine. "Okay then."

"Thank you," Alan said. "I think we'll take that tour with Simon and Marco now. If you and Hayden want to go over the rest of the details together, that would be perfect. I know that my publisher, Rich Higgins, should be arriving shortly, along with my son, Eli."

Sierra rolled her eyes. "What? You didn't tell me that Hayden's fiancé and Eli were coming. That's great. *Perfect.* I can deal with Eli, but Hayden with Rich? God! She'll be pouring on her holier-than-thou act. Give me a break. Why didn't you bring the entire family with us, Dad? Yo could have asked Aunt Fran, Uncle Joe, every cousin…"

Simon immediately wrapped his arm through Lulu's, obviously sensing the tension. "Shall we?"

Marco strolled up next to Sierra and almost forcefully wrapped his arm through hers. She squirmed, but then received a stern look from her mother and sighed, allowing Marco to lead the way. "Come now, Bellissima, there is so much to see here at the winery. Let me escort you," Marco cooed.

That was Marco—full of charm.

Alan got in behind the group, his hands clasped behind him, chin slightly down, as in either deep concentration, or else distress.

Hayden turned to Nikki. "Oh yes, this will all be perfect. You have no idea just how perfect this will all be."

Nikki didn't have a clue how to respond. She wasn't even

sure what the woman meant, but she figured that Alan
Sansi's definition of perfect was probably radically different from her own. From what she'd seen and heard so far,
this entire event was going to be less than *perfect*.

Butter-Sautéed Chicken Breasts

in a Creamy Walnut Cilantro Sauce with Nickel and Nickel Chardonnay

What a buzz kill that Rose Pearlman is! Poor Nikki. She handled her in stride, though. It's just too bad she didn't get a bit
more time to smooch with her guy before being interrupted by
the rude woman. One way to handle rudeness, though—food
and wine. Seemed to work like a charm with Mrs. Pearlman.
Nice job, Nikki!

This is a rich and delicious recipe. It'll please even the most
uptight, silly, sour person you know. Pair it with the Nickel and
Nickel Chardonnay, which is produced at True Chard Vineyards. It's a Napa Valley Carneros Chardonnay that is similar
to a French white Burgundy. It's not over-oaked, and is lean
and clean with good acids.

> 1 cup shelled walnuts, finely chopped
> ¼ tsp salt
> ½ tsp hot paprika
> 2 large cloves garlic, peeled and halved
> 3 tbsp olive oil
> ¼ cup sun-dried tomatoes
> 1 packed cup chopped cilantro
> juice of 1 lemon, or more to taste
> ½ cup half-and-half

4 chicken breasts (pound flat)
1 cup flour on a plate
2–3 tbsp clarified butter (see pork loin recipe for clarifying
       butter)

In a food processor, grind walnuts with salt and paprika. After walnuts exude their oil and the mixture is pasty, scrape into a small bowl. Crush garlic with a pinch of salt. Heat oil in a skillet over medium-low heat. Add garlic, sun-dried tomatoes, and cilantro and cook, stirring, until oil just begins to sizzle (maybe 2–3 minutes). Add to the walnuts along with the lemon juice and half-and-half.

Heat frying pan to high with butter. Salt and pepper chicken breasts, dredge in flour, shake off excess, and when the pan is very hot but not burning, place the chicken in and sauté for 1 minute on one side, turn, and sauté on the other side for a minute—the meat is done when just springy to the touch.

Remove chicken to hot plates and pour sauce over chicken. Grilled asparagus and roasted red potatoes make a nice accompaniment.

Three

IT was getting late in the day and Nikki needed to get home and change for dinner on the wine train. Plus, she wanted to see Derek again before he left for New York.

There were still a few guests who hadn't checked in, including Alan's son, Eli. The publisher, Rich Higgins, who was evidently engaged to Hayden, had checked in late.

"Sorry to get in so late. It was one of those situations where I got caught up at the offices and it took me some extra time to get out here with the traffic and all. I'm sure Hayden is wondering where I've been. I've tried reaching her, but either her cell is off or she's busy." Rich Higgins opened his leather briefcase and set one of Alan's books on the front desk. "His latest. I'm looking forward to showing it to him."

Hayden's fiancé and also Alan's publisher was a nice-looking man, probably somewhere in his thirties, with blondish hair, hazel eyes, and a decent build suggesting he worked out. He wore a coat and tie, which threw Nikki off, yet again. The group that had appeared throughout the day didn't strike her as New Age, feel-good types. Maybe she'd had this Alan Sansi guy wrong all this time? Maybe she'd been worrying for nothing?

She picked up the book. *Living Well in a New Age.* "Huh. Great. I should get you settled in. I think the Sansi family may be in their rooms but Alan is meeting with the owner here."

"Oh. Was there a problem?"

"No. They had a scheduled meeting." Nikki wondered if she shouldn't have said anything. Maybe Alan wasn't ready to tell his family or his publisher about his outside interests, like the aromatherapy line. "Where are your offices? Are you in New York?"

"No. Actually we're in Santa Barbara. Not too far away. Wine country there, too."

"Lots of it," Nikki agreed. "I've got your keys to your room here. The transportation for the wine train will be leaving at six-thirty tonight."

"Thanks. Just enough time to get settled and cleaned up. See you tonight, right? You've been working with Hayden on everything?"

"Yes. I'll be there." All she wanted to do was go home and curl up with a book, Derek, and Ollie. But there would be no Derek tonight, and by the time she got home from the event, she doubted even a good book would thrill her.

Rich nodded his thank-you, rolled his bag out of the lobby, and headed to his room.

Nikki closed her eyes and shook her head. She needed a break. She wished everyone would hurry up and arrive so she could get started on the evening's plans. Just then she felt a pair of hands on her shoulders and jumped back.

"Oh, God, I'm sorry. I didn't mean to scare you." It was Alyssa Pampas. Alyssa had joined the Malveaux team about a year earlier after meeting Nikki in an odd place—a strip bar in San Francisco. Alyssa's little boy had a heart condition and the young woman worked at the bar to make enough money to support her child while she attended school. She'd helped Nikki put some bad guys in their place and Nikki had taken a liking to her, suggesting she interview for the job at Malveaux as a taster. Alyssa had sailed through the interview and then accepted the winery job, where she more than proved she was skillful at her job and quickly climbed her way to a better position as a supervisor at the hotel and spa.

"I was lost in thought. I still have quite a bit to do," Nikki replied.

"Why don't I finish checking the guests in for you? I've already completed my reports and handled the charity event stuff. You'll have a late night being 'on.' I can do this."

"Really? You sure? What about Petie? It's almost four. Don't you have to pick him up?" Nikki asked, referring to Alyssa's three-year-old.

"No. He's staying a bit later with the day care. They had a little party for him today and his teacher called and said he's still playing and wants to stay longer. Kathy has been a lifeline for me. I get pretty tired, you know. She's really like a grandma for Petie."

"I know. She's a good lady," Nikki replied. She'd met Alyssa's day care provider a few times when she'd gone to pick up Petie with her. "But why don't you go home and rest? I know you're tired and stressed. You need to take care of yourself." Nikki laid a hand on her shoulder.

Alyssa shook her head. "No. Working helps me keep my mind clearer and off of things. Petie and I are so close that I'm realizing we need space once in a while. If we get through this..." She choked up.

"You will get through this. He will get through this. He's a strong kid, Alyssa." Petie lived with a heart disease called cardiomyopathy—a disease of the heart muscle where the heart loses its ability to pump blood effectively. He was currently on a heart transplant list, along with two hundred and seventy-five other children under the age of seventeen. Nikki knew the strain it had placed on Alyssa. Petie was sweet, silly, and from everything Nikki had seen of him, a fairly rambunctious and normal three-year-old boy. But everyone at the winery knew that Petie wouldn't live a long life if he didn't get the transplant. "You are a strong woman, and if you need anything at all from me or the winery—time off, whatever—you know all you have to do is ask. I would love to have Petie come stay with me and Derek for a weekend so that you can get away. Why don't you do that?"

Alyssa smiled even though tears dampened her eyes. "Maybe. Thank you. That might work. I don't know. I don't know if I could leave him for a weekend, but maybe a night. I would like to go and visit my sister in Vegas."

"Absolutely, and you should. We're here for you."

Alyssa wrapped her arms around Nikki. "Thank you. I'm so glad you're my friend."

"Hey, now. Come on. Why don't you go sit in the café and have a glass of wine or a cup of tea?"

"No. Maybe after I'm done here. I like checking people in and meeting them."

"You sure? There have been some strange birds walking in here this afternoon," Nikki warned with a grin.

"Oh yeah?" Alyssa laughed.

It was good to see her smile. Alyssa was by far one of the strongest women Nikki had ever known. She'd been through hell and back even before Petie came along and then she found out he was sick. She was a pretty, petite brunette, brown-eyed woman, who had just reached her twenty-fifth birthday. She'd handled quite a lot in her young life and she'd done it with elegance. Nikki admired her and also felt somewhat protective over her—like a mother hen. If given the chance, Nikki figured she'd probably make a decent nurturer. It was something she liked to do, and when Alyssa needed it, she was there for her.

"Oh yes. These S.E.E. members are, to say the least, interesting."

"I'm not surprised considering Simon and Marco are involved." Alyssa's comment made them both laugh.

Nikki gave her the list of those who still needed to be checked in and she started to walk back to Derek's place— oh yeah—Derek and what was also her *casa* now. She walked past the rose garden and waterfall that cascaded like slick glass against one of the stone walls of the hotel. Although she'd never been to Italy, she was sure there had to be sites there like the waterfall at Malveaux. It was pretty spectacular. She stopped to take it in for a minute. It was her moment of meditation. Alan Sansi had to be able to appreciate that. She took in a couple of breaths. What was that? Here she was breathing in, listening to the water, and . . . she could hear raised voices. Yes, that's definitely what they were. One was accented. Asian, maybe? Definitely both males. She peered around the waterfall wall and spotted Alan Sansi, hands on hips, facing an Asian man who had his suitcase in tow. Nikki didn't recall checking him in. She couldn't make out the words they were exchanging, but the guru did not look happy. He stood there shaking his head while the other man kept trying to hand him a DVD of some sort. Now this was interesting. No. No. Nikki stopped herself; this was none of her business. Ah, hell, but it was interesting! Alan the guru didn't strike her as one to argue with anyone. Didn't the guy just *breathe*? That seemed to be his prescription. Stress was not on his agenda.

And then, in a seemingly totally uncharacteristic Sansi move, Alan poked the man in his chest and said loud enough for Nikki to hear, "That is not what this is about, Iwao! I don't want to see the DVD. It's none of my business. I don't want to interfere and I would appreciate it if you did the same. Now leave me and my daughter alone. Take what you have there and get rid of it. Let's get back to our purpose here. Thank you!" Alan turned on his heel and stormed off toward his room, leaving the Asian man shaking his head and Nikki with her mouth gaping open.

Okeydokey. None of that made sense at all. Nikki hemmed and hawed before heading toward the man. She stopped as she passed him. "Can I help you, sir?"

"I am checking in. I am part of S.E.E. group. My name is Iwao Yamimoto." He bowed.

"Oh yes, Mr. Yamimoto. I'm Nikki Sands. I manage the winery here and have been involved in scheduling the week for all of the members." She remembered seeing Mr. Yamimoto on the list, along with a woman's name—Mizuki, presumably his wife. They were some of the last to check in. She wondered where his wife was. "The front desk is that way." She pointed. "Just go around the rose garden and in through the large archway."

He bowed again. "Thank you very much."

She smiled and nodded. It was all she could do not to ask him if there was a problem between him and Mr. Sansi. She literally bit down on her tongue as she turned and watched him head toward the front desk. Hmmm. *Leave it alone. None of my business.* Oh, boy, that was quite a task to ask of Nosy Nikki. She was aware that people in Napa had coined her with that nickname, but c'mon, it wasn't as if her curiosity had not been applied toward the good of all mankind. Or at least for the good of those in her neck of the woods.

To her dismay, Derek wasn't at home. She looked at the clock. Almost five. He really should have been getting ready for his trip back East. Then she spotted his suitcase packed and ready to go, and it was impossible not to feel sad. How silly. He would be gone for only a few days, but she didn't want him gone for even one.

Ollie was there to greet her, though. He didn't exactly get up, all one hundred pounds of him too comfortably tucked into Derek's leather chair to move. The dog raised his head and thumped his tail as best he could with it wedged between his rear and the chair. She walked over and gave him a pat on his head. He replied by closing his eyes and going back to sleep. "Nice to see you, too."

She sighed and headed to the shower. After a few minutes of warm water spraying her, she felt a bit refreshed. She slipped into the old standby black dress and stood in front of the mirror, unable to twist off a tube of mascara that was tightly stuck. Time for a new tube. Weren't you supposed to replace it every couple of months anyway? Not only did she need new mascara, but she realized she probably should've bought a dress with some color, some pizzazz, but her old accommodations had burned down several months ago along with all of her belongings. She had stayed in the hotel until Derek proposed living together a couple of weeks ago. Makeup and new clothes hadn't been on the top of her priority list. Until now.

Maybe she'd do some shopping next weekend when things would likely have settled down. She thought about calling Isabel and asking her to go. They hadn't seen each other in a while. Isabel was a good friend who owned a restaurant in Yountville called Grapes. The two of them had been bosom buddies until Nikki started dating Isabel's brother, Andrés, and then kind of broke his heart. Well, really broke his heart. Nikki had been torn between Andrés and Derek and had eventually followed her heart, which led her to Derek. Isabel claimed to understand. She and Nikki talked, and occasionally did things together still, but it wasn't like it used to be, and Nikki missed her and the close friendship they'd shared.

Derek came into the bedroom and shook her out of her thoughts. Many of her things were still in boxes stacked against the white wall. Derek's room—now hers as she had to constantly remind herself—was white and blue, continuing that Spanish, ranch feel the house had. "Hi. How was the rest of your day?"

"Good. You're running late, aren't you?"

"No. I'm ready. Alan and I had a good talk and then I had to wrap up a few things. It's funny. He's far more human than I'd thought."

"Tell me about it."

He looked at her and made a face. "What does that mean?"

"Nothing. It's just the way that Simon and Marco had made him out, I expected an angel with wings, halo, and all." She didn't want to reveal the conversation she'd overheard between Alan and Mr. Yamimoto. She knew how Derek felt about her curious nature. It definitely was not his favorite of Nikki's traits, and they'd gone rounds with each other in the past over her inquisitive nature.

"Yeah, I know those two do hold him right up there next to God. But he is a very down-to-earth guy."

"Uh-huh. I wish you didn't have to go to New York tonight," she said. "And I really wish I could drive you to the airport, but I have to do this wine train dinner. I'll have to listen to some psychobabble on elevating my soul through the S.E.E. program instead of spending extra time with you." Nikki did her best pout.

"Oh, don't be so negative about it. Like I said, Alan Sansi is a decent guy. Who knows? Maybe there's something you can learn from him."

"Not you, too? Don't go all Guru Sansibab'd out on me."

He laughed. "Come here."

She wrapped her arms around him and he kissed the tip of her nose. "I wish you could go with me, too. But I think you can handle all of this without me. I feel we're in a good position to go forward with an ad campaign with Alan. Simon and Marco have worked up some great ideas. I know they can drive you crazy, but when you put them together and keep them focused, they can do a great job."

"I know. That's good news about Alan Sansi and this ad thing. It sounds as if he's going to do the licensing agreement with us." She pulled away from him and finally got the mascara tube open, only to find it almost empty. She made a face.

"I was hoping you'd be able to meet with us today. I know you were overseeing the arrivals, but Alan and I aren't finished sealing the deal. I explained to him that, while I'm gone, you'll be in charge. I left some notes on my desk that I took while we talked. They're in the home office here. If you stay in touch with Alan regarding the key points, when I get back we should be ready to have contracts drawn up."

"Sure."

"And could you do me one more favor?" he asked.

"What?"

"Take off that dress."

"Jeez. You don't pull any punches. I know I've worn it a million times. I haven't had much of a chance to get many new things since the fire. Give me a break."

He smiled. "Oh no, I love the dress. It looks great on you. I just think it looks better *off* of you." He wiggled his eyebrows.

"I have to be ready in a half hour and you have a flight to catch. I still have to put my makeup on." She waved the tube of mascara in front of him.

"Makeup schmakeup. We have time. I'll make the plane." He grabbed her, kissing her.

She dropped the mascara tube. Nothing like going *au natural*.

Four

THE Napa Valley Wine Train is an experience no tourist visiting the area should go without. Nikki always thought of it like stepping back in time to an era of elegance and luxury. She always enjoyed a trip on the wine train. The décor alone made one happy to have come aboard. The mahogany paneling, brass accents, etched glass partitions, and brocade and velveteen fabrics were reflective of the finest early-twentieth-century trains, such as the Venice Simplon Orient Express and the Andalusia Express.

Being a sort of Renaissance woman, Nikki had taken time to learn about the train and the railroad in Napa. Local craftsmen had turned the train into a travel dome of splendor. The "turn-of-the-century" Dining, Parlor, and Chef du Cuisine Kitchen cars had been purchased from all over the United States and Canada.

The group would be riding in one of the 1915 Pullman

dining and lounge cars and milling in and out of the wine-tasting lounge, where Malveaux wine would be poured. The scenery alone would be something to die for as they rattled past vineyards, the grapes just now springing to life at the ends of healthy vines. Some had dark, thick, twisted branches, while others were longer, more elegant, their vines almost reed-like. It depended on the variety of grapes the vineyard grew. The passengers would pass large wineries with various motifs from the castle-like, Tuscan-like, redwood buildings, country and farm style to old stone wineries—there wasn't anything less than spectacular on this excursion.

That was why Nikki had suggested it for Alan Sansi and his followers, which tonight included Marco and Simon, the Pearlmans, Mr. Yamimoto, and the woman Nikki assumed was his wife, Mizuki. She was dressed in a red and black kimono, her hair tied back with long ivory needles into a tight chignon. She looked several years younger than Mr. Yamimoto.

There was also a nice-looking young guy who Nikki hadn't met who sat with Alan's daughter, Sierra, the problem child. The publisher, Rich Higgins, sat next to Hayden Sansi, rubbing her back. There were a few other people whom Nikki had yet to meet, but her gut told her this was going to be somewhat like summer camp; by the time this week was through, she'd know more than enough about each of the S.E.E. members aboard the train.

The Pullman car they were in held about sixty or so passengers, and because of the decent size of the car, people were able to get up from their seats, mill around, and get to know one another.

Nikki knew through her discussions with Hayden over the past week that the idea behind an elite week with Alan was supposed to be a combination of fun and learning. The fun part was on Nikki's shoulders. She'd had to plan a diverse itinerary of events for the group. Members would have access to Alan in a more casual atmosphere than they would at his larger events, and this also gave members a unique opportunity not only to grow spiritually, but to network with one another in different "lifestyle areas." Nikki found Hayden's wording amusing—"lifestyle areas"? Come on. Why not just say "network for business"? Or "socialize"?

Nikki had first suggested they do the murder mystery wine train where actors presented diners with clues after a "murder" takes place on the train. However, Hayden hadn't felt that would be appropriate considering that her dad was all about goodwill, and murder didn't pair well with the positive-thinking aspect of Sansibaba's teachings. Nikki could see her point, but wasn't there also a point to laughing a little? Not that murder was funny, but she knew that dinner theater shows typically played up the comedy. Then again, Nikki had had her share of murder mysteries. And not the dinner theater type.

So, with the train winding its way through wine country, a smile on her face, and the sunset spreading vast rays of pink and gold across the sky, she felt satisfied that things were going as planned.

Alan and his wife, Lulu, sat at the table with her, along with Eli Sansi—Alan's son, who had finally checked in— Iwao Yamimoto, and his wife. This could be interesting. Would the argument she'd witnessed between them come up over dinner on the train?

"How did all of you get involved in the S.E.E. group?" Nikki asked. Oh, there was her infamous curiosity off and running. She knew she should slap a hand over her mouth and make it stop.

Eli Sansi leaned in, setting a crisp glass of Sauvignon Blanc down. "Obviously, I didn't have much of a choice." He laughed. "Considering I'm his son."

"Eli," his mom snapped.

"He doesn't mean it negatively," Alan interrupted.

"Dad's right. I don't at all. I'm grateful that he's my dad." He slapped his dad lightly on the back of his shoulder. "I wouldn't be writing my book without Dad."

"Oh, are you writing a book?" Mr. Yamimoto asked, his voice heavily accented.

"Yes, on how teenagers can use the principles my dad teaches in their life. I've scaled it down so that the language is like theirs and they can get it."

"That is good idea. Inspiritus is publishing the book?" Yamimoto asked.

"We haven't gotten that far yet." Eli picked his wine back up.

"Rich will soon be a part of the family, and Inspiritus has always published Alan." Lulu leaned in and gave her husband a kiss on the cheek.

"Just because he's going to be a part of the family doesn't mean he has to, or even will, publish my book. Dad's the moneymaker."

"But you are his son, no? That make sense, but maybe you find another publisher? One who better for you."

What was Nikki missing here? Why was Mr. Yamimoto so interested in Eli's book? Maybe just food for fodder, but the look good old dad was giving to Eli gave Nikki a different impression. This was not a subject this family wanted to delve into with strangers or even within the intimate circle of S.E.E members.

"Maybe," Eli replied.

Nikki noticed that Mrs. Yamimoto never spoke a word, but kept her head slightly down and eyes averted.

"I like Mr. Sansison works a lot. I want to publish him in Japan. Maybe I publish you, too, in Japan, Mr. Eli."

"That sounds great," Nikki said. If she was in charge of

the Malveaux Estate right now, then she needed to wrap her brain around the business at hand—sealing the deal with Alan. And if Alan Sansi was going to go global, it could be very good for Malveaux. The possibility of running ads in Japan was also smart business; she'd recently read a report stating that wine consumption had tripled in the country in the last decade, and young adults, especially women, were making it their drink of choice. Tokyo alone consumed sixty percent of the premium wines in the Asian market.

"Yes, very good." He bowed his head. "We are talking good deal for Mr. Sansison and you, too, if you want to meet me and listen to what I offer."

"Iwao, my contract with Inspiritus is locked in and I honestly think that is the best way for Eli to go as well," Alan said.

Before Mr. Yamimoto could answer, they were interrupted.

"Hey, hey, finally I get a chance to come over and say hi to Alan Sansi. And is that Iwao Yamimoto? Hey, man, how's it going?" A large man in every sense of the word came over and smacked Iwao Yamimoto on the back. The much, much smaller man about fell out of his chair.

"Juan Gonzales." Alan stood up and pumped the man's hand. "Nice to see you. I saw you on the list but hadn't seen you yet."

Nikki had not checked Mr. Gonzales in. She'd already left the front desk when he'd arrived. Alyssa had done those last check-ins.

"Just got in from Mexico City. I had a business trip down there, then had to get back to L.A., wrap up some business there, and wouldn't you know when I got on over to LAX, my flight was delayed? All in a day's work. But I wouldn't miss this for nothing. I love you. And Iwao, haven't seen you in too long, man. I think it was Paris?"

"Oh yes, Paris, that very good time. Eiffel Tower so pretty, and you, Juan, you funny guy. Got your letter today. *Funny.*"

Nikki thought the way Iwao said the word "funny" the second time sounded sarcastic, and she couldn't help wondering about it.

Juan looked at him oddly. "What letter you talking about, man?"

Iwao pointed at him and laughed. "See, you be funny again. You bring pretty lady guest this time?" Iwao asked.

Juan started laughing. "Nah, it gets to be too much cash you know? Lots of dinero for pretty ladies. Lots. But you know that." He shook his head and looked squarely at Mrs. Yamimoto.

Alan sat quietly and seemed to be studying Juan.

"Oh hey, look here, we got fresh blood in the group." Juan stretched out his hand to shake Nikki's. He let out a low whistle. "Nice."

Nikki clamped down on her jaw, again asking herself how in the hell had this guy become an Alan Sansi follower. Then again, she glanced over at Marco and Simon and couldn't help wondering the same thing. Was this group really more about people who actually lacked the most in spirituality, life advancement, positive thinking—whatever it was being called these days—who searched it out and spent every last dime and minute trying to reach a state of Nirvana? Or was it about something else?

"Ms. Sands is actually our coordinator this week," Alan said. "She's done an amazing job from what I read of the itinerary. We're truly grateful for her participation in helping us all grow."

"Cool. You'll be converted yet. This stuff works. Ask Iwao. He knows, right, buddy?" He smacked him hard again on the back.

Iwao winced. "Oh yes. Sansi system work real good."

"Yeah, hey, you seen Rube? He's here with that wife of his. She's a treat, huh?"

Nikki assumed he meant the Pearlmans. "Good thing she isn't always around, for Rube's sake."

"It's always so nice to see you, Juan." Lulu picked up her wineglass.

"You, too, Mrs. Sansi. Nice to see everyone again. And the newbies, that's always good. New blood is always good. I better get back to my table. My stomach isn't working real good right now. I think I'm feeling starved," Juan said.

Nikki pointed to the servers, who were now beginning to come down the car's aisle and serve delicious entrees. Nikki had ordered the grilled prawns marinated in a Serrano lime sauce. "I think you must be right about the S.E.E. program." She knew she was schmoozing, but if that's what it would take to help Malveaux Estate, then she'd do it. Nikki had her own selfish reasons for wanting to pave the way for a deal to close between Alan and Derek. She wanted Derek to be proud of her. She didn't want to blow it. "You asked for food, Juan, and now you're receiving it."

Everyone laughed. "You're good. You'll get this," Juan said. "I better get back to my table but I had to come say hi. I got some new guy at my table, Kurt Kensington. Boy, that guy definitely needs some of the Sansi spirit. He's kind of full of himself. And you might want to watch him, Alan and Mrs. Sansi. He's coming on heavy to your daughter."

"It's not our job to interfere, Juan."

He pointed at him and laughed. "Right. Nice to meet you, Nikki."

Lulu grabbed and squeezed Alan's hand.

Alan maintained his complacent smile. "Interesting gentleman, working his way through the journey." He stood and excused himself for a moment to wash his hands.

It was possible that Alan had lost some of his cool there for a minute. Juan seemed the type to shake up a person, and maybe he'd shaken the guru a little.

There was an uncomfortable silence at the table for a moment. Eli Sansi finally broke it with, "Do you think the bar has anything stronger than wine?"

Nikki was kind of taken aback, but replied, "I'm sure they do. It's—"

He held up his hand. "I know where it is. Thank you."

"I think I'll head to the restroom as well," Lulu Sansi said.

What was it with the Sansis? Did they travel in packs? Kind of the way women friends did to the bathroom? A bit strange.

Nikki now found herself sitting alone with Iwao and his wife. Iwao said something in Japanese to her and she answered him in a bare whisper.

Nikki didn't know what to do. It was awkward being left there at the table with this strange man and his silent wife. "You've followed Alan Sansi's system for some time?"

He nodded. "Yes."

"And what do you love about it? I'm learning what it's all about. It's rather interesting."

"It horseshit. That is what you say in United States? Horseshit." He smiled.

Nikki stared at him, not certain if he was joking or not. "Excuse me. I don't think I heard you correctly."

"You did. This all horseshit. These people no want to improve. They want to think they better than everyone. They only want more money. Everyone always want more money. If they think there is easy way to do it because they listen to Alan Sansi, then that is what they do."

"But you said that you loved Alan and—"

"I do love Alan. He going to make me lot of money. I like

money, too. That is why I going to publish big-time guru. Lot of money in that." He rubbed his fingers together. "He good guy, but he like money, too. Don't let Alan Sansison trick on you. You American people all like money, do and believe anything for it. Alan and his son will make deal with me this trip. You see. I bring this horseshit to Japan."

Nikki was speechless. "Yeah. Okay." She stood. "I'll be right back. I think I'll check on the wine train. They're, um, serving our wines and I want to make sure that everything is good back there."

He nodded. The wife still never looked up.

Nikki glanced back at Iwao Yamimoto speaking in hushed tones to his wife. She shook her head. Something was brewing here. Nikki didn't know what it was, but it sure in the heck didn't smell of enlightenment. In fact, it reeked of downright nasty.

Serrano Lime Grilled Prawns
with Duckhorn Napa Valley Sauvignon Blanc

A little nasty brouhaha is mixing up there on that Napa Valley Wine Train. How will Nikki handle all of these enlightened souls? She might have to drink a couple of bottles of wine to make it through the evening. No. Then she'd become a big lush. That's not a good idea. Nikki will do as she always does— grin and bear it and drink a couple of glasses of wine instead of full bottles. Hey, what can go wrong at this point? She's eating grilled prawns and drinking Sauvignon Blanc!

Nikki loves grilled prawns, and with the spice from the Serrano marinade, the Duckhorn Napa Valley Sauvignon Blanc is an excellent pair. The Duckhorn has a little Semillon on it. It's not too herbaceous and is slightly rounder and fuller than many Sauvignon Blancs. This is a great summer dish.

⅓ cup peanut oil
2 tbsp olive oil
2 tbsp white wine vinegar
1½ tbsp balsamic vinegar
1 tbsp fresh lime juice
1 tbsp fresh lemon juice
1 small garlic clove, minced
2 Serrano chilies, seeded and finely diced
3 tbsp honey
1–2 tbsp minced fresh coriander
48 tiger prawns
salt (pinch of)

In a small bowl, combine the peanut oil, olive oil, white wine vinegar, balsamic vinegar, lime juice, lemon juice, garlic, honey, chilies, salt, and coriander. Whisk to blend well. Marinate for 20 minutes.

Preheat grill for medium-high heat. Thread prawns onto skewers, piercing each first through the tail, and then the head.

Brush grill grate with oil. Baste with marinade glaze on each side again while cooking. Cook prawns for 5 minutes, turning once, or until opaque.

Five

THE setup for the evening was a little different, but Nikki found herself having a good time. Okay, so the wine helped. But seriously, she was meeting new people, and although most were a little to the left of center, as far as she was concerned, they were all basically nice.

With each course, she found herself seated with a new group of people. The idea was to rotate tables as the separate courses came in and talk about what you learned in the past year about yourself and others. It was kind of difficult because it was on the train, but Hayden insisted it was the exercise her father wanted to do. Nikki and the wine train event coordinator made it work.

It was an exercise that Alan suggested everyone try, and "everyone" apparently included her as well. So she threw caution to the wind and, in true Sansi spirit, "went with it."

Luckily for her, as things turned to more personal-type questions, she found herself seated across from Marco when it was her turn to "share." The problem was she was also next to Sierra Sansi, who had put away plenty of wine, and kept leaning on Nikki. "You are so cool. Like a normal chick. I want to be your best friend. You know, BFF? I need a friend," Sierra slurred.

Sierra's sister, Hayden, was also at their table, looking completely disgusted by Sierra. Instead of friendship, Nikki offered the tipsy girl a bottle of water or some coffee.

Marco clapped his hands together. "Bellissima," he said to Nikki in his beautiful Italian accent. "You tell us what you learned this year."

"Oh God, I don't know."

"No, no." He shook a finger wildly in front of her face. "You know and I know you've learned many things about yourself and people around you."

Marco was her "go-to" guy. He knew more about her than most people, and that was because she trusted him to keep her secrets, even from Simon. Now here he was trying to expose her!

"Come now. Tell us."

She sighed and thought for a moment.

"Yes, come on. Tell us your life lesson for the year," Sierra slurred sarcastically.

"Okay. I learned that following my heart is better than following my head even if it means I might get hurt."

Marco nodded as if he approved.

"And I learned that people aren't always what they seem." She narrowed her eyes like a cat at him.

He laughed. "Oh, that is so true, isn't it, Bellissima?"

Sierra perked up a little. "Love, huh, and heartbreak? No. I think you should follow your head and not your heart. Because your head is smarter." She giggled. "And it does not get smashed into tiny shredded pieces. And I get what you meant that people aren't who they supposedly are. Let me tell you, do I get that."

Hayden stood up. "I think you and I should make a trip to the ladies' room, Sierra."

Sierra made a face at her. "I don't have to pee."

Hayden grabbed her arm. "It's time for a walk."

Sierra Sansi stood up at Hayden's demand. "You are such a bitch sometimes."

"I know, Sierra. I'm a total bitch."

"You and Rich, such the perfect couple. You must really practice this stuff Dad teaches because you seem to always get what you want."

"Bathroom. Now."

"Wow. What was that all about?" Nikki asked.

Marco closed his eyes for a second. "She has had too much to drink."

"I can see that. She's practically falling down. Her parents must be beside themselves. That young woman is a mess."

Marco nodded. "Ah, yes and no, as her father will say. It is her choice, her journey."

Nikki took that in for a moment. "Okay, so maybe it is, but isn't it also her family's or friends' choice to help her? Couldn't that be their journey? It seems like her sister is trying to help."

"It does look that way. It is all in perfect order, no?"

"I don't know about that," Nikki replied. "So far I haven't seen a lot of perfection out of any of this."

"That is the point. There is perfection in nonperfection. It's life."

"Oh, brother. Why are you spending so much money on all of this babble when you just made the best point yet? It's all life. Just life with its ups and downs. The moments that suck and the moments of bliss. You don't need this, and I'm telling you that Sierra Sansi needs some counseling, not all this huruguru crap."

"Such a skeptic."

"No, a realist," Nikki replied.

"You have to remember that Sierra Sansi is an adult and her parents can only do so much to see she gets help."

"Why do you think they brought her then?"

"Because I think they do want to help her."

"I think rehab would help," Nikki said.

"It's not our business or our journey, Bellissima. We are only a short chapter in all of this."

Nikki took a sip of wine. This was way too philosophical for her. If Sierra Sansi had been her kid—adult or not—she would have told her that she was going to take her ass to rehab and get some help, or else there would be consequences, like being cut out of her trust fund or something huge to give her some sort of wake-up call. "You want to know what I would do?"

"Tell me," Marco said.

Nikki did, and as Marco was reflecting on it for a few moments, Hayden came back to their table. "Did you see my sister?"

"No," Nikki said. "You were with her, weren't you?"

"Yes. I was. In the bathroom, and she kept insisting she wanted more wine. I told her the wine bar was closed."

"It probably is now." Nikki looked at her watch. They were into the dessert portion of the trip and she knew they closed the wine lounge down before serving dessert. "But I think the lounge up front is still open."

"No. She doesn't need anything else to drink. Oh God. I have to find her."

"I'll go with you," Nikki offered. "I've been on the train before and know my way around."

"Thanks," Hayden replied. "That would be great."

Marco waved them off and Nikki led Hayden throughout the different cars on the train and on up to the lounge. Sierra was nowhere in sight. They checked the bathrooms again, but no Sierra.

"That's odd. She couldn't have gotten off," Hayden said.

"There's maybe one other place, but she had to have gone looking for it," Nikki suggested.

"Where is that?"

"There's a small storage car in the back. It's where they load the wine."

"Yes. If she went looking for a glass of wine and she found that, then I'd say there's a chance she's in there." Hayden followed behind Nikki in and out through the people on the train. "Usually she doesn't drink so much. She never used to, but she's had a few problems lately and I've noticed she's started downing the wine a bit."

"Not good."

"No."

As they headed toward the back of the train, Sierra came running toward them, pale and blabbing, but not making any sense. Her sister took her by the shoulders. "Sierra? What is it? What's wrong?"

She kept shaking her head and pointing to the back of the train. "In there with the wine," she muttered.

"What? Yes, we figured that you might be having more wine back there. Sierra, you have to stop. I think you could have a problem."

"No! No!" she screamed.

Nikki pushed her way past the sisters and pressed the button on the wine storage car. Something was terribly wrong—drunk or not, Sierra Sansi was clearly upset.

When Nikki stepped inside, she could see why. Her knees wobbled, wanting to collapse, and the blood running through her veins chilled at the sight. There was Iwao Yamimoto on the floor between two boxes of Cabernet Sauvignon by Malveaux—his throat slit and the cork from a wine bottle shoved into his mouth. Iwao Yamimoto had been corked by Cabernet.

Six

NIKKI spied Detective Jonah Robinson before he saw her. He was talking to the uniformed police on the scene who were having people sit down and go through the interviewing process, which would be quite lengthy considering all the people who had been on the train. When he looked her way and locked eyes with hers, he shook his head. She mustered a weak smile.

He sauntered over to her. There was no other word to describe the way Detective Robinson walked, other than possibly *strut*. She couldn't help spotting Simon and Marco, slack-jawed and wide-eyed. They'd seen the detective before, but he was one of those men who took the breath away each time you saw him. He didn't possess drop-dead gorgeousness like Derek or Marco did. Hmmm—Nikki was a lucky girl. But the thing about Jonah Robinson was that he exuded mass sex appeal. Still there had been no love lost between Jonah and Nikki on their first encounter, despite his good looks. What Robinson had in the way of "hotness," he lacked in charm. Nikki first met him when Georges Debussey was murdered at the hotel, and they hadn't cared much for each other from the moment Robinson started questioning her in an accusatory tone.

But because of that case, they'd found a mutual respect for one another, and there was no denying it: whether or not you liked the detective, he was sexy. Lenny Kravitz sexy with mocha skin, deep green eyes, and a lanky leanness that reminded her of a cat on the prowl. And over time, Nikki had learned to like Robinson.

"Why is it that when a murder happens around here, you seem to be close by? Every time," he said.

"Hey, I've been trying to stay out of trouble. It's been what, a year or so? I've been good. Honest."

"I doubt that. You want to tell me what you know about the victim, what happened, what this thing on the train is all about? Someone said it's some cult group."

"Oh, my God, no. Who said that?"

"I'm not telling you, and..." He raised a finger. "Don't get messed up in this one. Don't, don't, don't."

"I don't plan on it."

"Sure you don't," he said. "Sonoma County is lucky I transferred here instead of staying in the city, so you don't need to be doing none of that snooping you're famous for."

She crossed her arms. "I resent that."

"It's true. Now, you ready to tell me what you're doing hanging out with a bunch of Hare Krishna types?"

He took out a small notepad and pencil. She explained to him who the group really was and why they'd all been on the wine train. "I had just met Mr. Yamimoto today and then he was at our table for a bit tonight. From what I gathered, he's a publisher from Japan wanting to publish Alan Sansi's books in his country. But Sansi didn't seem all that interested."

"Uh-huh. What else do you know?"

Nikki had learned from her past dealings with Robinson not to keep anything from him, and although she was notorious for crime solving, she didn't think she wanted to take a stab at this one. She told him what Iwao had said about Alan Sansi's system being horseshit and she also told him she thought the dialogue between Iwao and Juan Gonzales had some kind of hidden message in it.

"What do you mean?" Robinson asked. "What kind of hidden message?"

She shrugged. "I don't know. It was weird, though. Iwao was talking about some note that Juan left for him earlier, and then made a comment about him being a funny guy. I don't know... it struck me as odd."

Robinson wrote this information down. "Which one is this Gonzales cat?"

Nikki pointed him out. He was seated, speaking with one of the cops.

"I think I better talk with him, and we need to get access into Iwao Yamimoto's room. I doubt that will happen tonight. There's a lot of witnesses to go through, so I'd appreciate it if you got it locked up tight."

"Sure. His wife is also staying in there. She doesn't seem to speak any English."

"His wife?"

Nikki pointed to Mrs. Yamimoto. The woman was crouched against the chair she'd been sitting in at dinnertime. She was as silent as she had been earlier. The only sound she'd made was when she realized what had happened to Iwao, and she'd let out a cry so animalistic and pain filled, Nikki's heart literally felt a deep pang and ached for her. Now she seemed to be in shock. Initially Nikki had sat down and tried to speak to her, but she got no response and ultimately decided that the woman wanted to be left alone. Even if she didn't, the cops showed up quickly, before there was any real time to comfort anyone. Everyone sort of had that dumbstruck look on their face.

"I better find out. I may have to get an interpreter here."

Nikki nodded. "What do you plan to do with all of these people?"

"I don't know yet."

"I'm sure after this, they'll all want to go home," Nikki said.

"No." Alan Sansi had come up behind her. "No one is going home. This, this situation . . . Iwao's death is something we need to deal with as a group. We all signed up for this journey and I think we need to see it through."

"Mr. Sansi, I assume?" Robinson asked.

"Yes."

"You do realize that one of your followers—"

Alan interrupted him. "I don't have followers. They are members seeking a path of enlightenment."

"Right. One of your members may have killed one of their own tonight. It could have been someone on staff on the train or a passenger not associated with the group. We'll be checking all angles. The way Mr. Yamimoto was murdered was violent and malicious. I think you may want to reconsider continuing on with your week. There may be a killer amongst you."

Alan didn't respond for several seconds. His happy-go-lucky demeanor had changed since earlier that day. He was subdued and even strained. "I agree with that. But as I said, this is what we all signed up for. Is there a problem if we do continue with the program?"

Nikki found his choice of words strange. She knew she certainly hadn't signed up for murder on the Napa Express.

"The police department should not have a problem with it, but I think regarding the program for the week, well, that would be something for Ms. Sands and Mr. Malveaux to decide," Robinson said.

Oh no. Derek. Robinson had to remind her that her partner in love was currently radio silent—on a plane to New York City. How was he going to take this? She knew the answer to that. She glanced at Simon, who was seated next to Marco. They were both watching them.

"Derek is on his way to New York."

"I guess it's up to you then. I would suggest if you're going to continue, then you should hire extra security. I can place a uniformed officer at the hotel but, I have to tell you, with the cuts the department has recently taken, I can't afford any of my men to play rent-a-cop."

"All right. I'll see what I can do," Nikki replied. "If you really think we should and can continue, then I'll do my part, Alan."

With a nod of his head, Alan quipped, "Yes. I do."

"I'd like to speak further with you, Mr. Sansi. Ms. Sands, if you'll excuse us and maybe help calm nerves. I know murder doesn't get under your skin the way it does others." Robinson smiled slightly. "Right over there, Mr. Sansi. I'll be with you in a moment." He turned back to Nikki. "I'm probably going to regret this, especially since it's not exactly by the book, and I've already adamantly warned you away, but right now I could use your eyes and ears. You're actually above suspicion this time, I think."

"What are you asking me for, Robinson?" She placed a hand on her hip and tossed back her dark hair.

He sighed. "I'm short on staff like I said, and you did solve Georges Debussey's murder. You've got good instincts. I don't want you snooping per se, but I could use you to listen to your gut on this and tell me anything you might think or feel, even if it sounds whacked out. I think this group is probably pretty kooky." He spun a finger in circles around his right ear.

She smiled. "Let me get this straight. You're asking for my help?"

He studied her. "Kind of. But don't let it go to your head." He sighed. "I'm sure that I'm going to regret this. Don't cross the line, though. You know what I'm talking about. None of that breaking and entering you've done in the past, or following people in cars. None of that. All I want from you is information. You hear someone tell someone else something that don't sound right, you call me. You see something strikes you as odd, you call me. Your gut screams at you about something, you call me."

"All right, I got it. I'll call you."

"Good. You really okay with these folks staying at your place?"

"I've got a big dog, remember?"

"Oh yeah. The ridgeback." He laughed. "Good. Keep him close by. I'll be by your place tomorrow. I think you and I are through tonight. Like I said, play hostess for now. And keep your ears and eyes open. I'm going to talk to the rest of these people."

"Hey, Robinson, I forgot to mention to you that I saw a heated conversation between Sansi and the deceased earlier today at the hotel."

"Know what it was about?"

"No clue. But it looked like Iwao Yamimoto was trying to hand something to Sansi, like a DVD or maybe a small case of some sort. I don't know, but he told Iwao to mind his own business."

"That's what I'm talking about. Little gems like that." He pointed a finger at her.

She saluted him and he shook his head walking— sauntering—over to Alan Sansi. It was strange, she knew it was—a man had just been murdered and she felt rotten about that, but she couldn't help feeling a rush of adrenaline when Robinson asked for her help. Who would have ever thunk it? Things had certainly changed. Then again, things always change. Nothing ever stays the same. Jeez, now she could probably sell that to a ton of people and make millions just like Alan Sansi, who was now standing in the corner of the train being questioned by one intense detective.

Seven

BY the time Nikki and the S.E.E. members made it back to the hotel, she was exhausted but still running on adrenaline. Her mind raced, trying hard to recall her entire day, everyone she'd checked in, all the interesting nuances she'd learned, and the initial impressions she'd gleaned.

Alan asked for everyone to join him briefly in the room Nikki had allocated as a conference room. There were moans and groans from some, especially Rose Pearlman.

"I think this is insane to stay here, Ruben. There's a killer on the loose and I don't see the sense in staying."

"Rose, we're fine. We aren't hurt and I don't know if you heard that Detective Robinson say that no one is allowed to leave the county. Without notifying him, anyway. We aren't going anywhere."

Robinson had asked everyone to stay in town until he'd had a chance to go over their statements. Nikki was okay with it because she couldn't see herself in any danger. She

also didn't believe that anyone else was in any real danger.
Her aunt Cara, who had raised her, and was now a retired
LAPD homicide detective, had taught her quite a bit about
the criminal mind and various psychoses that killers hid so
well. Her sense was that someone had planned Iwao
Yamimoto's murder. The violent manner that he was killed
in, from what she could tell, almost looked professional.
Iwao had to have either been lured or planned to meet someone in that wine storage car; it wasn't as if people went
looking for it. As far as slitting someone's throat? That
tended to follow one of two trains of thought—no pun intended.

The first was that a true professional had done it. Even
someone with links to organized crime. It was that type of
brutality that organized criminals enjoyed inflicting. It
made a statement to anyone who might have an idea as to
why Iwao had been murdered—basically, keep your mouth
shut. If Iwao was into sketchy activities or business dealings, and he had a partner or partners, and this was an organized crime hit, well...any associates would know to shut
the hell up and back away quickly.

Thinking of shutting the hell up made Nikki glance
around the room for Mrs. Yamimoto. She wasn't there.
What did that mean exactly? Sure, Nikki had not expected
the wife to join the group. How were the cops handling her?
Should she move her from their bedroom? Robinson didn't
say, only that he needed to get into the room in the morning.
She wished she'd had more of an opportunity to speak to
Robinson about her. Nikki knew that if Iwao Yamimoto's
death had been an organized killing, then there was someone or several people who knew why he'd been killed and
what for. That first theory bothered her; could Mrs.
Yamimoto be in any danger?

The mafia theory felt a bit off, but it was still a consideration. Granted she hadn't learned much about Iwao

Yamimoto in the short time she knew him, but he was a publisher, not a drug dealer or arms supplier. Or maybe he was? What was the saying? You couldn't judge a book by its cover. Not only that, Iwao had turned from the goofy dogooder who thought highly of the Sansi system to a naysayer as soon as Alan turned his back. He'd quickly become a greedy money monger. She had to speak with Mrs. Yamimoto.

There were other angles to consider—maybe a vendetta. But why? Possible lust, murder for money, power… Oh, the options were plenty when it came to taking another person's life.

And there was a third theory tucked way back in her mind. It was one that could mean there was more trouble brewing at Malveaux Estate, and that theory meant whoever had killed Iwao was completely deranged, and didn't have much of a reason to kill other than for pleasure. Now, that type of person could have been anyone on the train. This wasn't someone who was just a tad crazy, but a total nut case. And that type of person was never easy to weed out. Unfortunately, psychos didn't hold up signs announcing their mental imbalance.

She'd have to listen and look hard as Robinson asked her to, to see if anyone fell into this category amongst the S.E.E. members. Spotting insanity was not easy because people with pathological personalities often appeared completely normal, even charming and likable. Nikki would have to dig out some of Aunt Cara's old books on psychopaths versus sociopaths. The boxes full of books were still in the garage. When her aunt had retired, she'd let Nikki pick through the lot of the books before she carted them off for donation. Being that Nikki was an actress starring as a detective in a cop show that was pretty much pulled from the network before airing more than a season, she'd chosen a handful of books that, ironically enough, had proven handy over the past couple of years. Far handier for her as a winery manager than an actress.

If the psycho theory that Nikki wanted to shove back into the deep recesses of her mind was possible, then it could mean more trouble ahead for the members of S.E.E., Malveaux Estate, and herself. It could mean that one of the members was a good old-fashioned serial killer.

Nikki scanned the room again where everyone was settling into chairs waiting for Alan to say something soothing or earth-shattering—anything. From what she spotted, none of them looked like serial killers. Then again, what does a serial killer look like? Typically the guy, or occasionally gal, next door. Unremarkable. A chill went through her. Not a great thought.

Simon started a fire in the fireplace and the group seemed to divide into two categories—the group that sat stunned and silent and the group that chatted quietly about what had occurred that evening. Nikki had noticed that Sierra Sansi had been taken to her room by her mother. Sierra had been the first one to find Iwao, and even in her inebriated state, it had not only sobered her up but horrified her to the point of speechlessness. That was understandable.

Alan Sansi walked up to the front of the room and everyone stopped speaking in their hushed tones, all eyes on him. He clasped his hands together and looked skyward, then down at the floor, pacing back and forth for a minute before he ever spoke.

"Tonight a horrific event occurred. We lost a fellow human, a member of this program, and someone I considered a friend. Many of us here, I'm sure, want to go home, where things may feel safe to us. It's comfortable at home. I want you to rest assured that Iwao is *home*. He followed the principles in S.E.E. He believed the philosophies, and knew they worked." He took a deep breath.

Little did Alan know that Iwao thought it was all "horse-shit." Or maybe he did know? Oh, great. Nikki's mind raced in circles. Why did Robinson have to ask her to look, listen, and learn? Who was she kidding? Even if Robinson hadn't asked her to pay attention, she'd be doing exactly what she was doing now. Allowing her mind and theories to run away with her.

"Iwao would not want us to go home. He would want us to continue this journey. He chose his path, and possibly someone in this room was the catalyst to his achieving the end of this journey here on earth in his vessel of a human body."

Oh, no, no. He was not going to tell this group that Iwao Yamimoto had decided and wanted to die by the sword and whoever had done this to him was simply *the messenger,* now was he?

"Whether or not the person who took Iwao's life will be revealed is going to be his or her decision along with the decision of those who are trying to find the truth. It all works in accordance to the laws of the universe. What I do know is that we are all meant to stay this week and learn from one another. There is meaning behind what happened tonight, and together we will find it. I plan to continue this journey tomorrow morning at breakfast with everyone. I believe Ms. Sands has a hike planned afterward." He looked at Nikki.

She nodded and tried to smile for the morose group. "Yes. I've planned for us to set out at ten o'clock. We'll be hiking the Ritchey Canyon Trail and Upper Ritchey Canyon Trail, which is about four point two miles and it makes for a moderate hike. It's located in the Napa Valley State Park and there are redwood groves and all sorts of gorgeous flowers and plant life. We may even see some deer or fox. It is very nice." It sure was hard to play touring hostess with a murder in the back of the mind.

That got some oohs and ahs and a groan. Nikki knew that the unhappy member could be none other than Mrs. Pearlman.

"Nikki and Hayden have arranged for a picnic, and our discussions will take place out there. There is no better place to feel your soul soar than out in nature. We have a free time scheduled for the afternoon, and then a wine tasting in the evening with a talk on how wines are created. Correct?"

"Yes. I'll be teaching the class tonight as our vintner is currently on vacation with her family in France."

She couldn't believe how this was all playing out. It was weird and kind of disconcerting. It almost had that "But the show must go on" feel to it. Yet she really did believe Alan was sincere. And in a way, the man was right. No one could do anything for Iwao now. It was terrible, but what could be done other than to achieve some kind of justice? And as always, Nikki had a passion for justice. Maybe she'd inherited it from Aunt Cara, maybe it had been because of some of the cruelties she suffered as a child, but whatever the reason, she did believe Iwao Yamimoto's murderer needed to be found and brought to justice.

Eight

SURE, it was late, and Nikki had pretty much had enough of the night, but dammit, she had to go and check on Mrs. Yamimoto. It was the right thing to do. It troubled her that not one of the S.E.E. members had mentioned her. True, Mrs. Pearlman had asked where she was, but Alan had shushed her and said that the woman Iwao had been with was not a S.E.E. member and should be left alone by the group.

"Oh, so she can go home, and we can't?" Mrs. Pearlman stood.

"That is up to the police, and Rose, I am not making you stay here. You are welcome to leave any time."

Nikki witnessed Ruben tug on his wife's sleeve, pulling Rose close, and delivering an earful. No one heard the exact words, but whatever he said was enough to silence the Oompa Loompa imitator, who quickly closed her mouth and sat down.

Leaving the meeting area, Nikki checked the time. Past midnight. Maybe she shouldn't bother. What if the woman was asleep? Doubtful. A nice gesture of a pot of tea could be soothing. Oh, who was she kidding? Yes, she felt rotten for anyone who was in Mrs. Yamimoto's situation—losing a spouse, especially in such a horrific way, had to be devastating, but even worse was knowing the killer got away with the crime. Nikki did not want to see that happen and she was sure neither did Iwao's wife. She headed to the kitchen in the café and fixed a pot of Sleepytime tea.

Ten minutes later she stood in front of room twenty-three. The rooms were set up in sections at the hotel. Here were a few rooms on their own—cabin-like, and like this one, there were some that from the outside had the look of a town house, with one room being below the other. She had a fondness for this room. It had been her suite for several months after the fire. It was private, large, and comfortable. Nikki's free hand shook as she rapped on the door. No one answered, and after a minute, she knocked again. Two thoughts ran through her mind—either the Mrs. had skipped wine country *or* she was asleep. She might have taken a sleep aid.

The room faced rows of Chardonnay grapes set on rolling hills, but tonight what Nikki noticed was the silence. Really noticed it. Sure, this location was always silent. It was the wine country. But it was the witching hour and dark, really dark. She should have grabbed Ollie before doing this. Just as she'd freaked herself out and was turning to hike back down the stairs, the door cracked and Nikki practically jumped out of her skin while trying to hang on to the hot carafe. This was why she'd never make a real detective—she knew how to wind herself up to the point that fear took over.

Her nerves settling, Nikki faced Mrs. Yamimoto, whose ivory face was tear and mascara stained. "Mrs. Yamimoto. I am so sorry to bother you. I brought you some tea." She held out the carafe.

The woman shook her head. "No. No."

"I understand. You don't want the tea. I'll leave you alone." This had been a stupid and insensitive idea.

The woman took hold of Nikki's sleeve and then bowed. Nikki did her best to bow back and then say good night. "I can leave the tea with you, Mrs. Yamimoto."

"No, no."

"Okay. I'm sorry to have bothered you."

Again the woman grabbed her sleeve. Did she want her to stay or go? "Do you speak English?"

"No English. No Mrs. Yamimoto."

"Huh?"

She motioned Nikki into the room. She followed, set the tea down on the console where the hotel daily replaced both wineglasses and coffee mugs. She held up the carafe and Mrs. Yamimoto nodded. Nikki poured the tea and handed her the first cup, then motioned for them to sit down in two cushy, velvet-covered chairs in front of the fireplace.

"I can turn that on for you if you'd like," Nikki said, a little louder and slower than normal, thinking maybe somehow the translation would get across. She realized by the look on the woman's face that she wasn't registering it. Nikki took it upon herself to light the gas fireplace and do it so that Mrs. Yamimoto could see for herself how to do it, for future reference. It was chilly in the room and even the warm earth tones on the walls seemed cooler than usual.

The recently widowed woman bowed at Nikki again. They both sat down. Now what?

Nikki made a gesture and touched the woman's hand. "Mrs. Yamimoto, I am so sorry."

She frowned. "No. No Mrs. Yamimoto." She pointed to herself. "Mizuki."

Nikki pointed back at her. "Mizuki?"

She smiled. "Mizuki."

That was nice of her to want Nikki to call her by her first name. "Mizuki, I am so sorry for your loss." How in the world was she going to talk to this woman, especially get any information out of her? "Have the police talked to you at all?"

Mizuki cocked her head.

Nikki made her fingers into imaginary guns. "Bang, bang. Police."

"Oh, bang, bang. No."

"Yeah, well," Nicky struggled for something to say. She took a sip of her tea and stood. "I just wanted to bring you the tea." She pointed to Mizuki's mug. "Good night."

Mizuki stood and held out her hand. "No. Uh." She brought her hands up to her face as if she were searching for the words. "Jen."

"Jen? What?"

"Jen. Jen. Sierra."

"Sierra?" Now that caught Nikki's attention and Mizuki had said it loud and clear. "Sierra Sansi?"

Mizuki nodded.

"Jen? Who is Jen?"

Mizuki held out both hands and waved them at Nikki. With frenetic movements, she opened up a laptop on the desk and motioned for Nikki to come over. She did. It took a couple of minutes for the laptop to warm up. Jen? What was she trying to say?

Once the computer was on, Mizuki opened a file of photos and clicked through several. Most of them were of Iwao in different locales, a few of them were of Mizuki. And then there were a couple of Iwao with a handsome young man. He had an athletic build, high checkbones, dark hair, and had to be related to Iwao because there was quite a resemblance to the dead man.

"Is this your son? Jen?" Nikki made a motion like she were rocking a baby. She pointed to Iwao, then Mizuki, then this man she called Jen.

Mizuki eyes grew big. "No Mrs. Yamimoto!"

Then it hit. Mizuki was not married to Iwao. Now things were coming together. She did look too young to be this Jen's mother, but he was obviously Iwao's son, and if Nikki had it right, she wanted her to contact him. He should know that his father had been murdered. But what was this about Sierra Sansi?

"Mizuki. What about Sierra?"

Mizuki did a few more clicks on the computer screen, and there in a photo stood an unhappy, stern-looking Iwao, and this Jen hugging Sierra and planting a big kiss on her cheek.

Nine

AFTER leaving Mizuki's suite, Nikki sprinted back to the house. What did this new information mean? Things were already getting messy and she knew she'd have to befriend Sierra for some answers. Did Mizuki think Sierra was connected to Iwao's murder? Sierra had found him initially, but she didn't strike Nikki as a brutal killer at all.

She stopped halfway to the house, breathing hard. The night air was crisp, and with only a sliver of a moon in the sky, stars twinkled like diamonds. She ran regularly but the day was catching up with her. Bending over with her hands on knees to catch her breath, she was caught off guard when she looked up. What the . . . Who was in her house? All the lights were on, blazing like headlights on a semi, and she'd been caught in them. Again—what the . . . She knew she'd only left the porch and family room lights on. Oh, no. What if Derek had somehow caught wind of all this and come home? No. That would be impossible. His flight was out of San Francisco at nine. Well, it's true the murder had already gone down and they were being questioned around that time. Maybe Robinson had called him, or even Simon. He'd probably be pacing the floor and worried sick that she hadn't shown up yet.

She picked up her pace again until she reached the front door and hesitated slightly before opening it. There was a killer on the loose. But it was highly unlikely he or she would turn on all the lights in the house. Plus, even though Ollie didn't have a mean bone in his body, the sight of him was pretty intimidating. The UPS guy still didn't believe that he was harmless. What the hell. She walked through the door and immediately knew that it wasn't Derek awaiting her. She recognized the woodsy scent of Allure by Chanel.

It was Simon, of course, accompanied by Marco.

"Oh, Bellissima, where have you been?" Marco rushed to her and held out a brandy snifter.

"I see you two haven't wasted any time getting comfortable."

"We knew you'd have the good stuff," Simon said.

"Give me a break. That mansion you live in has bottles worth thousands in the cellar, not to mention you could have gone into the warehouse for a nice bottle of wine."

"Sure, Snow White. Do you really think my mommy dearest left us the key to the cellar? And besides, we weren't about to head into the warehouse with some bogeyman in the hood."

She rolled her eyes at him. Simon did have a point about his mother, Patrice. When the boys' father died, she inherited the home and the boys inherited the winery. Patrice was not exactly mother of the year by any stretch of the imagination, and since Nikki had first arrived at the winery, she'd done what she could to chase her away. Eventually Nikki won that battle and Patrice was currently residing in Greece. Simon and Marco promptly took over the big house on the hill, while Derek remained in the ranch style he'd built by using the frame from an original barn that stood on the property.

Nikki eyed Ollie standing over his dog dish, ground beef in his bowl. "I see they tempted you with the good stuff, huh, Cujo? Nice going, letting the riffraff in."

"He seemed hungry," Simon said and sneezed. "I just took my allergy pill."

"I don't know how you could really be allergic to him. He hardly has any hair at all."

Simon dismissed her comment. "It should kick in soon. I always forget he's like a permanent fixture here." He pointed to Ollie.

Guilt flooded her upon realizing that in her afterglow of the late afternoon events with Derek, she'd forgotten to feed Ollie. Bad mommy! She bent down next to him and he looked at her like he was definitely pissed off at this faux pas. "I'm sorry, bud. My bad. Aren't you lucky the boys stopped by? And now that I'm home, you two can skadoodle on up to your place."

"Skadoodle? No way. We want the scoop. What gives? Like, where have you been?"

"Taking care of a few things. And what are you talking about? Scoop about what?"

Marco frowned. "At this hour, and after this evening, you were taking care of things. What things?"

"You can do better than that," Simon said. "We've been worried about you."

"Worried about me?"

"Duh. Killer on the loose? Marco and I *do* worry, you know."

"Yeah, right. You two don't worry about me. You know that I can take care of myself."

"Yes, we always worry, Bellissima, but the honest truth is we want to know what Detective Robinson was talking to you about." Marco brought his snifter up to his nose and took a long whiff.

Simon frowned. "Yeah, so what gives with you and the hot detective hanging out in the corner talking all hush-hush-like?" He rubbed his hands together. "Now dish, dish. And what did take you so long to get back here? Sansibaba let us out almost an hour ago."

She sighed. There was no way of getting around this. These two were relentless, and when they wanted an answer, she'd learned that either she'd have to eventually lie—and that typically meant some long, convoluted bullshit story—which she didn't like doing but at times found necessary. Or she'd have to give them the real scoop, and in this instance it could behoove her to tell them the whole truth and nothing but.

When she was finished, both of them were speechless. At first.

"Whoa, there, Snow White. Back up an eensy-teensy second," Simon said.

The slack-jawed silence couldn't have lasted. "Yes?"

"That part about this Jen who has to be Iwao's son and Sierra Sansi, and then the Sansibaba—"

"Alan," Marco interrupted. "He wants to be called Alan."

"Whatever. Okay, so you're not thinking that somehow Alan or his daughter is tied into this?"

She shrugged. "I don't know what to think. It's some strange stuff, boys."

Simon shook his head. "No, no, I don't think so. We're so not going there. We are all enlightened people, not killers, especially not Alan or any of his family."

"I disagree," Marco said. "I do think it was one of the members. I think that people can be fantastico at hiding who they really are. And that is what we are looking at. A person with a mask."

"Maybe so. Tomorrow I'm going to dig out my books from my aunt's library—they're still packed away—and read up on sociopaths and psychopaths. Two slightly different personalities but both could be killers, and if we can find one basically wearing a mask, Marco, then we're on to something. Let me ask you, how well do you two know any of these people?"

"Not very," Marco admitted. "You know we are some of the newest members."

"I can't believe you would think that someone who follows Alan Sansi would do such a thing," Simon said. "Much less Alan himself." Ollie had come over to where Simon sat on the couch and nudged Simon's hand, whining. "Go away. You can't have the couch. Go. For God's sake, we fed you ground sirloin."

"Go lie down, Ollie," Nikki said. Ollie looked at her and then came over and plopped himself on the floor next to her feet.

"You obviously have had some contact with Alan. What do you know about him on a personal level?" she asked.

"He's who he says he is, Snow White. He is the real dealio," Simon said. "And I am appalled that you would think the worst."

"Really?" she asked.

"No. I take that back. Cynicism seems to be in your nature."

"That is not true. I'm a very positive person. What I don't do is always take people at face value."

"His son is strange," Marco muttered.

"What do you mean?" Simon asked. "I didn't think so. I found him delightful just like the Sansi—er…I mean, Alan."

"I sat by him for some time tonight, and he's not like his father. I get the feeling he wants to be his father, but he doesn't feel real to me," Marco replied. He snapped his fingers. "Like the mask. I think Eli Sansi wears a mask."

"I kind of get a strange feeling from him. I guess he's also writing a book, and then Iwao was offering to maybe publish the book, but Alan shut that down quickly, basically saying that their loyalty needed to remain with Inspiritus. That's understandable, considering that Rich Higgins is his publisher and soon to be his son-in-law. But Iwao was determined to get Sansi's business, at least the foreign rights to publish his stuff in Japan," Nikki said. "Did Eli do something in particular that made you feel this way, Marco?"

"No. He...I don't know. It is a feeling that I have. Like it is...What do you say? An intuition thing." He rubbed his gut. "Right here. You know? I get this sense he has jealousy toward his father."

"Oh come on." Simon wrinkled up his nose and took a long sip off his brandy.

"No, no, really. I watched him watch his father tonight, and in his eyes I see a man with a jealous soul. Children can be jealous of their parents, and his father is a great man."

Nikki ran some ideas by the boys of summer. "If Eli is jealous of his father and Sierra is one angry, resentful daughter, for reasons that could possibly be tied into Iwao Yamimoto, maybe we have a family affair on our hands. Maybe one of them did it? Or a couple of them? Or one planned it out and one executed it. This could not bode well for Sansi's public relations. Could one of his family members be looking to actually sabotage their dad? Once this hits the press, you know what will happen. There will be speculations and accusations. Even Robinson himself asked me if the group was a cult."

"That rat bastard." Simon crossed his legs and stretched out onto the sofa. "Awfully cute rat bastard, but all the same, how dare he? We are not a bunch of Tom Cruises waiting to jump on Oprah's couch declaring our devotion to our loved ones, although I'd do that for you." He looked at Marco who smiled. "Maybe for you, too, Snow White."

"To be so lucky," Nikki replied.

"Yes, well, and Scotty didn't beam us down from the *Enterprise*. We are the real deal."

"I know. I know you're the real deal, Si. Look, let's take this a step further with the Sierra Sansi angle. She apparently knew Iwao, and she and this Jen, who looks to be his son, were more than friends from that photo I saw. They looked pretty cozy. I wish I could have understood Mizuki better. I know Robinson is tracking down an interpreter, but something tells me he won't make me privy to what she tells him. And she may not tell him what she's told me. Robinson can be intimidating and Mizuki may not want to talk with him around. Maybe we could find a private interpreter on our own."

Simon studied her. "I don't like the sound of any of this. I can see the brain going zoom, zoom, zooma zoom in there, and you just need to chill and let that detective do his job. Quit being a Nosy Nikki."

Nikki ignored his comment and continued on, more for herself than for the two of them. She was fleshing thoughts out and they were coming out fast and furious and she had to tell someone. If she forgot her ramblings, maybe Simon and Marco would be able to prod her later. "I haven't figured Hayden out. Although she kind of fits the normal mold. She's polished and sophisticated, and from my conversations with her, pretty much in charge of a lot of her dad's business and definitely his financial affairs. Lulu Sansi also appears pretty down to earth, but again, looks can be deceiving. What we don't know is when the killing took place. We need to narrow that down. Where had Iwao said he was going when he got up from the table and who did he say it to? My guess is Mizuki."

"It is interesting," Marco said. "I agree with you that maybe the Sansi family had skeletons to hide in their closet."

"Marco," Simon said in a tone that could only be interpreted as *shame on you*. "You're encouraging her."

"No. Think about it for a minute. Alan is rich and famous because he is this supposed spiritual genius. His one daughter seems to have many problems, and his son is a jealous man. Does that not make you think it is strange?" Marco's face darkened.

Simon shook his head. "No. It doesn't. *You* think about it. Each of us is our own individual and because of that we have choices. His children are not a reflection of who he is."

This was kind of an ironic twist because Marco had been Alan Sansi's staunch supporter when Simon had strayed, wanting nothing more than shopping sprees at Barneys and mimosas aplenty at breakfast. If Marco could see the *real* light here, why couldn't Simon? Dysfunction junction resided at the Sansi family's castle.

"Possible." Marco shrugged.

"How about anyone else? Did you notice anyone who seemed kind of off, or who may have been missing for any period of time while we were on the train?"

Marco nodded. "Kurt Kensington. He's a new member, too. He sat with me in one of the groups tonight. I could not understand who he is. Another hard man to figure out. I asked him what his business is, and all he said was that it was his own."

"Stop it. Stop it already. You're indulging her. Jeez Louise, don't you see what is happening here? She's slipped right into her Little Miss Detective mode. Stop it, both of you. No good can come of it," Simon remarked.

This time they both ignored him.

"That is kind of strange," Nikki replied. "Was he the guy

that was hanging on Sierra for a while?" She remembered
Juan Gonzales telling Alan and the group seated with her
about it. It was shortly after that everyone had excused
themselves from the table for various reasons, and Nikki
had been left alone with Iwao and Mizuki. When had Iwao
gotten up from her table and whom had he been seated with?
Nikki could not remember. They'd all been moved so many
times from table to table. When Alan had started off the evening, he'd said that people could move around freely and
settle in where they felt comfortable with each rotation. She
thought she'd met everyone that evening, but it would be
Mizuki who would know when Iwao left the table and how
long he'd been gone.

"Oh, I think that Kurt guy is so cute," Simon said.

"He's an ass," Marco replied.

"I thought we were enlightened and didn't make judg-
ments." Simon pouted.

If Nikki had had a glass of wine to suck down at that second, she would have either choked on it or swallowed it at
once. She'd already finished off her brandy, and in conjunc-
tion with the Sleepytime tea and the late hour, she was
growing tired. But the thing about Simon not being judg-
mental? That kind of jolted her. She'd watched his transfor-
mation since becoming an Alan Sansi member and he'd
definitely mellowed, but judging others was one of his favorite pastimes. It usually drove Marco crazy.

Marco waved a hand. "We are. We really are, but I am
telling you, Kurt Kensington was filled with ego."

"That's why he is here, then, and we are supposed to help
him."

"You two, stop. Look, Iwao Yamimoto died tonight. He
was murdered! Okay? And between you and me and
Ollie…" She glanced at the dog, and knew she probably
shouldn't share this with any of them, except for the dog,

but decided to do so anyway. "Detective Robinson has asked me to keep my gut in check and see what I can learn about these people and who might have wanted to kill Iwao."

Simon sat up straight and slapped both hands on his knees. Marco's eyes widened and they simultaneously said, "Oh!"

"So all that talk going on between you wasn't flirting?" Simon asked.

"You can't be serious," Nikki replied. "Sometimes you are so ridiculous. I'm in love with your brother. You know that. Robinson is not my type even if I was single."

"Right. Robinson is everyone's type, honey." Simon rubbed his hands together. "Let me get this straight, you're playing Robin to Robinson's Batman?"

"The beautiful detective's sidekick. This sounds like a problem, Nikki," Marco added.

Simon nodded and she gritted her teeth.

"You two. You both have dirty minds. Get the smut out of your head, because I'm going to need the two of you to help me to help Robinson."

"Nikki! What would Derek say?" Simon asked. "You have been involved in these types of situations before and I know my brother dear isn't too keen on you playing Sherlock Holmes. He really won't like you playing Watson to Detective Luscious."

Nikki had already thought about what Derek might say. She knew she'd have to call him first thing in the morning and tell him what had happened. It was almost one o'clock in the morning California time and she needed to get to bed in order to even think clearly tomorrow—although technically it was already tomorrow. Yes, she did need to get to bed. Derek still had an hour in the air and then had to get checked in at his hotel. She wished he hadn't taken the red eye.

"I'll talk to Derek as soon as I can, and like I said, get your mind out of the gutter. Robinson needs help and he asked me because he knows I have good instincts."

"He knows you're a good snooper," Simon said.

Nikki didn't even respond. "I want you two to think about this. There is likely a killer in this group. It's not a huge group of people. You two are now on the *inside*, so to speak. I am the coordinator, but I think since you two will be involved in everything going on this week from journaling and crying out your feelings..."

"We don't cry, we breathe through them," Simon said.

"Whatever. While you're *breathing* through your feelings, you can be listening and watching the others. I'm going to bed now and then when you two get up, which will be when I get up at the crack of dawn—doesn't matter that it's almost the crack anyway—we will have coffee together and go over each one of the members. Then the three of us are going to get buddy-buddy with them. We'll each take a handful and see what we can come up with."

"I don't want to do that. It feels so icky wrong," Simon said.

Marco nodded. "It does feel wrong, Nikki. I do not think that it is a good idea."

"Oh yeah. Here are your choices, boys. Let a killer run loose on the vineyard. That's one choice. Or help me help the police and I won't tell Derek about the hundred thousand dollars you spent to become members of this group."

"You wouldn't," Simon said.

"Try me."

Marco looked at Nikki, then to Simon. "I think she would."

"See you in the morning. Coffee is at seven. I'll have the list already made."

Marco turned and smiled, giving her a little wave. Simon slammed the door behind them. She laughed, knowing that both the boys of summer were as in on this as she was. They just had very different ways of expressing themselves. Simon liked to use his dramatic flair and Marco played coy and sweet, but she knew when the coffee was steaming hot in the morning, her pals would be right there with her going over her list of suspects and ready to track a killer.

Ten

THE boys had joined Nikki for coffee as she'd predicted. She'd gotten up earlier than usual, even though she'd had only a few hours of sleep. It was just past six when she woke up, much to the dismay of Ollie, who'd slept on Derek's side of the bed. Nikki hadn't fought him. She'd been too tired and he was a warm body.

She hemmed and hawed about calling Derek. It would have been past nine in New York. He'd gotten in, in the middle of the night, so she justified holding off giving him a call and apprising him as to what had happened. It was possible, even likely, he was still asleep. She knew that he wouldn't be meeting old man Vicente until lunchtime. Deep down she knew that the real reason she wasn't making that phone call just yet was because of the reaction she would likely get on the other end; Derek was going to come unglued when he heard about what happened.

She'd had time alone while drinking her first cup of coffee to consider what she knew about the murder.

First, there was Alan Sansi. It seemed like the logical place to start. She opened up her laptop and set up a new document that she titled YAMIMOTO MURDER. Aunt Cara would be proud. She really should call her and get her professional input, but she wasn't even sure which country Cara was in these days. Since her retirement, she'd become a whirlwind traveler. Her aunt saved a lot of money during her years on the force and had herself a nice sum in her 401(k). She deserved to be enjoying it. But it was times like these that Nikki really missed her and wished she could get her input.

She typed in Alan Sansi's name and her first impressions of him: TRUE TO HIS CAUSE. Then she asked herself the question she would ask herself about each one of the members. What could be a possible motive? With Alan, Nikki wasn't sure. But he'd behaved oddly and had had that argument she'd witnessed with Iwao. And it seemed to have something to do with his daughter, who, from all angles, Nikki figured had to be Sierra. She'd been in that photo with his son. *Iwao's son.* Nikki would have to get in touch with Robinson and tell him the latest she'd learned and that he needed to find out where Jen Yamimoto was located. She should have tried to ask Mizuki if Jen was in Japan or the United States.

There was another thought that came to mind about Alan, but it was so far out there. Then again, nothing about murder was ever really logical. Maybe so in the killer's mind, but not for anyone else. Could Alan Sansi have killed Iwao because Alan knew Iwao didn't believe in his theories? Could Alan's *ego* be the culprit? Wouldn't that be ironic?

Maybe he knew that Iwao thought his philosophies were "horseshit," as the dead man had so eloquently put it. Could that have bothered someone like an Alan Sansi, a man who supposedly had no ego and lived only from the soul? It was a thought she'd have to dig deeper into to see if there was any merit to it. There were a few angles with Alan Sansi, but first she'd have to find out if the guru had even disappeared long enough from the train car to murder Iwao.

She listed everyone else she could think of, and the next suspect to stand out was Juan Gonzales. Not because Nikki knew of any concrete motive, but because of the way Iwao had reacted toward Juan. There had been some kind of underlying irritation coming from Iwao toward Juan. She wasn't sure if Juan had even been aware of the hostility Iwao seemed to be emitting, but she was pretty sure Lulu and Alan had picked up on it, and she would find a way to bring the subject up with them and see what they had to say. There was also this business of a note that Iwao had received from Juan when he arrived in the hotel. Nikki would have to ask any of the Housekeeping staff if they had seen a note.

Juan had acted clueless when it came to the note. If she could get inside Juan Gonzales's head, maybe she'd learn something. Or better yet, she would get into Iwao Yamimoto's room to see what she could find. She thought she'd made a decent impression on Mizuki and that in itself should get her in the door. But the snooping around could be another story. Maybe she could send Alyssa in as Housekeeping. No. Probably not a good idea. She'd already employed the boys in this situation; she couldn't risk Alyssa getting herself into a bad spot.

Once she'd made the list and the boys had gone over it with her, Simon looked up. "You seriously want us to infiltrate these people's lives?"

"I wouldn't call it that. Give me a break. Get to know them. That's what you're here for anyway, and then report back to me with anything you learn, like oddities, their idiosyncrasies, fears. Their lives, basically. If you fill me in, then I can analyze them and maybe come up with something."

"This is bad karma, Snow White."

"Karma shmarma. Face it, boys, I'm not the next Dalai Lama. Now, let's get out here and get this hike going."

Simon stood from the table. "I can't believe you gave me Rose Pearlman to pally up to today. She's so unpleasant."

"That's what you get for being nasty to me." She gave a flippant toss of her dark hair.

"Wait. Remember that we do have a purpose here and that is to enlighten ourselves," Marco said. "Have an open attitude toward Mrs. Pearlman, Simon." He crossed his arms. His melodic voice and accent always sounded so sweet no matter what he said.

Nikki shook her head. "You two throw me off. What? Do you change identities when you sleep at night? You know one day, you're the sage." She pointed to Simon. "Then the next day it's Marco's turn."

"We do balance each other out nicely." Marco laid a hand on Simon's shoulder.

"Yes, we do."

The three of them headed up to the conference area, and before long, Nikki's plan was rearranged because Alan Sansi had formed his own groups. She figured that the boys would know to roll with it and investigate whomever they were grouped with.

Alan came to her outside the bus that intended to take them to the park where they would begin their journey.

"With Iwao gone, I would like to have even numbers in the groups so everyone can participate fully in today's event. Is it possible for you to be a team player today?"

"Well, I guess I can do that, but I thought you wanted me to lead the group on the hike and point out the various sites."

He laid a hand on her shoulder. "There are no specific

leaders. I'm not even a leader necessarily. We are all each other's teachers."

Nikki really didn't want to hear any more of the "I teach you and you teach me" rhetoric. If there were no leaders in the world, it would be total anarchy. "Sure. I can do, be whatever you need." Agreeing was far easier than trying to argue her point.

Before they began the first leg of the hike, Alan addressed everyone again. "Last night was difficult. Today is a new day, yet we don't forget yesterday, but instead we move forward and breathe through our intentions today. You may dedicate this hike and what you learn today to Iwao and his life, or to yourself, or to someone else. Feel free to share, talk as you walk, or simply absorb the nature around you. Whatever you are guided to do is what you are supposed to do."

Oh, brother. Was there no structure? No basis in reality here? It was like Gestalt therapy gone wild. Nikki liked Alan fine, and she knew this was what he believed in and preached. But come on, sometimes you *had* to do what needed to be done and not just go the way the wind blows.

They reached their destination and Nikki momentarily played head of the class by describing some of the native plants and possible wildlife they might come across. A glance at Alan told her to let everyone go off willy-nilly, except for the pairs he'd come up with. Nikki was paired with Ruben Pearlman, who did not come across as either a sociopath, psychopath, or really any type of killer. However, she reminded herself of something Aunt Cara would tell her, "Information can come from the most obscure places and people. And when it comes, you may not recognize the value in it until somewhere down the line."

The hike through the park happened to be one of Nikki's favorite pastimes. She wished she could've brought Ollie because he enjoyed it, too. The typically lazy dog would finally spring forth to life with all the scents surrounding the area. A lushness swept across the area and displayed itself in green, gold, and auburn foliage. The earthen scents that covered the park could be detected only in the wine country, reminding one of a simple, light, and fruity dessert. The redwoods gave off their own heady, earthy scent. Nikki couldn't imagine ever leaving Napa Valley. This was her home now. She'd finally felt like she had roots after having none for so long. Aunt Cara had given her some stability in Los Angeles and she'd been the only parent Nikki remembered. She vaguely recalled her biological mother, who she knew was still alive in the hill country of Tennessee, but she shoved away any memories of that woman (and pretty much her entire family, sans her aunt) because they weren't exactly people she wanted displayed in picture frames on her wall.

After about fifteen minutes of everyone doing as Alan suggested, which was taking in the beauty and meditating on it, silences broke with pairs of people as they began talking and asking each other questions. Nikki did find that fascinating about human nature—people were ever curious. She just happened to get a double dose of curiosity when she entered the world and had been that way since she could remember.

"Do you like living in New York?" Nikki asked.

Ruben Pearlman, whose breathing was somewhat labored, nodded. "Yes and no. I've lived there all of my life. I'm newly retired and would like to move somewhere less fast paced."

"Like here?" Nikki asked.

"This would be wonderful, but probably as expensive as Manhattan or close, and Rose wouldn't have it. I had to beg and plead with her to come on this trip with me. A tad too country for her. I'm sure she's not exactly enjoying the hike, but it's good for her, and I keep thinking that with time she'll come to appreciate the lessons Alan teaches us."

"Haven't you been members for a while?"

"Yes, but Rose has only visited the places she's really interested in, like Hawaii or Fiji. She likes the travel part of this deal, not necessarily the workshops. She wanted to go to Bali, where we were supposed to go on this event, but since they had to cancel the locale and have it here, she wanted to hang back home. I told her it would be wonderful and begged her to join me still. My wife doesn't realize that we may not be able to travel as much as we used to, and we may have to move from Manhattan no matter what she wants. I hate to admit it, but I might also have to withdraw our membership in the group." He looked down and kept walking.

"Do you mind if I ask you why?"

"Finances. Money is tight for us. I made a bad deal not that long ago that has hurt us, and our lifestyle will have to change."

"I'm sorry about that."

Ruben waved a hand. "It's okay. It really is. If there is one thing that I have come to realize by being a part of this group, it is that it does not matter how many dollars are in your bank account, or if you have designer furniture or clothes, or drive a Mercedes, or whatever it is that you think floats your boat. None of it matters all that much if you're not happy in here." He pointed to his heart.

Nikki stopped for a moment and he halted along with her. "You get this, don't you?" He did. Ruben Pearlman was for real, and for the first time since she'd heard all of Alan's philosophies, she believed that Ruben Pearlman was enlightened.

"I hope I do. It took me a long time to understand that. My wife is still out there floating around in her Donna

Karan outfits and spa treatments, none of which are wrong or bad, but they don't make her happy. Nothing makes her happy. If she gained the happiness that I finally got, then all of the fringe would be icing on the cake."

"You're pretty cool," Nikki said.

"Thanks." His face turned red. Could that have been from embarrassment or from how hard he was working on the hike?

"What did you do before retirement?"

"I've been heavily involved in various media productions. I worked for years in the record industry, but with the transition it's taken over the last few years, I had to branch out a bit. At my age that wasn't easy. I dabbled in some movie production stuff and that's when things turned sour for me. Not that long ago I kind of had to back out of that."

"I understand that. I used to act."

"Tough business," he replied.

"Don't I know it." How was she going to get him to talk about the other members? His background was interesting and he'd been confirming her first impressions of him as being a stand-up guy. Now she wanted to know if he had any insight into any of the others. The best way was to ask. She glanced up ahead of her and saw that Simon was jabbering away with Marco. Okay, that was not what they were asked to do. She gritted her teeth. They knew plenty about one another and neither of them was a killer.

She needed to swing for the fences here. "What do you think about the other members in this group? You obviously are getting Alan's message loud and clear, but how about everyone else?"

He laughed. "Everyone goes at their own pace, I suppose. I don't know. My wife, who I love, obviously has a way to go."

"What about Iwao Yamimoto? What do you think about what happened?"

Nikki noticed Ruben's upper lip twitch at this question. She'd looked at him while asking because when trying to get information out of others, facial expressions could give a lot away, and his expression surprised her. He actually seemed nervous about the question. But couldn't that be because she was speaking of the recently dead—the murdered dead? Could be.

He took a minute before answering and she got the impression that he was thinking about the best way to answer her question.

"I knew Iwao fairly well, and he was a decent man and a hard worker. But enlightened? My impression was that Iwao still had quite a trip to make."

"Really?"

"Iwao was not in this thing for enlightenment. He was in this for money."

Either Iwao revealed this to Ruben like he had with her, or else Ruben had his number. She couldn't help wondering how well they knew each other and started to ask when Rose Pearlman huffed and puffed herself right up next to them.

"Ruben? Ruben? Can I talk with you? I need a rest. My feet are killing me. Why don't we trade partners for a while?"

Ruben looked from Nikki to his wife and to Hayden Sansi, who shrugged and said, "Fine with me."

"Okay," Ruben replied but not sounding all that enthused about this new pairing.

Nikki wasn't too happy either. Although she hadn't figured Ruben to be one to have anything to offer as far as Iwao's life and death at first, she now felt that she was wrong. Ruben Pearlman did have information that could come in handy somehow somewhere. Again Aunt Cara's saying sank in: You never know where information might lead you.

Hayden came up by her as the Pearlmans hung back.

"Thank God. Her husband is a saint to keep putting up with her. That woman is a total bore. All I heard about was how plum wine is so much better than California wines, and how when her husband would do business in Japan he'd come back with her wine from there. Boring."

"Ruben Pearlman does business in Japan?"

"I think so from the way she talked. But if I hear another mention of plum wine, I think I'll kill her. Oh, God." She brought her hands to her mouth. "Bad choice in words."

Nikki didn't even hear Hayden for a few moments, her mind whirling with this new revelation. Okay, so Ruben had admitted knowing Iwao outside this group, and yes, a lot of people do business overseas, but could the connection between Iwao and Ruben be tighter than Nikki's initial impressions? Had they done business together? Was Ruben going to tell her that when his wife interrupted them? And if not, what did that mean? She needed to find out exactly what ties, if any, Ruben and Iwao had between them.

Eleven

WITH her brain still in overdrive, Nikki tried hard to switch gears. The Japanese connection between Iwao and Ruben could be completely fruitless and simply wishful thinking, and right now she needed to turn her focus on Hayden Sansi. She could not waste this opportunity. Befriend the woman. Get her talking about something she'd surely want to talk about.

"You're getting married. When is the wedding?"

Hayden lit up. "Only three months away. Rich is wonderful. Look at him up there."

Rich Higgins was walking alongside Alan, and they looked to be in an intense conversation.

"He wanted to get married sooner, but he knows how important it is for me to have the perfect wedding."

"Sounds like a good guy. We all dream of the fairy-tale wedding, I think. At least women do." She thought about Derek for a minute. Was there a wedding in her future?

"And Rich has been so helpful. He's right there with me, planning away. He's going to fit so well into my family. My mom and dad adore him and think he's perfect."

What was it with Hayden and perfection? By the way she made that comment about her parents loving her fiancé, Nikki wondered if she was trying to convince herself of this. "That's great. I guess you met him because he publishes your dad's books."

She nodded. "He's only recently taken over the active role as publisher. He's always been involved with the business, but it was his mother who started the company, and that's who my dad's relationship was with. His mom lost her battle to cancer last year and Rich had to fill in for her. He and my dad are still negotiating how their relationship works on both a business and personal level."

"Really? I don't understand. They get along, don't they?"

"Sure, sure." Hayden nodded emphatically. "But Rich does things differently from his mom. He's a better businessperson in reality. He understands bottom lines and how to manage marketing campaigns. He knows how to grow a business."

"His mother didn't?" Nikki was perplexed by what Hayden was telling her. "She must've understood business to some degree. She seems to have built a good business with so much of it around your dad's work."

"Yes. True."

That was all she added.

"Right," Nikki said. "I don't mean to pry." Sure she didn't. "But you're kind of indicating that the waters are troubled between your dad and Rich."

"Am I? That's not what I said. I said that Rich does things differently from his mom and that kind of makes my dad, I guess, irritated at times."

Nikki did know how to twist words, but she also knew

how to read between the lines and when she was pushing the envelope—like now. "I did gather your father is pretty loyal to Inspiritus. In fact, last night Iwao had been talking to your dad and brother about publishing their books in Japan."

She laughed. "My dad would never do that, even if he thinks that Rich is a little too marketing oriented and isn't prone to *allowing things to go and flow*. He finds Rich to be not as sage-like as his mother, Jade, had been."

"Jade? Kind of a different name for an older woman."

"She changed it back in the seventies. I think it used to be Amy or something."

"Ah," Nikki replied. "Your dad then had a strong loyalty to Rich's mom and he'd never consider another publisher?"

"Not in a million years."

"Your brother seemed interested in speaking with Iwao about it."

Hayden laughed at this, too. "Yeah, my brother, Eli. He wishes he was another one of my dad, but he's no carbon copy. Dad keeps trying to convince him that he has to follow his own dreams and not try to pattern himself after him, and Eli keeps trying to convince Dad that being like him is his dream. No one's buying it, though. The facts are that Eli wants to be like Dad because it's lucrative."

"Doesn't sound too enlightened."

Hayden nodded. "Well, not all of us can be like dear old Dad, and I can't blame Eli for seeing a good thing and wanting to hang on to it. My father helps us all out, but at a certain point he and my mom have to cut the financial ties between us and let us flop or soar."

"And you look to be soaring." Nikki wondered about the nepotism in the family.

Hayden seemed to sense what she was getting at, even though Nikki tried to keep the edge out of her tone. "I soar because I've proven to both of my folks that I'm worth working for their business. I keep things organized. Believe it or not, organizational skills aren't what my parents are great at. I'm a Virgo, so it's by nature that I can keep things together."

"You do seem to be pretty together. How about your sister, how is she today?" Sierra Sansi had not joined the hike that morning.

"My sister could be better. Last night when she found Mr. Yamimoto, it was difficult and horrible for her, for more reasons than just finding him."

"What do you mean?"

"Well, Mr. Yamimoto was almost family about a year ago."

"What?" Nikki practically rubbed her hands together, like this was about to get really good.

"Sierra was engaged to Iwao's nephew, Jen."

"Nephew?" Not his son?

"Yes. Jen Yamimoto met my sister through martial arts actually. It's a long story, but basically Jen broke my sister's heart and she's been on a downward spiral ever since."

"That's terrible. She's a martial artist?"

"Yes. An excellent one, too. Black belt. The whole nine yards. It's a shame for her to be where she's at in life. There's no need for it. She was really doing great. Sierra had some substance abuse problems when she was a teenager. Then Dad got her into karate and kickboxing. It mellowed her out and focused her, even though she could totally use her skills and knowledge to really hurt someone. I wish she'd get off of the direction she's going in and get back with it. My dad even lined her up with a major movie studio, like Paramount or something. She was helping choreograph different moves for dancers and even stunts for martial arts–type movies. That's how she met Jen. That was also what he did. Or does.

I'm not sure what he's doing actually. I think he could have gone back to Japan."

"Was he in L.A. before?"

"There and New York. Sierra insists he went home."

"Shouldn't he be told about his uncle?"

"Yes, I suppose that he should. Don't you think the police would handle that? Or his mistress?"

"Mizuki?" Nikki was kind of surprised. She'd understood that Mizuki was not the missus, but a mistress?

"Yes. Come on, everyone knows or knew that Mizuki was Mr. Yamimoto's mistress."

"I didn't. How did you?"

"I sorta figured it out. Then Sierra confirmed it, but my dad wouldn't let us talk about it. He doesn't like gossip. Says it can ruin the soul, because it is too difficult to determine what is truth and what isn't."

Nikki could see that Hayden didn't follow that philosophy and frankly, for her, that was a good thing at the moment. "It's interesting, the six degrees of separation. Sierra met Iwao's nephew and they were involved, and Iwao was a part of this group."

"No, Mr. Yamimoto actually didn't join until after Jen and my sister hooked up. Mr. Yamimoto is really the only one who has been able to get a place as a member because he pulled the 'we know each other' thing."

"How does someone get to be a member of the elite group anyway?"

"They apply. They put down a deposit, send in their applications, and then my father makes decisions on who is accepted."

"Do a lot of people apply?"

"You bet. Thousands."

"Thousands?" Shocking. There were thousands of people willing to part with a lot—*a lot*—of money all to be graced by Alan's presence and words? "How does your dad decide, out of these thousands of applicants, who gets in and who doesn't, and how often do they rotate in and out?"

"Good questions. But why do you want to know? You're not thinking of applying, are you?" Hayden asked.

"No. I'm curious how my two pals made it in." She laughed. "They aren't exactly as light-filled as some others I've met here." Only one actually showed any hint of enlightenment—Ruben.

"That's the ticket. Dad chooses people who probably need it more than anyone else. He can read between the lines in everyone's application and he can tell who is serious about it, who needs the most growth, and who will work hard at it. He likes to choose couples because many times there is more growth for an individual if their significant other is also on the same journey."

"Ah, makes sense. But Iwao used his connection with his nephew to join the group."

"Sort of. Yes. I shouldn't have said that but it's true. My dad knew he wasn't here for all the right reasons. Then again most members here aren't. They discover the real reasons once they belong."

"So, your dad knows everything there is to know about these people."

"I suppose. But Dad is funny. He forgets half of it. His focus is much more on the present than anyone's past or future. I'm the one who keeps everyone's information together."

"You do?"

"Yes. Someone has to," Hayden replied.

"You have everyone's application that's in this group?"

"I do."

"Do you read them?" Nikki asked.

"No. That's private."

Nikki wanted those applications. "I suppose you keep them back at your parents' offices?"

"No. Not the members that are with us. I bring them. There may be an occasion where my dad needs them for some reason." Hayden stopped and bent down to retie her shoe.

"Right." A faint twinge of electricity shot through Nikki's gut and out through her extremities. She could not outright ask Hayden to see these applications. Before she got too excited, she'd have to ask Simon and Marco what exactly existed on them. They would know. It had to be more than name and address. Thank you very much.

Everyone made it to the turnaround point, and fortunately, it had turned out to be an amazing day—clear and crisp, which helped on the hike, keeping everyone from getting overheated. Nikki had been concerned about Ruben Pearlman on the hike up. He'd appeared pretty out of shape.

At the turnaround, waiting for everyone was a picnic lunch that a catering company had prepared. They'd brought the food up ahead of the hikers and a group of waiters were now handing out the lunches to them.

While Nikki planted herself on a boulder and ate a veggie sandwich, Hayden moved and gravitated toward her fiancé, Rich. Now there was a man Nikki needed to talk to. Really she needed to talk to all of them, but what if she could get ahold of those applications each of them had filled out? Could be worthwhile. She had to figure out how to do it. She could go straight to Robinson and tell him about them. He'd get a search warrant or whatever they needed to collect classified material. Were those applications even classified? It wasn't as if Alan Sansi was a psychiatrist or doctor of some sort. There had to be a way and she'd find it.

Hayden Sansi had filled her with tons of food for fodder, from the Sierra-Jen-Iwao connection and the way Iwao manipulated his way into this group, to information about Rich and his mother and Inspiritus. But the coup was the applications. There were answers there. Nikki knew there had to be. There were lots of answers she'd already learned. The problem was figuring how to fit them into the questions and put it all together. Once she accomplished that, the last piece would appear—the one that revealed to her who had murdered Iwao Yamimoto.

Twelve

WHEN the group made it back to the winery at about two o'clock, they were all given an hour break before the afternoon "dream board" session would begin. Nikki wasn't quite sure what this dream board session consisted of, but Simon and Marco were excited about it.

"It's a lot of fun. It's where we put our wants and desires in every aspect of our lives onto a poster board, frame it, and there you have it. The universe grabs hold and everything you put out there manifests itself in its own way," Simon said, walking with Nikki toward the hotel, where she wanted to check on things with Alyssa.

Marco had gone ahead to make sure the room where the dream board thing was supposed to take place was set up properly.

"Sounds great. But guess what I need you to manifest? A killer. You two lovebirds were too busy sharing each other's dreams and visions to chat with the suspects while on that hike, and that was not our deal."

"Hush your mouth, Snow White. While you were busy digging deep into everyone's life, and not for the reasons we're here for—"

"Uh-uh-uh. Let me correct you there, my friend. You may be here for other reasons, but not me."

"As I was saying." He crossed his arms and kept walking. "You didn't notice that I had a little talk with Juan Gonzales and he is an interesting guy."

"Really? Look at you. Good boy." She had not noticed Simon talking with Juan, but she'd been wrapped up, first with Ruben and then Hayden. "What did you find out?"

"That Juan produces low-budget movies and usually makes them down in Mexico. Foreign film stuff."

"That is kind of interesting." Nikki remembered that Jen Sansi and Sierra met on a movie set, and that Sierra's father was the one to help her get involved in that. Was there a connection between any of them and Juan, and if so, what?

"You think that is good. Check this. Juan and Iwao did a movie together, set in Japan. One of those kung-fu types. Juan still distributes the DVD. He said that it didn't do too well in the States, but in Mexico and Japan it's done a decent job."

"Now we're talking," Nikki said. "This is good stuff. You're right."

Simon clucked his tongue. "I know."

Nikki had to think all of this through, but there were streams of connections here with some of these people and they were outside of the S.E.E. group themselves and she couldn't help thinking those connections were what might have gotten Iwao killed.

"What else did you find out from him?" Nikki asked.

"What more do you want?"

"Like how did the business go down between Iwao and Juan? Were they still on good terms before, you know..."

Simon sliced his finger across his neck.

"Yes, before Iwao was murdered. Do you have to be so crass?"

"I'm not crass, Snow White. I'm honest, and that's what we all should be."

No comment.

"I'm sorry but that's all I've got. It's not so easy to drag personal info out of people, you know."

Nikki never seemed to have that problem. "You're getting the knack of it, though. Good for you. Okay, keep snooping. I appreciate the work, Watson."

"You're high, Sherlock."

"I wish," she said.

He raised his eyebrows. She socked him in the shoulder. "Not really. Stay the course." She touched the side of his right eye. "Keep on the lookout." Then she touched his ear. "And keep on listening. I have a question for you."

"Why am I not surprised?"

"The application process that you went through to become a S.E.E. member—can you tell me a little bit about that?"

"You thinking of joining us?"

"No. But I do know that Hayden Sansi keeps all of those applications and even has them on hand here at the workshop."

"How do you know that and what are you thinking?" Simon asked.

"She told me herself. I'm thinking that there could be some answers in those applications."

"How do you figure? You don't think someone is going to write in their application, 'I have a tendency to think homicidal thoughts and may act on them.'"

"Of course not. But a lot of times when you read between

the lines, you can see some issues standing out. What did the applications consist of?"

"We answered a ton of questions about why we wanted to be involved, our background, all of that. Each answer we filled in was almost a page, sometimes more."

Nikki nodded. "That's what I'm talking about. Have to get ahold of those applications and see if I can find a clue of sorts."

"How do you plan to do that?"

"I'm not sure." She shook her head. "This is one of those things I'll have to think on. Right now, I have to see how Alyssa is doing, holding down the fort, and I really should try and get ahold of your brother."

"Oh boy, I wouldn't want to have that conversation."

"I'm not exactly looking forward to it myself."

"Good luck. I'm going to go prop up my feet and relax a little before I start dreaming some more. I think I'll go rest my weary head on one of the tables in the spa, maybe get one of the girls to rub my temples. It's hard work being a snoop. I don't know how you do it."

"Yeah, you better go and get those temples rubbed," she replied. Where did he come from? But she loved him all the same. She couldn't imagine life without him getting on every last one of her nerves.

NIKKI was surprised not to find Alyssa at the front desk, and the reception phone hooked up to one ring on the voicemail. Something was wrong. Alyssa never took off. She was one of the most responsible people she knew. Her sixth sense kicked in. She dialed Alyssa's cell phone number and it also went immediately to voicemail. What was going on? While Nikki was pacing back and forth, trying to think of what to do, the phone rang. She picked up immediately before it could go to voicemail.

"Malveaux Spa and Winery. How may I help you?"

"Nikki?"

It was Alyssa. "Oh my gosh, where are you? I'm at the front desk and you're not here. Is everything okay?"

"I'm sorry. I had to go. It's Petie. We're at the hospital."

Thirteen

NIKKI sat next to Alyssa in the treatment room inside the hospital, holding her hand and watching Petie get a cast wrapped around his arm while a nurse demonstrated talking Elmo for the tyke. Thank God he'd only broken his arm. When Nikki had heard the words "hospital" and "Petie," she'd thought the worst. But the little guy had apparently been playing on the jungle gym when another toddler decided to be malicious, as toddlers can be, and pushed him off. That toddler had been punished with a time-out, but Nikki would still like to bend him over her knee. Petie wound up landing wrong and making a clean break in his arm. However, with his condition, he needed to be monitored and looked after with a bit more care than the average child.

"Thank you for coming. I'm sorry I had to take off suddenly and leave the hotel."

"Please don't be sorry. He comes first. The hotel is fine.

You know that. Most of the guests were with us anyway, and those who weren't would have found help if they needed it. I'm just happy Petie is going to be okay. How are you?" Nikki realized that this had to be stressful for Alyssa, even though there was relief that her child was not hurt worse than he was. Alyssa and this baby had been through more than enough, and any hiccup along the way had to be hard to deal with.

"I'm okay. I really am. Look at him. He's so precious."

Petie was laughing his head off at Elmo, while the doctor wrapped the cast. "Yes he is."

"How about you? How are you with all the craziness at the hotel? I haven't even talked to you about last night's murder. I heard about it this morning from one of the members. He brought down a suitcase that didn't belong to him, he said. I forgot about it with all of this. I stored it in the back room."

"Oh. That shouldn't be a problem. Did anyone else come down and claim it?"

Alyssa shook her head. "No."

"Who brought it down?" Nikki asked.

"Cute guy. I don't know, maybe thirty, in good shape. Dark hair, on the tall side, and lean build. Nice guy, kind of weird, though, because he wouldn't look me in the eyes, and that always gives me the heebie-jeebies."

Nikki figured Alyssa was talking about Kurt Kensington. She'd checked him in yesterday and noticed the same thing. He was either busy fiddling with his hands, looking down, or looking away. "Well, do you know who the suitcase belongs to?"

"He didn't say. After he left, I pulled back the cover on the plastic info card and it read IWAO YAMIMOTO."

Nikki sat up ramrod straight. "Yamimoto? You sure?"

"Don't think I'd forget a name like that."

"Iwao Yamimoto was the man who was murdered last night."

"Oh. I didn't know. Oh, my God!" Alyssa replied.

The doctor looked up at them.

Nikki lowered her voice. "Yeah. I think that must have been Kurt Kensington, one of the S.E.E. members, who brought down the suitcase. What I want to know is, why did he have Iwao's suitcase and why did he only bring it down this morning?"

Fourteen

BY the time Nikki made it back to the winery, the dream board session was in full force inside the meeting room. Round tables had been brought into the room, which already contained sofas, a fireplace, and books that served as the winery's library. It was the oldest room besides the mansion on the property and was the room that the rest of the hotel had been built around. Derek and Simon's dad had built this separate room outside of his home so he could boast about having a private library. He'd had it constructed in that same Italian style that the now surrounding hotel and spa had been done in and it used to double as a party room.

Alyssa stopped by with Petie to see what the dream board thing was all about. Nikki had mentioned it to her in the hospital. Everyone turned and looked as they walked into the room. Simon and Marco saw that Petie had a cast on and immediately came over.

"What happened?" Simon asked.

Alyssa told him about the unfortunate jungle gym incident.

"That's terrible. Poor boy." Marco's accent sounded even more charming when directed at a little guy. Marco kissed Petie's cheek and retrieved an ink marker off one of the tables. "Can I draw something on the cast?" he asked Alyssa.

"Of course."

Marco drew a smiling monkey and signed his name. Petie watched, curious as he drew it, and started laughing along with the adults when he was finished and then made goofy monkey faces.

Simon then took over and drew an elephant next to the monkey. This was a big hit, too.

"This looks interesting." Alyssa nodded in the direction of the room.

It was pretty strange. Here were adults flipping through magazines, writing down affirmations on note cards, and cutting and pasting their "wants and desires" onto their poster boards. It looked like a preschool classroom only with bigger people. Petie wanted down from his mom's arms and was ready to charge toward the art supplies.

"I don't think so." Alyssa pulled him in tighter. "I better get him home. I wanted to see it for myself, though. Not such a bad idea. Maybe I should do one."

"You should," Simon said. "It's so much fun. We're all really exploring our creative sides."

Marco nodded. "It is a good time. Come and join us."

"I'd love to, but I can't. I should get Petie down for a nap. It's been a hard day for him."

"Wait a minute," Simon said. "Do you have magazines and markers at home?"

"I'm a mother. I have both," Alyssa said.

Simon went back to his table and brought over a rolled-up poster board. "Maybe while he's taking a nap, or even another time, you can do one for yourself."

"Thanks, Simon. I think I will." Alyssa took the poster and tucked it under her free arm.

"What are you going to put on your dream board?" Nikki asked.

"Oh, I don't know. I suppose for starters a heart—a healthy one for Petie."

Petie pointed to his heart and said, "Heart."

"You're so smart," Nikki told him, choking back some emotion. He was so sweet.

"Then who knows? Maybe a mansion on the ocean." Alyssa laughed. "And a photo of some hot guy."

Nikki laughed. "Who do you think is hot?"

"I don't know. I'm kind of into rock stars." She laughed.

"Oh honey, who isn't?" Simon said.

"You know who looks like a rock star? That cutie Detective Robinson. He's *soooo* sexy. Nikki even said once that he looks like Lenny Kravitz."

"That is true." A vision of Detective Robinson came to mind and Nikki had a lightbulb moment. "Hey, what are you doing Sunday night?"

She shrugged. "I don't know. At home with this guy." She tickled Petie's tummy.

"No. You're not. I'm having a little dinner party at my place. You and Petie are coming." She turned to Simon and Marco. "And so are you two."

"Oh goodie. I love dinner parties," Simon said. "They're so chic."

"We should get back to our projects. Nikki, you'll join us, no?" Marco asked.

"Sure."

The boys said their good-byes to Alyssa and Petie and went back to their table.

"You're doing a dinner party while trying to run this charade?" Alyssa asked.

"I'll burn off some steam with some friends. Besides, the members are on their own for dinner that night."

"Great. Count us in. I better get going. Looks like you're being summoned."

Nikki spotted Alan motioning for her to come over. What now? She said good-bye to Alyssa and Petie and made her way over to the great guru, rubbing her hands together. She knew it might wind up being a lot on her plate, but it would be worth it because not only could she be good at playing detective, she might also make a decent matchmaker.

"HI, Nikki. We were concerned about you. We started on the dream boards about an hour ago," Alan said.

"I'm sorry. My friend Alyssa's little boy broke his arm and I met her at the hospital. He has some health problems and she needed the support."

"You're a good friend," Alan said.

"I did what anyone else would do."

"No. Not everyone else is kind, and I can see that you are kind and always concerned about others."

For some reason, Alan was making her nervous. What was it? She couldn't pinpoint it, but it was there. "Thanks. Well, is there anything you'd like me to do?"

"No. I don't think so. You're more than welcome to do your own board or see what others have done and help them put their intentions out into the universe."

"Right." Had these people forgotten that a man had been murdered less than twenty-four hours ago? Nikki moved away from him quickly. What was bothering her about him? Was it the attitude?

She decided to pass on the board, and headed on over to

where Simon sat flapping his lips with Rose Pearlman, Eli Sansi, and Kurt Kensington. Now there sat an interesting group of folks. Wonder if Simon still had his radar on?

She pulled a chair up to the table.

"Oh, Snow White, good. You're joining us. Poor Petie and his mommy." He frowned. "I hope Alyssa really does do her own board. It'll be good therapy for her. She needs some mommy time. So, we were just sharing our dream boards with one another."

"Great." Nikki mustered a smile.

"I'm going first." Simon stood and held his board up to the group. "This here is my dream home with Marco."

Kind of surprising to see it wasn't set amongst the vineyard. Simon had cut and pasted on a photo of an ubermodern apartment.

"See here. It's in Manhattan." He pointed to a view through a window of Central Park. "And we would shop at all the best stores with our baby, right here."

Nikki's jaw dropped. *Baby?* Simon pointed to a cherubic-looking baby.

"You want a baby?" Rose asked, sounding as astonished as Nikki felt.

"Of course. What? Just because we're gay, you don't think we might want children?"

"I do think that a mother and a father should be involved. Not two daddies," Rose replied, staring him down like a grizzly bear readying for the kill.

Simon's eye back was just as evil. Oh, no. This could be trouble. "Let me tell you what children need . . ."

Nikki interrupted, hoping to head off a full escalation here. She stood and put a hand on Simon's back. "Children need love, and I am sure someone as spiritually devoted as Mrs. Pearlman would agree." Nikki flashed a huge smile.

Rose Pearlman recoiled some and looked to be pouting,

but she shut her trap and that was the outcome they were all looking for.

"How about you, Kurt, is it?" Nikki looked straight at the man with the crew cut and beady ice green eyes that seemed to sear through her. She could see how Simon found him attractive because the man was edgy—almost intimidating—and Simon had a tendency to be attracted to the intense types. Lucky for him, Marco could be intense but balanced it out with his charm and good nature. He certainly didn't have that edge this guy did. "Let's see your dream board." It was really strange to be asking grown men to see their dream boards. Maybe she should have called it something a bit more masculine—vision board, maybe?

Kurt hesitated, then slowly stood and picked his board up from the seat next to him. There was an audible gasp. Even Nikki caught herself.

The only word to describe Kurt's board was "violent."

No one spoke for a few seconds.

Once again, it was Rose Pearlman who took a stab at it. "What the hell is that?"

Kurt glared at her. "My board," he muttered.

"I understand that. But what does it represent? I understood his," she said, gesturing at Simon, "although I still think he and his partner, or whatever they call each other, are nuts for wanting a kid."

Simon tensed. Nikki grabbed and squeezed his arm.

Kurt shifted his weight to one leg. "I want to be a novelist like Stephen King, man. I want to write horror books and flicks."

Nikki studied the board. It had images of people on the board, but then next to them, Kurt had written words like, "monster," "slaughtered," "kill." One of the photos was...Wait a minute...She squinted. "Excuse me, but that looks like Iwao Yamimoto," she said.

Kurt shrugged. "Maybe it is." He smiled.

Like ice being dropped down the inside of her shirt, Nikki's body grew freezing-ass cold. "That's wrong."

"Why?" Kurt asked.

Simon and Rose Pearlman looked at each other, and this time it wasn't with mutual dislike, but mutual fear.

"Well, because the man was just murdered last night. That's why. And you have a photo of him and next to it you wrote 'slaughtered.' Don't you think that's wrong?" Nikki asked. She wasn't afraid of this bully.

"How do you know that Iwao Yamimoto was not a terrorist and that a hit man from the CIA needed to take him down? Huh? Have you ever thought of that?" Kurt stared at her.

Was this guy serious? "A terrorist? He was Japanese," Nikki replied.

"Do you know that for sure? Maybe he was Chinese."

No one said a word. Then Kurt Kensington started cracking up. "Oh, my God, you people don't think I'm serious, do you? I told you that my dream and goal is to be a bestselling horror or even espionage-type author. And I want to write horror movies. Freddie Kruger type. That's all there is to it. Sorry you don't find my humor amusing."

"I'm afraid I don't." Nikki figured at this point she had nothing to lose by being straightforward. She had witnesses in case the guy went berserk or she was later found dead— not a comforting thought—but at least Simon and Rose Pearlman would know whom to point a finger at. "By the way, were you the guest who brought down Mr. Yamimoto's suitcase to the front desk this morning?"

Kurt didn't say anything for a second, but rather glowered at her. "Yes. So? The hotel obviously mixed our bags up."

"Why did you wait until the morning? You must have needed something from your bag last night, I would think."

"I had two bags. One I carry books in, like the one Mr. Yamimoto had. Last night we got in late and I didn't exactly feel like reading. I discovered it this morning when I went to get one of my books out."

"You actually carry an entire suitcase filled with books? And didn't you realize you had two of them in your room?" Nikki questioned.

Everyone at the table watched the ping-pong dialogue go on between them, heads flipping from one person to the next.

"I told you, I'm working on being an author. As far as the two look-alike suitcases, I can answer that. When I checked in, I asked the bellhop to bring my things up. I wasn't in my room when he did so, so he set them in the closet. I assume that's your protocol."

It was. Nikki nodded.

"Okay, then we went out for the train ride. I never changed so I never went into the closet. When we came back from the ride, I spotted the bag downstairs in the lobby set down by those palm tree plants you have, and that was where I'd set my things when I checked in. I figured the bellhop forgot the smaller bag. I picked it up and brought it into my room."

"What, and you fell asleep with your clothes on then?" She wasn't buying this at all.

"If you want to know, Ms. Sands, I sleep in the buff."

She wrinkled her nose, but remained quick on her toes. "Okay, then, what about the bag itself? A bag filled with books I would think would be pretty heavy. Couldn't you tell by the weight you had a different bag?"

"It was late. I'm strong. I work out a lot. I don't think about a pound or two here and there. Are you finished questioning me, Detective Sands? Or would you like to come to my room and see all of my books?"

Simon looked over at her warningly. Going alone to

Kurt's room was definitely not something she desired to do. "I believe you, Mr. Kensington, and trust me, I'm no detective." But the police might think it was odd. The first chance she had to speak with Robinson she would be sure and get this idiot on the detective's radar.

"Call me Kurt, please."

"Kurt, then." She tried to smile, but it was impossible. This guy epitomized creepiness and again Nikki had to wonder how he'd become a part of the S.E.E. group. She needed to get ahold of those applications that Hayden had told her about and find out what she could dig up on Kurt Kensington because at that moment all she could hear in her mind was David Byrne of the Talking Heads belting out "Psycho Killer" and the part where he sings *Run run away.*

Well, that was exactly what Nikki desired to do. Get away from Kurt the psycho.

Fifteen

STILL shaken after the dream board session by Kurt Kensington, Nikki had an hour and a half to get prepared for the winemaking event she was to host. Not a lot of time and still quite a bit to do. She needed to get ahold of Derek. What time was it in New York? Almost eight. He was probably at dinner. She also really needed to speak with Mizuki and see how the woman was faring. The lady knew more than she'd been able to tell Nikki. If only there was a way to really communicate with her.

She'd try. Sooner or later she'd get ahold of Derek. It wasn't as if he could change things here anyway, and he'd worry needlessly. He needed to work out the business between him and old man Vicente and she didn't want to distract him. Oh boy, though, if he caught whiff of what was going on around here without her being the one to tell him, she knew there'd be hell to pay.

What to do?

Her question was answered when she spotted Robinson coming down the stairs from the top room suites.

"Hey," she called out.

Robinson turned to her as he slipped his aviator sunglasses over his bad boy green eyes, same color green as the ivy that grew up the side of the walls of the hotel. He nodded in her direction and smoothly moved down the stairs. "Hey, yourself."

"How's it going?" she asked.

"Not great. I've got about a hundred-plus tourists who were on that train last night in different cars and several of them have plans to leave today. I've got as many men as I can conducting interviews and working on this thing. I've got my boss breathing down my back and I was upstairs trying to get something out of that geisha of Yamimoto's. I tell you my head is pounding."

"Geisha? She's not a geisha!"

"Isn't that what they call them in Japan? I don't think it's 'hooker.'" He looked at her over his shades.

She took a step back. "No. She's not a hooker or a geisha."

"What the hell is she then?"

"I don't know." God! Why did he fluster her? "Girlfriend?"

He laughed at that. "Yeah. No. Not a girlfriend, Sands. I'll give you 'sweetly paid mistress.'"

"Did you confirm then that he had a wife?"

"Yes, he does. But she's loco in the *cabeza*, like kamikaze style."

"What are you talking about?"

"She lives in some kind of mental institution there in Japan. From what I've been able to find out, the poor woman barely knows her name, much less who her husband is or was. She tried to slit her wrists a half dozen times before Yamimoto had her committed."

"Huh."

"Huh, what?" Robinson asked.

"I don't know, just, huh. I got the impression that Mizuki really loved Iwao."

Robinson crossed his arms and rocked back onto his cowboy boots. "Mizuki and Iwao? When did you get on a first-name basis with the vic and his, uh, mistress?"

"I did help coordinate this thing and so it's kind of natural that I would call people by their first names, not like you, the cop. Everyone is a last name to you. Even me."

"Even you? What am I supposed to call you?"

"My name might be good for starters. We are friends, sort of."

He pushed the shades back up onto the bridge of his nose. "I suppose we are sort of friends. So, friend. My gut says you got some info for me because I'm not buying the deal about you being the coordinator and having to get to know everyone on a first-name basis. What can you tell me?"

She breathed a deep sigh. "I don't know much from Iwao's *friend*. She doesn't speak any English."

"I noticed. An interpreter was supposed to meet me here, but hasn't shown. I'll have that guy's tail when I get ahold of him. She gave me nada. All I know is she ain't the wife. You got more?"

"I know that Iwao Yamimoto's nephew Jen Yamimoto dated Sierra Sansi and the breakup was ugly."

"I think we better sit down and do some talking."

She checked her watch. "I don't have much time right now. I have to get ready for this winemaking event I'm supposed to do for this group."

"Really, and how does winemaking enlighten?"

"You'd be surprised."

"Why don't I help you set up and you give me your scoopage?"

"I could use the help and I suppose I have gathered some *scoopage* together."

"Cool," he replied. "After you, Sands."

ROBINSON helped bring in boxes of wine for her while she set up the glasses inside the tasting room, which usually just smelled of cedar wood and wine but right now she could smell musk mixed in—it had to be Robinson. Simon and Marco would be bringing in the food shortly for her. They were doing appetizers for the evening to go with the various wines she'd chosen.

Nikki filled the detective in on all that she'd learned, or thought she'd learned, placing an emphasis on Kurt Kensington's odd behavior.

"That doesn't make sense, Sands. Here this guy is shoving this shit in your face with his dream board. That sounds kind of stupid. Killers are not typically stupid and in your face, unless they want to get caught. But a guy who does what he did with the poster thing is more like a wannabe. It's like someone who sees a mad guy in the media and writes in an anonymous note or calls in and says that he's the killer. It's an attention getter, but not the real deal." Robinson pulled a couple of bottles of Cabernet out, setting them on the counter in the tasting room.

The private tasting room was by far Nikki's favorite room at the winery. Painted in a dusky color, it felt warm and cozy, especially with a fire stoked in the corner fireplace. The area by the fireplace was set up like a living room with leather seating and shelves of books in the built-ins. It wasn't filled with books like the library, but it still contained some classics and also some newer fiction. The best part of the room was that the walls displayed the finest artwork Nikki had ever seen. There were acrylics, oils, and watercolors as well as some bronze sculpted pieces on tables throughout the room. When Derek's family built the place decades before, no expense had been spared, and Derek maintained that tradition, currently purchasing many local artists' pieces.

"Don't you think that Kurt displayed some really bizarre behavior? Shouldn't you check it out?"

"I plan to. But he's showboating, Sands. He's trying to get under people's skins. Freak them out, because that's what he is, a freak. I doubt he's a killer."

"I have to ask about the cork thing. Whoever is sick and demented enough to slice a man's throat and then stick a cork in his mouth, could be sick and demented enough to boast about it, even in a roundabout way. Couldn't that be what Kensington was doing?" Nikki saw some water spots on a few of the glasses and grabbed a towel to clean them off.

"We're looking at that angle. We're looking at all of it."

"But what do you think about the cork itself? Could it be a symbol, like, you know, 'Put a cork in it,' or 'Shut up'? Think about that. Maybe the killer murdered Iwao because he wanted to reveal a secret or he had something on the killer."

Robinson crossed his arms and rocked back onto his heels. "I only asked you to keep your eyes and ears open, not to go theorizing on me. It'll get you in trouble."

"All I'm saying is Kurt Kensington is not all there, and someone who puts a cork in their victim's mouth has a few screws loose."

"Killers do."

Nikki sighed. "I know that. It only seems to me like he's a decent suspect here."

"That's why I'm the real detective here and you're not. But you are doing a fine job. You keep it coming, friend. I gotta few more leads to check out, especially on that Pearlman cat."

"Ruben?" She stacked the glasses neatly in a row.

"Another first-namer with you, huh?"

She frowned.

Robinson ran his hands through his hair. "Yes. Pearlman may not be all that he seems to be. I'll let you know if I find out anything more than that. For now, take it at face value."

"That doesn't seem fair. Here I am, all eyes and ears and giving you good information out the ying yang, and you're not going to tell me what you've got?"

He pulled his shades from his front shirt pocket. It was one of those tighter-fitting, almost western-type shirts that the hipper young guys wore nowadays. Robinson was no spring chicken, but he still looked decent in the latest fashion. "That's the way it goes. I'll be in touch."

It would be a waste of her time to try and fight him on this, so she shook her head and went back to her business. She had only about ten minutes and neither Marco nor Simon was there yet with the food. Where were those two when she needed them? Probably a good thing they didn't see her with Robinson. She hadn't exactly filled the detective in on their part in the scheme of things. She doubted he would agree to her Three Muskateer–ing it, and knowing Simon, he would come into the room, see Robinson, and ramble on about his own ideas as to who, what, why, when, and how.

"Hey, Robinson?"

He turned around, reaching the door. "Yeah?"

"Tomorrow, um, I'm having some friends over for dinner and I thought maybe you might want to come."

He looked at the ground and then turned back to the door, his back facing her. "What time?"

"Sixish."

"Why not? I guess that's what friends do."

She laughed when he shut the door behind her. He was a

strange duck, but a duck one couldn't help liking. She wondered if her powers as Cupid would work. And she had a few more guests to invite. Nikki knew her dinner party would be far from dull. And who knew? There may even be a killer amongst them.

Sixteen

SIMON and Marco set platters of stuffed mushrooms, shrimp scampi skewers, beef Wellingtons, and various cheeses, fruits, and veggies out for the members.

"I didn't expect all of this," Nikki said. "Did you get it from the restaurant?"

"What? No. Marco did all of this himself. He slaved away over the last few days, prepping and then freezing the Wellingtons."

Marco blushed.

"You did all this?" Nikki asked.

He nodded. "I wanted everything to be perfecto, and I know how hard you have worked to help us and the S.E.E. group. We are grateful."

She knew that Marco was a fantastic cook. He ran the café and he and Simon did the breakfasts together in the morning, but Nikki had an inkling that Marco would have liked to take over the chef position at the gourmet restaurant on the property, Georges at the Vineyard. Since Georges's death, they'd gone through a few chefs and none of them had worked out spectacularly yet.

"I should really talk to Derek about you being the head chef at Georges."

"You would do that, Bellissima?" He batted his long eyelashes.

"I told you to put the idea out there and our little Goldilocks, Snow White of a girl would come through." Simon wrapped an arm around Marco's shoulder.

"Hold on, you two. I said that I would talk to him, but try not to put the pressure on. Be realistic, okay? Derek may say that Marco already has enough to shoulder here, which is true."

"I can take over his duties."

They both looked at Simon and, without saying a word, started setting food out for the members, who would be arriving shortly. He opted not to fight their silence, probably knowing that the underlying meaning beneath it was accurate—everyone knew, including Simon, that he'd much rather be getting a facial or massage, or working on enlightening himself, than tackling any real work.

"I need you two to do me a big favor." Nikki lowered her voice and looked from side to side to make sure that no one else had entered the room.

"I thought we already were." Simon smirked.

Give him his kudos. "I know, hon, and you have been awesome. But I've got a little break-and-enter job for you."

"Oh no. After that time in San Fran, I don't think so," Simon replied. "It's enough that we're pretty much phonies here at our first intimate S.E.E. gathering and now you want us to be common criminals."

"Didn't seem to bother you before." Nikki picked up the plate of tropical fruit and set it on the serving table they'd brought in.

"What do you need?" Marco asked.

"Kurt Kensington is superstrange," she said.

"I'll concede to that," Simon added. "Cute, but strange."

"I told you two that last night," Marco said, lighting the burner under the buffet server that held the Wellingtons.

"Did you tell him about the vision board session?" She glanced at Simon.

"My word, I can't believe I forgot to do that." Simon did a quick replay of what had happened with Kurt during the session.

Marco shook his head in disbelief. "Not a good man. He must need a lot of enlightenment."

"So now that you two know what a strange bird we're dealing with, I need you to get into his room and see if there is anything completely off. Anything at all out of the ordinary."

"Like what?" Simon asked.

"For starters, see if the guy really does have a suitcase that looks like Iwao Yamimoto's, but filled with books."

"What does Iwao's look like?" Marco asked.

"I don't know. I haven't been in the storage room yet," Nikki said. "But take pictures of his luggage and then I can compare."

"Do you see how her mind works? Take pictures. With what? My DCS Pro Back Plus? Am I a photographer now?"

"Use the camera on your phone. I just need a visual to compare. And I have a feeling that nut job might have something that will stand out to you." Nikki knew that Robinson could be right that Kensington was simply one of those strange types who sought attention any way he could, but Nikki still thought he should have taken her story a bit more seriously. What if Kensington was less of an attention getter and more of a deranged killer?

"A feeling? Okay, so you want us to get into the creep's

room, take some photos, and check it out all CSI style, just based on your funny feeling." Simon walked back over to the wine and poured himself a glass of red. "When is this shenanigan supposed to go down?"

"You said so yourself that the man is a weirdo. I'm thinking a good time might be during the wine tasting. Everyone will be focused on the wines, they may even get a bit tipsy, and your presence won't be missed. And if it is, I'll explain that you're grabbing a few more things for me."

"My presence is always missed." Simon took a sip of his wine.

"That wine is for the guests, you know," Nikki scolded.

"I am a guest. Remember? I'm a S.E.E. member. I'll probably get kicked out, because now I'm a traitor, thanks to you." He pointed at Nikki.

"Leave the guilt trips for someone else." She looked at Marco.

"Not me. I don't like them either. Come on, Simon. Nikki needs our help."

"Fine." He shook his head. "She's spoiled. You're spoiled." Simon pointed at Nikki. "We spoil you. That's the problem. No boundaries."

"Okay, Dad. And one more thing," Nikki said.

"Oh, just one more thing. It's never only one more thing with you, Snow White. It's like ten, twenty, two hundred fifty."

"You'll like this one." Nikki flashed them a smile in hopes of appeasing their display of irritation. "Since you have been a good mom and dad, boys, I am going to make your favorites for the dinner party tomorrow night."

Both men raised their eyebrows. "Chili and cornbread?" they both said.

"That and some other treats."

"You are up to something. You only do chili for a lot of people. Who else did you invite besides us and Alyssa?"

"I thought I'd ask Alan Sansi and his family."

"You are?" Simon was looking at her dubiously, his voice rising.

"Yes. I thought that it would be good to get to know everyone a little better for myself in an intimate setting," Nikki replied.

"You are not telling us something. You don't want us there to get to know us better, you want us there so you can keep snooping. I'm telling you that Alan had nothing to do with Iwao's murder."

"Maybe not, but one of his clan might have and I want to get to know everyone and see how they react. I also have another motive. You actually gave me the idea, Simon, when Alyssa mentioned liking the rock star look and then you brought up Detective Robinson."

Simon twirled around her. "Oh, you! I get it. *Matchmaker, matchmaker, make me a match,*" he sang. "You are so sweet, but Snow White, arranging romantic liaisons is not your forte. It's never a good idea to try and get involved in other people's love lives."

"This coming from Cupid himself?" Nikki strained to keep the incredulous sound in her voice at a minimum. "You practically stood over me and Derek with an arrow aimed to fire."

"Yes, but *I* am good at it." He bowed.

"He is," Marco said in serious agreement.

"Debatable," Nikki replied and grabbed his wineglass from him.

"You two live together, don't you? I sort of had something to do with it, I think. Before you know it, there will be love, then marriage, and then one baby or two in a baby carriage." Simon clapped his hands excitedly.

"Aren't you moving a little too fast?" Nikki commented.

"No. You two are moving a little slow if you ask me." He

tapped his wrist with a finger. "You don't have a lot of time on that clock."

"Simon!" Marco and Nikki said in unison.

"What? It's true. Forty is on the way, baby, and you know that is middle-aged and not exactly perfect for chasing babies around. Your back starts hurting and then the knees go. Before you know it, you'll be a mess. It's time to get that brother of mine with the program. Come on, get a ring on that finger, start doing some baby making. I am ready to be an uncle." He snapped his fingers in the air.

"I thought you wanted to be a daddy," Nikki said.

Marco looked at Simon with a stunned expression. Uh-oh. Looked like Simon hadn't shown his better half the dream board.

"I like babies, and I want to be an uncle, and yes, if I could be a daddy and Marco wanted to have a baby, too, then I would say yes to that."

Nikki could tell that Marco didn't know how to respond. "Look, here come the Pearlmans." This was the first time Nikki had been relieved to see the cranky wife.

"Goody gumdrops," Simon said while Marco continued staring blankly at him. Simon felt his eyes on him and said, "I know. Shocker. Can we talk it about it later? Don't we have to go play Agent 007 or something?"

Marco nodded and went around to the bar to pour small tastings for the guests. Nikki could tell by the change in his demeanor and how silent he'd become that Marco's dream board probably didn't replicate Simon's. Where might that lead? She also couldn't help wondering about her own fate—the whole marriage and baby carriage thing. That sure sounded good. In fact, more and more it sounded exactly like the vision she had for the future. The near future. She only hoped Derek shared it, too.

Seventeen

"WINEMAKING is really like making art," Nikki said, speaking to the group members, who were all seated with two separate flights of wine in front of them. Flights of wine were several glasses of wine with a few sips poured in them, designed simply for tasting. One flight would be white and the other red. For the whites, Nikki had a Sauvignon Blanc, Pinot Grigio, Riesling, Viognier, and Chardonnay. For the reds, she'd selected a standard Pinot Noir, Merlot, Cabernet Sauvignon, Syrah, Zinfandel, and a nice Malbec the winery had started producing a couple of years ago.

"It begins with the soil. At Malveaux we grow the majority of our grapes but we do buy some grapes from vineyards in Sonoma and Monterrey counties. Many of you may be aware that we recently partnered with a wonderful Australian winery, the Hahndorf Winery. The Sauvignon Blanc and Viognier you will be tasting in the white wine flight is from the Hahndorf Winery. The Australians grow those grapes nicely and blend them well. In the red flight, you'll be tasting Aussie wines in the Pinot, the Malbec, and the Syrah."

One of the S.E.E. members interrupted her. "What makes one region better than another in terms of grape production? For instance, why do Sauvignon Blanc grapes taste better from Australia than from here in Napa? Same goes for the Zinfandel. I heard one of your employees talking about the old vine Zin grapes you blend here. What goes into that?" It was Rich Higgins. Next to him stood Hayden—less Chanel today and more J.Crew with her pressed jeans, button-down, and argyle vest.

"Excellent question," Nikki said. "It's not necessarily that the wine tastes better, because that all depends on your palate. There are so many factors that go into the winemaking process. As I mentioned, it starts with the soil and with the quality of the grape. And the quality can be affected by the soil, the weather during growth, the way the grapes are pruned, and if they're harvested correctly at the right time. After the harvest, we look at sugar levels, which we call Brix, acidity levels and pH balances, the color, the seeds, the taste. It's all well thought out and created in hopes of making a superior product. There is a strong science aspect to wine production, but there is an equally strong creative aspect. Blend the two together and you can get an outstanding wine. Once the harvest and science are planned out, the grapes go through the crushing and primary fermentation process." All eyes were on her and everyone looked interested. She enjoyed speaking to groups of people. Maybe that came from her acting days.

"Basically crushing is liberating the fruit from the skin. Did you ever see the *I Love Lucy* episode where Lucy stomps on the grapes?"

Everyone laughed.

"Right, that's not typically how it's done now except for

maybe the really small operations or a few in Europe. We have a mechanical crusher and destemmer. Red wines get their color from the grape skins, so during fermentation of a red wine, the skin of the grapes needs to be in contact with the juice. Most white wines are processed without destemming or crushing and are transferred from picking bins directly to the press." Nikki went on to explain the fermentation process, how cultured yeast is typically added even though grapes already have a natural yeast on them, and how that yeast feeds off the must. The must is made up of skins, stems, seeds, fruit pulp, and when it comes in contact with the yeast, together they produce CO_2 gases and alcohol. She also explained the second fermentation and the aging process. She hoped no one had become bored as most of the members were not oenphiles, only enlightened souls. "That's a real basic how-to on winemaking. If you have other questions, I'll walk around and we can talk, but please eat and drink and enjoy. I know that Alan is going to talk about how winemaking and the growing of grapes are akin to soul growth." Nikki stifled a giggle. She wasn't sure how he'd tie it all together, but knew he would in some bizarre fashion.

Even during her talk, in the back of her mind, Nikki felt the dark cloud of murder hanging over her, and she knew when people began drinking and loosening up, that she'd go in for the kill. So to speak.

Nikki sidled over to Juan Gonzales, wanting to see what information she could get from him. "You having a good time?" Nikki asked.

"Sure. I love wine. Love food, too." He rubbed his paunch, and smiled. Nikki noticed for the first time that he had a couple of gold teeth on the bottom row. There looked to be some cheese caught in them, and she tried not to stare at it. Juan was probably somewhere in his late forties. He ran his hand through his slicked-back dark hair and smiled at her.

"What's not to love?" She smiled. Get friendly. Get into this guy's head and find out about the note he sent to Iwao. She raised her glass.

"Good talk, by the way. You sure do know a lot about wine."

"Oh well, it's my job. And how about the enlightenment sessions? How are those going for you?"

"I still have plenty to learn, that's for sure, but Alan is wonderful. He's so patient with all of us misfits, you know."

"He seems wonderful. I don't know him that well, not being a member and all, but you must, I assume. Everyone in the group must." Nikki did her best to appear casually interested.

"No, no. I don't know most of the people, but there are a few new guys, like your friends Simon and Marco, who I'm getting to know."

"How about Iwao? You knew him pretty well. At least it seemed like you did last night on the train when you came over."

He frowned. "Yeah, man." He shook his head. "That was wrong, you know, so wrong that happened to him. I did know Iwao. I'm pretty shaken up about it."

"I can see that." Nikki tried to sound sincere, but come on! This guy was slamming back the vino and hardly thinking twice about Iwao Yamimoto. Those were the facts. "Did you two know each other outside of the group?" She already knew that they did. He'd told Simon that. Would he have the same story for her?

He was slow to answer, as if he was searching for the right words. "We did. We met through the group and had some things in common. And you know we did some business together."

"Yeah? What kind of business?"

"We did some film work together. Why all the questions?"

"I don't know. I find it curious that everyone here seems to have forgotten that this man was murdered last night and some of you knew him rather well."

He laughed but Nikki didn't think there was anything slightly humorous about their conversation. "You have a curious nature, don't you?"

"I suppose that I do, but more than that, I find the situation disturbing, especially considering that you knew Iwao and did business with him."

"What am I supposed to do? Sulk? Is that what we're all supposed to do, Ms. Sands?" His tone turned nasty and Nikki didn't care for it at all.

"A little mourning couldn't hurt," she said pointedly.

"You didn't know Iwao Yamimoto, did you?"

"No. I only just met the man."

He picked up another glass of wine on the table next to them. "Right. Let me tell you something. Iwao was not always the most ethical of human beings. In fact, he'd screw anyone over if given the chance."

"Sounds like you two had some difficulties. Is that why you wrote him a note when he arrived here?" Juan frowned at Nikki's question. "I remember Iwao mentioning it to you on the train and I got the feeling it wasn't a pleasantry or a welcome card."

"I feel I'm being attacked here. I never wrote Iwao a note, a card, nothing. I was confused when he said that to me."

Nikki studied him. Was he telling her the truth? She remembered the night before when Iwao made the sarcastic remark to him about the note; Nikki had sensed something was off between the two of them. Neither one wanted to be around the other. "I'm not attacking you. I apologize if you feel that way. I suppose it's what you said—I'm curious is all."

He nodded. "Right. I didn't write nothing, like I said. He

had to have misread the signature. You know, everyone who did business with Iwao had difficulties, even his nephew. There are at least a few people in this room who would agree to that. Not me. I hate to be rude, but since the police have interrogated me, I don't feel like having this conversation again in a social situation. I'm here to have fun." Juan Gonzales walked away from Nikki, leaving her dumb-struck.

Most people didn't walk away from her, not even when she was digging for information. She had to find out what his problems were with Iwao and why he clearly didn't like the man. Not only that, she had to find the note that had been left for Iwao, and see if it had been Juan who'd written it—or someone else, as he'd insisted. How was she going to do that? Could it still be in Iwao's room?

A note. What did you do with a note someone wrote to you? Especially if it was someone you didn't care much for? Throw it away. That seemed the logical explanation. Unless it was a threat—maybe you kept those? The police had gone through Iwao's room this morning, but what if Housekeeping had gone through it before that? She had to ask Mizuki if Housekeeping had been in their room, before she'd been moved out of there. If so, then that meant there was only one place a note could be: the Dumpster. She was not going there. No. First things first. See if she could some-how communicate with Iwao's mistress.

The police had asked the hotel to move Mizuki out of the suite she'd shared with Iwao so that they could check the room out further. Alyssa had taken care of the switch that morning. Nikki could use the excuse that she wanted to be sure everything was suitable in the new room. How she would do that, Nikki wasn't sure. The loud, slowly spoken English she'd tried last night hadn't gone over too well. But dammit, she had to try.

Maybe she could get away and check on Mizuki right

now. Where were Simon and Marco? They should have been back by now. Had they found anything more incriminating against Kurt Kensington, who was now busy chatting up Sierra Sansi? Sierra, Nikki noticed, did not seem to be pouring the booze down like she had the night before. Was there a reason for that? Sierra was a martial artist who had worked on films. Was she also a great actress? Nikki sighed. What she needed was some time to sit down alone and analyze last night's events by herself. Something was amiss but she was having trouble putting it together in the middle of this wine tasting.

She was not done picking at Juan Gonzales. She didn't care that he thought she was rude. She'd try a different tactic, because she planned to find out what his beef was with Iwao.

Juan was now engrossed in a tense-looking conversation with Ruben Pearlman. They glanced at her as she came toward them.

Juan started to walk away and Ruben smiled awkwardly at her. Then her cell phone rang. She could hear it from behind the counter—even over the din of people's voices. And she also knew it was Derek. She'd set a certain ring tone for him—ABC's "The Look of Love." Yes, she was a teenager in the eighties.

She grabbed the phone off the counter and took a deep breath before answering. "Hi, sweetie." Oh, no, now she was doing the endearment thing that they *so* did not do, and surely it would tip him off to the presence of winery shenanigans.

The tone in his voice told her that he'd already been tipped off. "Hi, yourself. I just got off the phone about five minutes ago with Simon."

Shit. Boy, when she got her hands around Simon's neck, she was going to wring it as hard as she could.

"Yes," she said, hearing the hesitation in her voice.

"I understand that there is a situation out there."

"Can you give me a sec? I have to walk outside. I'm actually doing the wine-tasting event for the S.E.E. members right now."

"I can wait," he replied, his voice stern.

Nikki grabbed a glass of wine from the table before heading out and took a larger than usual sip while making her way out the side doors. She brought the phone back up to her ear. "I can hear you now." She could also hear noise in the background where he was and decided to try to change the course of the conversation. "Where are you?"

"I'm at a restaurant that one of the Salvatores' relatives owns in Manhattan."

"Oh, Italian. Good. What are you having?"

"Ravioli. I think. Stop what you're doing and tell me what's going on out there, Nik."

She sighed. "Well, there's been a hiccup with Alan Sansi's event here."

"A hiccup? My brother told me that hiccup was actually a murder."

She cringed. Man, when she found Simon ... Where was he anyway? He'd obviously spent some time on the phone with his brother. *Thanks for the heads-up!* "Yes. One of the S.E.E. members was murdered last night on the wine train."

"Jesus, Nikki. Could you have called me?"

"You were on a plane," she protested. "And then I knew you had meetings and were busy, and what could you do anyway?"

"Not a whole helluva lot considering I'm stuck here in the city. Have you seen the news?"

"No. I've been kind of busy myself. What's the problem?" She leaned against the stone wall that housed the tasting room.

"Only the biggest snowstorm the East Coast has seen in fifty years. The planes are grounded. I don't know when I

can get home." Nikki heard the frustration in Derek's voice.
"As soon as Simon told me what happened, I called all the
airlines, but I already knew no one was getting out of here
tonight. It's been all over the news. It started early this
morning and hasn't let up."

"That's terrible, *honey*." *Terrible, my ass.* Secretly, she
couldn't help being a little glad that he was stuck out there.
If she knew him the way she thought she did, he would have
already been on his way to JFK if he could to get the first
flight home. Nikki was not ready to give up playing
Colombo anytime soon; there was a killer in Napa and she
hadn't earned her Nosy Nikki name for nuthin'.

Derek returned the sarcastic nickname exchange and
said, "That's right, that's terrible, *sweetie*."

"Derek?" Nikki heard a woman's voice in the background. "Your ravioli is on the table. It'll get cold."

"Hi, Sophia. I'll be with the table in a moment. I have an
important call here."

"Sophia? Who is Sophia?" Nikki asked, her blood pressure rising by the second. Anyone with a name like Sophia
could mean nothing less than trouble with a capital T.

"She's Vicente's daughter. She's also the family attorney
and is going over these contracts with us. She's a real stick-
ler."

"Okay." Nikki didn't have a more intelligent response in
her repertoire. She hated when she sounded jealous. For all
she knew, the woman was an ugly hag. "Is she pretty?" Ooh.
She closed her eyes tightly. Now why on earth did she have
to go there? That was even stupider than responding with
the "okay."

"She's attractive, I guess. If you like her look."

Not the answer you want to hear from your boyfriend.
Her look? Don't even pursue this one any further, Nikki
warned herself. In fact, talking about the murder suddenly
appeared like an easier conversation to have.

"I can't believe this happened on the wine train. Do they have any idea who did it? And Simon says that the workshop is still taking place."

"Yes. Alan felt that was the best way to go. And no, Detective Robinson really isn't sure who did the crime, or if it was one of the members or someone who worked on the train. My guess is that he's exploring all the angles."

There was silence on the other end for a few seconds. The only way Nikki could tell that Derek was still there was by the background noise.

"Jonah Robinson is investigating the murder?"

"Yes."

"Okay."

She shifted uncomfortably against the wall. "Is that a problem?"

"No. He's kind of different, and I thought when he was investigating Georges's murder that he kind of had a thing for you."

She laughed. "You're kidding, right?"

"No."

"Derek, we really need you at the table." Nikki heard Sophia's voice again.

"I'm sorry, babe."

Another freaking endearment. Bad sign. "You have to go, I know."

"I do, but listen to me. I know you too well, and this is not the ideal situation here. You there, in the middle of a murder investigation. Me here, not watching your back. It's not good. You better not be poking into this thing. Keep Ollie with you and promise me you'll stay out of Robinson's way and let him do his job."

She bit her lower lip. "I promise," she muttered. Crap. She hated when he made her make promises that she absolutely knew she couldn't keep. That was like holding a cookie jar out to a five-year-old and saying, "Now promise me you won't eat one when I go back and clean my room. You be a good boy, Johnny, and watch *Sesame Street*."

Please! And that was the problem: Derek knew she couldn't keep that promise and she knew she couldn't keep it, but she made it anyway.

"You better not be crossing your fingers behind your back, Nik. I mean it this time. Keep your word, and just stay away from Robinson. I love you."

"I love you, too. Enjoy your ravioli."

And with that, he was gone and she was left standing outside the tasting room, cell phone in one hand, empty wineglass in the other, knowing she'd made empty promises to the man she loved. What a scoundrel! How to live with herself? She looked at the empty glass. She could refill. That might make it easier. No. No. She couldn't do that.

Okay, since the empty promises had been made and she already knew she'd break them and feel all that guilt and shame, she figured, what the hell? Nikki went to see if she could talk again with Mizuki.

Cheese Ravioli with Sweet Italian Sausage
and Bracco Chianti Classico

Sophia! Sophia! That could not be good. All women named Sophia are sexpots and gorgeous. It's a well-known fact. And Derek is having ravioli with her at an Italian restaurant! Hmmm. Well, the only consolation Nikki can have in this moment is that she knows she makes the best ravioli around. So, when Derek takes a bite of that ravioli he's eating there with

Sophia, he won't be able to help remembering Nikki's divine cheese ravioli with sweet Italian sausage.

Got to have a good bottle of Chianti when eating ravioli, right? Yeah, well, Derek better not be with that Sophia! When he gets back to Napa, Nikki will have to make him her ravioli and pair it with her favorite Chianti by Bracco Wines owned by Lorraine Bracco of *The Sopranos*. The Chianti Classico is an elegant red wine with flavors of black cherry and plum. It's aged in new Slovenian oak barrels for a year. It's a fantastic wine for pasta and meat dishes.

> *12 oz fresh sweet Italian sausage links*
> *1 cup beef broth*
> *1 cup chopped onion*
> *3 cloves garlic, minced*
> *2 tsp olive oil*
> *28-oz can whole Italian-style tomatoes*
> *¼ cup tomato paste*
> *¼ cup dry red wine*
> *2 tbsp snipped fresh basil*
> *1 tsp dried oregano, crushed*
> *¼ tsp crushed red pepper*
> *12 oz dried or 16 oz fresh cheese-filled ravioli*

In a large skillet combine sausage links and broth. Bring to boiling; reduce heat. Cover and simmer for 15 minutes. Drain off broth. Cook sausage links, uncovered, for 2–4 minutes more, or until brown, turning frequently. Remove from skillet; cool. Slice into ½-inch pieces. Wipe skillet clean with paper towels.

In the same skillet, cook onion and garlic in hot oil till tender but not brown. Stir in tomatoes, tomato paste, wine, basil, oregano, and crushed red pepper. Add sausage to skillet. Bring to boiling; reduce heat. Cover and simmer for 20 minutes, or to desired consistency.

Meanwhile, in a large saucepan or pasta pot bring 3 quarts water to boiling. Add pasta. Reduce heat slightly. Boil, uncovered, 15 minutes for dried pasta or 8–10 minutes for fresh, or till al dente, stirring occasionally. (Or cook according to package directions.) Immediately drain. Return pasta to warm saucepan. Pour sausage mixture over hot cooked pasta. Serve immediately.

Eighteen

NIKKI peered back inside the wine tasting and saw that Alan Sansi had taken center stage again. This was good for her. It meant she could head over to Mizuki's suite.

She knocked on Mizuki's door, hoping no one from the wine tasting was wandering the halls, but there was no response. This troubled Nikki. Where would Mizuki have gone? Maybe she was resting. Both Robinson and Nikki agreed that Mizuki had information to share. The problem was, no one had been able to get that information because of the language barrier. It was too bad the interpreter that Robinson had requested hadn't come by when he was supposed to. She knocked again before giving up. It was dark. Ollie needed to get out and be fed. Poor guy. He was used to a lot more attention than what he'd been getting over the past couple of days.

Thoughts of Ollie led to thoughts of Derek. She didn't like the way their conversation had ended. She figured he was angry and frustrated, which she understood. Here he was, stuck in New York, when this horrible thing had happened. But really, what could he do? The strangest thing about it all was what seemed to be Derek's jealousy toward Robinson. He had nothing to be jealous about. The detective was just doing his job. Yes, he'd asked her to help and she'd omitted telling Derek that part. Boy, wouldn't that have really gotten under his skin! She wouldn't have wanted that.

Speaking of jealousy, what about that Sophia chick who'd been with Derek? A woman with a certain *look*. Hmmm. Nikki would have to Google this Sophia Salvatore character later. Right now she had to find out where Mizuki was. Nikki couldn't believe that she'd left her room. Maybe she went to the restaurant for some dinner? Nikki checked but she wasn't there.

Simon and Marco typically helped run the front desk during the evening, but since they were busy doing her dirty work—at least they were supposed to be—and Alyssa had taken off to be with Petie, one of the part-timers, an elderly woman named Edna, was at the desk for the evening.

Edna reminded Nikki of what a grandma should be—sweet disposition, gray hair, crepe-like skin that framed pretty blue eyes, and always wearing pastel colors. She walked with a little hunch to her back, which Nikki figured had to be osteoporosis setting in. Edna was a doll. The only negative was that Edna could be forgetful, and Nikki at times wondered if she was fighting senility. But she was always willing to fill in when they needed some extra help.

"Hi, Eddie." Nikki used the nickname everyone around the winery had for Edna.

"Hi, Nikki. Beautiful night, isn't it?"

"It is. I'm sorry to bother you, but there's a guest staying here named Mizuki, um, gosh, I don't know her last name. She's staying under the Yamimoto reservation, I believe."

Edna brought her hand up to her mouth. "Oh! That was the man who was killed on the wine train."

Nikki nodded. "Yes. I'm looking for his, his . . . well, I'm looking for Mizuki. She's probably about five feet, very petite, a Japanese woman. Doesn't speak any English. Did she by chance stop by here, or did you notice anyone like that?"

"No. I'm afraid I haven't, dear."

"Hmmm. Okay. I'm worried about her is all."

"Why don't you try calling her room?" Edna suggested.

"Good idea." Nikki picked up the house phone and dialed the suite number. The phone rang until it went to the hotel voicemail. She decided to try again. Still no answer. She could understand Mizuki not answering the phone because of the language barrier, but still Nikki redialed the number enough times that anyone would have picked it up had they been in the room. Nikki placed the receiver back on the phone.

What to do? Here was the thing: there could be something in Mizuki's personal belongings that could help find the killer, and if she was not in the room, Nikki would have an opportunity to check it out. It seemed like Robinson would have already searched the room himself. He could do that, couldn't he? Probably not without a search warrant, but had Mizuki's room been a top consideration yet? Nikki didn't believe so. Nevertheless, searching private belongings really was wrong—plain and simple. Yes, she'd asked Simon and Marco to do it, although for some reason having them search Kensington's stuff hadn't seemed as wrong as it would be to go through Mizuki's things. She was a nice woman who'd been thrown into this horrible mess. Robinson should really let her go home. Man, she was overthinking this stuff. Her frazzled brain only made everything more confusing and complicated.

"Are you okay, dear?" Eddie asked.

"Fine. I'm fine." She smiled at her. "You know, I think I

might check on her, take her some tea. If she isn't in her room, I can leave it for her as a treat."

"That would be nice," Eddie said. "I'll get you the key to the room. You know a funny story. I left my house keys here the other day, and when I got home, I couldn't get into the house. My neighbor came over and reminded me that I keep a key under a potted plant." She laughed but looked kind of sad at the same time. "Getting old is a bitch."

Nikki put an arm around her. "Aw, Eddie. Come on. You're not getting old. Don't be so hard on yourself. Everyone gets forgetful sometimes."

"I am getting old, hon, and it's not sometimes. It's happening more often. Soon I may have to retire for good."

"I hope that's not the case, but we'll understand. You let me know what you need from me and Malveaux, okay?"

"You're a good girl."

A few seconds later, Eddie came from the back room with a key for Nikki to enter Mizuki's suite. "Here you go."

Nikki told her they would have coffee next week when the event was over and talk about the future. She thanked her and went outside to head back up the stairs. Then she knocked again on the hotel door. Still no answer. She looked around, put the key in the hole, and turned. The door opened and she pushed it slightly, calling out Mizuki's name. She opened the door wider. No one was there, but Mizuki's suitcase was on the bed and looked to be half-packed.

The clothes in the suitcase all looked expensive. Nikki peered down at them—designer labels, including the shoes. Was Mizuki headed home? Had Robinson told her that it was okay to go?

She hesitantly lifted up some of the clothes. Wait a minute. Here was a DVD case. Maybe this was the DVD that Iwao kept trying to hand to Alan. There was no one around so Nikki opened the case. There was a DVD in it, but there was no label. It was just blank. What could be on it?

Nikki wanted to know but she couldn't do that. This was the woman's private belonging. She squeezed her fists together and closed the case up, placing it back down on the clothing.

Nothing in the room seemed out of the ordinary. It was quiet except for the roaring of the gas fire. Why had she left that on? She must not have gone far. Nikki also spotted a silk robe over one of the chairs facing the fireplace.

Nikki looked a little closer around the room. Typically, in every room, a bottle of Malveaux wine would be on the console table. Every day, if it was empty, a new one would be replaced by the staff. There wasn't one there. Nikki looked around the room; it wasn't anywhere. She'd have to talk to Housekeeping about this. She ran her finger over the desk for dust. There was a little. Whoever had been cleaning this room would have something to answer for. While she was at it, she figured she'd better check the bathroom and make sure they'd replaced the towels.

When she came around the corner, she stopped. The room started that spinning thing it did whenever this type of thing happened to Nikki—which was becoming far too often. There, lying on the floor, with her eyes wide open with a corkscrew lodged into her chest and a wine cork stuffed into her mouth was Mizuki. Dead.

Nineteen

ROBINSON looked as disgusted as Nikki felt. He had to be thinking exactly what she was: how could this have happened right under their noses? He was in the room now with the investigation unit that consisted of himself, a crime scene investigator, another homicide detective, and a few other people—Nikki hadn't a clue what their roles were, but she knew to stay out of their way.

Nikki leaned back against the wall outside the suite trying to remain calm and not conjure up that image of Mizuki dead. Nikki now felt confident that whoever had killed both Iwao and Mizuki was involved with the S.E.E. members. It hadn't been a deranged killer loose on the wine train. Nope, the killer was right here at the hotel and in plain sight. Why would that person seek out Mizuki?

If the motive was clearer as to why Iwao had been murdered, then the motive as to why his mistress was now being zippered into a body bag would also become clearer. But as of now, Nikki hadn't figured out any concrete motives.

She figured Mizuki had had information that might have led to the killer and the killer had also banked on that and silenced Mizuki before she had a chance to communicate her tale in her native tongue. That had to be why she'd been killed.

Once Nikki had found Mizuki and placed the 911 call, and the police had first arrived, an officer went down to the tasting room, where the fun was still going on. He'd informed them there had been a death and that all the members were to go to their suites until someone came by to interview them. They hadn't a clue as to what had happened at that point. Nikki figured at least one of them would have some idea, because one of them had to be a killer.

The members were all accounted for, except for Simon and Marco. Where in the heck were those two, and what if something bad had happened to them? She picked at her nails and worried herself sick.

Robinson came around the corner. "We need to talk."

"Okay."

"Not here," he replied. His face drawn and unsmiling, he grabbed her arm.

"Hey."

"Hey, nothing. Come on."

She wasn't about to argue with him. They went down the stairs and headed to the café. No one was there and they went back into the kitchen, passing the hanging rack of pots and the professional gas stove and oven. He finally stopped in front of the wood fire oven, let go of her arm, and turned toward her. "I thought you were hiring security," he said.

"You suggested it, but no, I haven't had a chance. I didn't think this psycho would kill someone else."

"He did."

"No kidding. Why am I getting the feeling that you're blaming this on me? You're the cop." She put her hands on her hips.

He crossed his arms. "I'm not blaming you, Sands. But here's the deal. You run this place, and from what you told me, you coordinated this whole event. Okay, so I got one dead guy on a train. I've been working every angle of this investigation on Yamimoto, talking to everyone I can who was on the train that might have seen something. Then I got the CSI people on the train, and I can tell you the train company isn't too happy with having to shut down a train and lose business. I thought maybe I had some decent leads, thought there could be answers there. I put myself out and asked for a little help from a *friend*, and now the dead guy's geisha winds up corked to death on the bathroom floor. What up?"

She made a face at him. "What up? I don't know what up. I've done everything you asked me to do. I've looked, listened, and told you everything." She didn't like his tone at all. "What up? God, why don't you tell me?"

He rubbed his face and blinked a few times. "Sorry, this is not going to go well back at the department. I gotta take the heat for it. I know I asked you to help and you're not even a trained cop. Hell, if we could get some support from all the taxpayers' money, that woman in there might not be dead. I could have had a detail on this place."

"Detail?"

"Trained officers watching."

"Oh."

"Man, I really thought that Yamimoto's death was isolated. I even suspected Mizuki of killing him."

"You did?"

"Yes. What I haven't been able to rectify is everyone's whereabouts at the time of his death, which I've narrowed down to be between eight and nine that night."

Robinson looked tired. "What do you know about this Juan Gonzales cat?"

"He's different and he did some business outside of the S.E.E. members with Iwao." She didn't want to tell him that it was Simon who'd initially provided her with this information. "He and Iwao did some king-fu-type movie together that Juan helped produce and distribute in the States and Mexico. But I don't think the deal benefited Juan much. Actually this evening at the wine tasting, he made no bones to me about his feelings toward Iwao, and they were not exactly positive. Then he clammed up. Even got angry at me when I tried to pry." She told him about getting the call from Derek and how it had interrupted her from further pursuing a discussion with Juan, but that she noticed him talking to Ruben Pearlman and they looked to be tight.

He nodded. "Good. That's confirmation of what I've learned. There is a connection between the three of them. After you told me what Pearlman told you on the hike about his being involved in media and music production, I checked him out. I made some calls. Looks like Yamimoto, Pearlman, and Gonzales did that movie venture that bombed together, and Yamimoto took more money from these guys than he needed. Looks to me like Yamimoto was stealing money from them. I don't have the full scoop yet, but I'm bringing them both in for a little talk. Any idea if either one of them went missing while this tasting event went down?"

"No. Is that when you think she was killed?" Again she couldn't help thinking about Simon and Marco. Had they seen something and had the killer taken them out, too? That was too horrible even to consider. Damn, where were they?

"I think she was killed earlier this afternoon."

"That would be far more feasible. It could have happened when we were setting up the tasting."

"That's what I'm afraid of. Here I was on the premises and this went down, right after I interviewed her. Or tried to." Detective Robinson looked understandably distraught and angry.

"Did she give you anything that you could go on or even understand?"

"Nothing. She gave you more by showing you those photos of Yamimoto, his nephew, and Sierra Sansi. I tried to ask her about that and she acted like a deer caught in the headlights."

"That could also be an angle to explore—Sierra and the nephew. Something isn't kosher there."

He nodded. "Yeah. You think you can talk to her?"

"I could try. I've hardly seen her at all since she found Iwao. Didn't you interview her?"

"I did," Robinson replied. "She was pretty shaky last night and I haven't had a chance to talk to her today. It might be easier for her to talk to you than me." He picked up the long pizza handle next to the oven and twirled one end of it. "Whoever did this wanted to be sure Mizuki wouldn't be able to tell us anything else. This killer is cunning. He's laughing at us right now, and this is the second time with the cork in the mouth. That's some type of signature or symbol. My guess is it represents something you've already mentioned—put a cork in it."

"He? You think the killer is a man?" Nikki asked.

"I do. Take Yamimoto first. The guy was taken out by slicing his throat. He had to have been jumped from behind and by someone strong. The cut is clean. I've talked with the medical examiner and she agrees with me. Then you have this killing here with the mistress. Granted, she was a petite thing, but the killer stabbed her with a corkscrew. Here's the thing with that, again—you need strength and either he got lucky and hit the heart muscle or he knew exactly how to hit it. The cork is the icing on the cake for him to taunt us with."

"It makes sense. So, you're narrowing in on Gonzales and Pearlman?"

"I'm checking their background right now, and I'll be questioning them personally again. I think they could even be in cahoots."

"What about Kurt Kensington? Maybe he's deranged enough that he thinks he could get away with it." Nikki crossed her arms.

"You're right. Everything I have so far on someone like him would be only circumstantial evidence. Maybe he's a pro of some sort and knows it's hard to build a case based on circumstances. This is a tough one, and now we have some serious safety issues. I need to talk with Alan Sansi. I can't make him shut down his workshop for the week, but I'll suggest it again. The problem is that I need these folks to stay around here. I can't have them leaving Napa and going back home. Not until I've thoroughly interviewed them and checked them out."

"What do you suggest?"

"Let me see what I can do about having an officer here at the winery. If there is a police presence, it should deter this guy from killing again. But something tells me he won't. He's done his job. He killed Yamimoto for one reason, which I will figure out, and he killed the mistress to make sure that if she knew anything at all, she couldn't tell anyone."

Nikki wondered. Robinson's reasoning made sense. She hoped he was right that whoever had committed these murders was finished.

But Robinson had been wrong before.

Twenty

NIKKI knew that the members were in their rooms. Some had already been interviewed. She had to finesse those member applications that Hayden told her about on the hike out of Hayden's hands and now was the time to do it.

She knocked on Hayden's door. Rich answered. "Hi, Nikki." He shook his head. "We can't believe this. Hayden and I are shocked."

"Have the police already spoken with you?" she asked, figuring they had because she doubted Robinson would allow anyone who was a part of the S.E.E. group to spend any time with another member or facilitator until after they'd been questioned.

"Yes. It's really unbelievable. First Mr. Yamimoto and now his..." Rich fumbled for the appropriate term. "His other half."

That was a delicate way of putting it.

"Would you like to come in?" he asked. "We were having a glass of wine, trying to digest this."

"Sure. Thanks. That would be nice."

Nikki entered the king suite. Like all the rooms at the hotel, this one was nothing short of pure elegance. It was a two-bedroom suite and had a fireplace, as all of them did. The room had been painted a soft peach hue, and candles were lit on the end tables. Maybe she'd interrupted something. Hayden was curled up n one of the chairs, wineglass in hand.

She turned as Nikki came in and looked about as tired as Nikki felt. "Hi, Nikki. Rich and I were sitting here talking about what happened with Mizuki and how horrid all this is. Even my father is completely shaken and nothing shakes him up." Hayden took a sip of the red wine. She'd changed clothes since the wine-tasting event, where she'd had on an argyle-type vest over a white button-down and a nice pair of pressed jeans. Now she wore a pair of gray pajama bottoms and a T-shirt that read SANSI KNOWS THE WAY.

Rich still had on his khakis and button-down. The two of them defined yuppiedom from the nineties.

"Here, Nikki." Rich handed her a glass of wine and sat down on the edge of the fireplace. "Have a seat." He pointed to the empty chair next to Hayden.

Nikki thanked him and sat down.

"What do you make of all this?" he asked.

"I don't know. My guess is that the police are looking heavily into the members here. It was one thing to have Iwao murdered last night on the train with the belief that it was someone outside the group being a killer...but now with this second killing, I'm sure the focus will turn to the members and our staff."

"No," Hayden said. "No one in this group would do such a thing. I can't believe that."

"You don't know, Hayden. Anything is possible. I think the best thing we can do is allow the police to conduct their investigation."

Nikki really didn't want to bring up the applications in front of Rich, but she didn't have a choice. It was now or never. She took a sip of the Pinot Noir, which reminded her of strawberries and of all things leather. "I don't know how to broach this with you, so I guess the best way to do this is be honest." Of course, Nikki couldn't even count these two out as suspects. The likelihood seemed low and the applications wouldn't pertain to them anyway. They certainly hadn't had to fill one out.

"What are you getting at?" Hayden asked.

She set her glass down on the table. "We are a bit of small town in a large county, and, well, I don't know if anyone said anything to you, but from time to time, I've been known to help the police out with their investigations. I grew up with an aunt who was a detective, and being around her, I kind of developed a knack for it."

They were nodding their heads. Her story was not entirely true. Yes, she'd helped out the police before, but not always by invitation. At least in this case, Robinson wanted her assistance. Granted, she was only supposed to look and listen since she hadn't overnight become an official member of the department, but Robinson was bogged down at the moment. There may be nothing to those applications at all, and if that was the situation, then Robinson need not waste his or any of his employees' time. But if there was something in one of them, then she could alert him and still have saved him and the department time and money.

"I don't think we're understanding you here," Rich said and motioned to Hayden.

"I know I'm not." Hayden took another sip of wine.

Nikki sighed. "Okay, on the hike, Hayden, you said that you hang on to the applications the members fill out."

"I do. So?"

"I need to see them." There it was, out on the table.

"Why?" she asked.

Rich looked from Hayden to Nikki.

"Because I am helping the police, as I mentioned, and they will be asking for them anyway, probably with a subpoena, and I don't know that you want everyone knowing that the police are looking at the applications. It could save you a lot of drama with the members if you gave them to me now." She threw in that "subpoena" word figuring the legalese might get their attention.

"I don't understand what you think you'll find." Rich took a sip from his wine.

She gave them the same spiel she had given Simon.

The engaged couple exchanged looks after she finished. Rich shook his head. "I'd hate to see Hayden get in any trouble with her dad for this."

"That won't happen. If anything stands out in the applications, I'll let the police know. If not, then no harm no foul."

"I suppose," Hayden said.

"I'll bring them back tomorrow. I promise. You have them here, don't you?" Nikki nodded and smiled at her.

"Okay," Hayden replied reluctantly. "But I need them back tomorrow. Early."

"I think that would be good," Rich said.

Hayden got up and went into the bedroom, which Nikki knew had paintings of vineyards on the walls and a white silk duvet cover on the bed.

"You help out the police then?" Rich asked.

"Sort of." She crossed her fingers that Rich wouldn't ask Robinson about it. If he knew what she was up to, he'd flip out.

"I sure hope they find this creep soon. I'm a bit afraid to stay here." He got up and refilled his glass.

"I believe the police are posting a man here for the night, and from what I've heard, they believe these killings were targeted. I don't think you have anything to be concerned about."

"I suppose. The police asked me all about Yamimoto's publishing dealings and his wanting to publish Alan's books in Japan. I explained that we have various foreign subsidies that do our publishing overseas and neither Alan nor myself was interested in going with him in that direction."

"Did you know Mr. Yamimoto very well?"

"No. This is the first time I ever met him. He'd called me a few times, but I knew Alan's stance and I agreed. Inspiritus has done a fantastic job for him. My mother really helped him build his image."

Hayden walked out with a stack of folders and handed them to Nikki. "Please do not tell anyone about this."

"I won't." She stood up. "I appreciate it, and I'll be by tomorrow."

Nikki walked out of their room, applications in hand, knowing she had a long night ahead of her.

Twenty-one

TWO murders in two days. Derek would be thrilled to hear this news. Thank God it was too late to call him in New York. It was already eleven o'clock in Napa when Nikki walked back to their house, and with the three-hour time difference, she doubted he'd even be awake. Police were still busy at the hotel, and Nikki hated that she had not heard from Simon and Marco.

Once inside her home, and with Ollie at her side, she gave a deep sigh of relief. She set the folders on the kitchen counter and bent down to hug the dog, who looked at her like she was crazy but enjoyed the attention all the same. "Hi, kid. How's it going?" Nikki patted his head.

Ollie wagged his long tail. Nikki went to the cupboard and took out a can of wet food and fixed him a bowl to eat. She then poured herself a glass of wine, sliced off some cheese, and put a piece of bread in the toaster. While the bread was toasting, she tried to call Simon and then Marco and got no response. She then went out into the garage and located the box with the books her aunt had given her and pulled a few out that looked chock-full of information. If she was going to stay up reading, then not only would she get to these applications, she could refresh her memory of what constituted a sociopath and a psychopath. She would do that first because reminding herself about what makes up the behavior and mind-set of a killer might help her when reviewing the applications.

A few minutes later, feet on the coffee table, bread and cheese in hand, and Ollie next to her on the couch, Nikki started flipping through a book called *The Mind of a Killer.* She found the definitions of a sociopath and a psychopath.

Both personalities have no empathy for others. Neither feels remorse or guilt. They are self-serving and seem to lack any conscience. They routinely disregard rules, social mores, and laws, unmindful of putting themselves or others at risk. Sounded like a wonderful type of human being— just like Derek's first wife, come to think of it.

Nikki went on to read that the sociopath was less organized in his or her demeanor, nervous and easily agitated— someone likely living on the fringes of society, without solid or consistent economic support. A sociopath was more likely to spontaneously act out in inappropriate ways without thinking through the consequences. A psychopath would think them through and figure out how to get away with it.

Nikki took a sip of wine. Was there anyone she could think of in the group who was steadily nervous or could be considered living on the fringe of society? Kensington did not strike her as nervous, but of all these people, she could see him having a solid lack of empathy. How about consistent economic support? Everyone who was a member had that. They had to in order to be able to afford the membership fee.

She gave Ollie a pat on the head and read further, learning that a psychopath tends to be extremely organized, secretive, and manipulative. The outer personality is often charismatic and charming, hiding the real person beneath. Though psychopaths do not feel for others, they can mimic behaviors that make them appear normal. Upon meeting, one would have more of a tendency to trust a psychopath than a sociopath.

Okay, now that could fit almost anyone because all someone had to do was put on a good act. And what better outlet to do it in? Who would think that anyone involved in an enlightenment group would be a psychopath? It was a good cover. Robinson was sure that the killer was a man, but there was Sierra Sansi to consider. She was a martial artist, had done some acting, dated Iwao's nephew. Nikki had seen enough photos to prove that. She'd been drunk—or had she?—the other night. Was Sierra Sansi putting on an act for her family and the entire world? Was the young woman more than just confused and a little messed up? Was she, in fact, a psycho?

There was more information about the psychopath that could fit Sierra. "Listen to this, Ollie." Ollie lifted his head. How she loved this dog. " 'Because of the organized personality of the psychopath, he or she might have a tendency to be better educated than the average sociopath, who probably lacks the attentive skills to excel in school. While psychopaths can fly under the radar of society, many maintaining families and steady work, a sociopath more often lacks the skills and drive for mimicking normal behavior, making seemingly healthy relationships and a stable home less likely. From a criminal standpoint, a sociopath's crimes are typically disorganized and spontaneous, while the psychopath's crimes are well planned out. For this reason, psychopaths are harder to catch than sociopaths, as the sociopath is more apt to leave ample evidence in his or her explosions of violence.' "

"What do you think of that? Could be we've got ourselves an old-fashioned psycho here at the winery. Speaking
of psychos, I wish the boys would call me." She leaned her
head back against the couch and closed her eyes. It was almost midnight, and she couldn't help drifting off.

She wasn't sure if it had been fifteen minutes or fifty, but
just as she'd started dreaming, Ollie jumped off the couch
and gave one of his low growls startling her awake. He
slinked toward the front door. "What is it, boy?"

He gave another growl and Nikki knew that someone
was lurking outside her home.

Twenty-two

SHE got up and inched behind Ollie, who maintained his low growl. Ridgebacks were traditionally hunters used in Africa to hunt lions, so when Ollie was on alert, as he was now, he did not go into the barking guard dog mode like a Doberman or German shepherd might. Instead, he went into a focused mode, slinking low to the ground, and Nikki knew that if someone tried to come through that door, they would have one hundred and ten pounds on them before they knew what hit them. Yes, she loved the dog even more at that moment. Her body shook and adrenaline pumped through her until she heard, "Snow White, open up the goddamned door. It's freezing out here."

Nikki swung it open to see the boys standing there. "I'm gonna kill you two!" She pulled Simon inside and Marco slunk behind him with a Barnes & Noble bag. She should have known they'd gone shopping. "Where have you been and what have you been up to? Do you know how worried I've been? It's past midnight."

"That's so cute, she was worried about us," Simon said.

"You are so sweet, Bellissima." Marco kissed both of her cheeks.

"Sweet, my ass, and don't you Bellissima me and do the kissy face thing." She wagged a finger in front of Marcos's nose. "Do you have any clue what has gone on here to-night?"

They both looked at each other. "No," they replied.

"Let me tell you then." She relayed the entire evening while they stood in the doorway with Ollie sniffing at them. She finally let them pass through in numbed silence. When she was finished and they were seated in the family room, she stared back at them. "And now, do you want to tell me where you have been and why you come a-knocking on my door at midnight?"

"That poor woman," Marco said. "This is terrible. What will we do?"

"Tell me about it," Nikki replied. "Robinson has been all over this place. This is not good at all, but I want to know where you two were. I was seriously worried after I'd had you go into Kensington's room and then you never showed back up, or called, or anything, and with Mizuki and all, God, I thought . . . well, I thought that maybe something bad had happened to you."

Simon shuffled his feet. "No. We're sorry, hon. I forgot my cell phone and Marco turned his off while we were out because we were talking." They glanced at each other.

What was going on between them? They were keeping something from her.

"But we did what you asked and then we went and did some more investigating because of what we found in Kurt's room."

"What do you mean, what you found?" Nikki asked.

"Show her the photos, Marco."

Marco pulled out his cell phone and scooted in next to her. "These are the books he had. The ones you asked us to look for."

Nikki looked at the thumbnails of the photos. "I don't understand." She was looking at a photo of a book. It looked to be some type of comic book.

"They're graphic novels. Very popular in Japan and the cool thing for teens in this country. They read from the back to the front, and when you look at the photos, they tell a story. Look at these." Marco brought out a handful of books from his shopping bag. "We think we got copies of every book that Kurt had stored in his room."

"You guys are smart, but tell me what caused you to do that? What about the books made you think to go out and buy copies?"

"Look at this one." Simon tossed her one of them.

Nikki started from the back as they suggested. It showed a GI Joe–type hunting a businessman who had wronged a group of people.

"Interesting."

"We thought so. See, we can be like you, too." Simon kicked his feet up on the coffee table.

"Like me. What does that mean?"

"I think he means smart," Marco answered.

"No, I meant snoopdavilicious."

"Snoopdavilicious?"

"Come on, Snow White. You're snoopy. We all know it. All of Sonoma County knows it, and your davine and delicious."

"I think it's divine," she said.

"No. It most definitely is not. It's davine."

"I guess I'm flattered." She shook her head. "Okay, so since you two are so snoopdavilicious, what is your gut telling you about these books?"

"That Kurt is a total flipped-out comic book nut," Simon said, sounding proud of himself.

"Beyond that."

Simon took his feet off the table and leaned forward, his face turning so serious it almost made Nikki laugh. "Okey-dokey. Here's what we think, because we talked about it." He looked at Marco, who nodded. "Kurt lives in a fantasy world, a violent one. He reads these Japanese comics, then he comes here as part of the Sansi group. He sees Iwao. Ooh, he thinks. Bad Japanese man just like in my book. I must take him out, like the hero in the book." Simon leaned back, clearly pleased with himself. "What do you think?"

"I think you're nuts, too," she said.

"No, really. Think about it."

"We forgot to tell you, Bellissima, that Kurt has dog tags."

"Dog tags?"

"Yes, like the kind you wear in the army," Simon said. "He's a trained killer. Now that's a theory. Oh, ding, ding, ding." He tapped the side of his head excitedly. "This just came to me. What if Kurt Kensington is a trained killer who was hired by someone else to kill Iwao and Mizuki?"

"I think I could believe that, but what about the taunting of the police with the cork-in-the-mouth thing?" Nikki asked.

"Maybe whoever hired him is beyond prosecution. Maybe Kurt is being protected by someone untouchable, like a government agency, and Iwao really was a bad guy or someone trying to harm our country and now Kurt is trying to plant diversions by doing the crazy stuff." Simon was talking at warp speed, caught up in his titillating theories.

"Okay, Jason Bourne, say that's true, why kill Mizuki?"

"Because she's also bad." Simon propped his feet back up on the coffee table. Ollie sidled up to him and Simon shooed him away. "I'll be Jason Bourne any day, by the way. I *looove* Matt Damon."

"I thought you loved me," Marco said.

"Don't be silly. You know what I mean."

"Guys!"

They both looked at her.

"You could be on to something." Nikki *had* thought of the organized crime angle before. What if Iwao did have some kind of bad business deal? From all accounts with Juan Gonzales (and possibly Ruben Pearlman), he'd done so. What if he'd screwed over someone he shouldn't have and Kurt Kensington was simply a hired gun, or like the other two men, Kurt had a direct link to Iwao? Had Iwao done something to piss him off, too, and Kurt, being a loose cannon, snapped? "Hold that thought." Nikki jumped up from the couch and took the applications off the counter. "We have work to do, boys."

"Wait a minute, are those what I think they are?" Simon asked.

"Yes, and I don't need a scolding. Let's start with Kensington."

"What does she have there?" Marco asked.

"The S.E.E. applications," Simon said.

Marco brought a hand to his mouth. "No!"

"I do."

"Bellissima, you have gone too far."

"No. I have not. Maybe we can read these over and find the crazy person who did this. It's worth a shot and I say we start with Kensington."

"Don't fight it, babe. It's a losing battle." Simon knew that there would be no stopping Nikki now. "At least you know that you can remove ours from that pile. Go ahead and hand me some."

"You are a quick study, my friend," Nikki said.

Simon shrugged, and took a handful from the stack of folders.

Marco followed suit and Nikki opened up Kurt's file. She skimmed over the usual name and address stuff and then read the essay section. The first question was, *Who are you?* Kurt's first sentence was, *I am a killer.*

"Okay, guys. I think I may have something." Nikki continued reading and shared the content with her now captive audience. "Kensington was in Iraq with the special forces. He killed a civilian and was put on trial for it. He says that he was guilty of the crime but thought the man was a terrorist and he was discharged from the army after the trial. He has since been seeing a shrink, who suggested he find his soul and spiritual side again—thus his application to become a member."

"Oh, that's good," Simon said.

"Good? Good? No. The guy is an admitted killer," Nikki said.

"He thought the man was a terrorist," Marco interjected.

"Yes, but the thing is, this guy knows how to kill, and from reading this, he does seem a bit unstable," Nikki said.

The boys couldn't disagree with that. Over the next couple of hours, way late into the night, they all read over the applications. Nothing else really stood out. Yes, everyone had some kind of dysfunction and turmoil. They were all seekers of enlightenment, but nothing screamed at Nikki the way Kensington's application had. Combine that with his horrific dream board, and as far as she was concerned, he appeared certifiable.

The three of them lay back on her couch looking stoned and feeling wiped out.

"You did good, boys. Thank you. I needed your help. But I have to tell you that you scared me to death tonight. You can't tell me that it took you five hours to break and enter the suite and then head on over to Barnes & Noble."

"It did take some time to locate the books," Marco said. "But that's not the only reason it took so long."

"Oh," she said. "I get it." Oops. She did not need any intimate details.

"You have such a dirty mind, Snow White. It's not what you think."

"It's not?"

"No," they both said.

"After Marco heard about the vision board and the baby idea I've been mulling over, he was kind of surprised. We needed to talk."

"Yes, we did," Marco added.

"And after we talked, we had a wonderful dinner of grilled salmon in this amazing Pinot sauce, and some champagne. Then we went to the bookstore and found the books, and then we came straight here."

"That's all you're going to give me?" she asked. "What's the champagne all about?" They drank champagne only on special occasions or to celebrate.

"Well, Snow White." Simon looked at her with tears in his eyes. "Marco and I are going to have a baby. We are going to find a mother to have our child. In fact, we want to know if you'll have our baby."

Twenty-three

NIKKI slept soundly through the night with Ollie at her side. Visions of babies and their toys weaved in and out of her dreams. She was happy for the boys but also a little concerned. A baby was a huge responsibility and she wondered if they were truly up for it, or only following what seemed to be the latest fad, adopting. She had told them gently but clearly that, for her, being the mother of their child was absolutely out of the question. She explained that if she had a baby, she was keeping it for herself. Marco understood right away, but it took Simon a little time to get it through his thick skull that she would not even consider the idea.

It was a little past seven when she poured her first cup of coffee and moved onto the porch with Ollie to drink it and soak in the serenity the valley gave her and so many others who lived there. But as peaceful as the valley was at that moment, a dark cloud of murder continued to hang over her and the winery. When she finished her coffee, she would have to call Derek and let him know about this latest murder. She also needed to get ahold of Alan and find out his plans. This morning was supposed to be free time for the group anyway and then the afternoon was to be spent in meditation with the option to take a yoga class. She also had to get those applications back to Hayden as she'd promised.

Thinking about Alan, Nikki remembered that she needed to go over the notes Derek had taken during their meeting the other day. Regardless of the situation, she still wanted to approach Alan on the product deal he'd discussed with Derek. With all the ickiness that had gone on, she'd almost forgot that one of Alan's reasons for choosing the vineyard as a replacement location to hold the workshop at was because he was interested in working out a licensing agreement deal for the spa products and the organic wines that Malveaux made.

She went into the house, took the notes off Derek's desk in the study, and walked back outside with the coffee. Ollie hadn't changed positions. She would really have to get him up for a run today. They could both use it to burn off some steam.

Nikki started reading over the notes. Luckily for her, she'd learned to read Derek's chicken scratch and then could write things out on a separate piece of paper so they were legible and made sense to her.

Derek had written down what type of payment there would be to Alan and what Alan's responsibilities to the winery and spa would be. He'd notated a basic marketing campaign and put Marco and Simon in charge. This was all stuff he'd mentioned to her. A note at the bottom of the second page was what caught her eye and made her go "Hmmm." Derek had written down VisionScope and next to that Iwao Yamimoto's name. What was that all about? VisionScope? Nikki knew she'd heard that name before, but maybe she was thinking of the dream boards? No. VisionScope. Nikki wracked her brain. Wait a minute. She got up and went back into Derek's study, scanning the books on the shelf. There was one on organic viticulture. She pulled it out. She'd thumbed through it before because Malveaux grew their grapes and processed through organic means. She looked on the side of the book; the logo read VS. She knew that didn't stand for Victoria's Secret. No half-naked women in this book. She turned to the inside cover and found the copyright and the publisher to the book. There it was: VisionScope. They were located in Ontario, Canada. What did any of this mean? And how could she call Derek up and ask him? She had to call Derek and tell him what had happened to Mizuki. How could she in the same breath try to tie in this note he'd written in a more nonchalant business discussion? She closed the book. Impossible.

She took the book back outside and closed her eyes for a minute. What was it she was missing?

"Ah, you do breathe."

Nikki's eyes shot open to find Alan standing over her, dressed in a pair of blue jogging shorts and white T-shirt soaked in sweat. "Hi. I see you've been out for a run."

"Beautiful morning. I needed the exercise and to think."

"I'm sure. Hey, would you like a cup of coffee? It's fresh."

"Normally I would turn caffeine down, but today I feel more human than I have felt in years. I didn't sleep last night at all. I suppose there's still quite a bit of ego left in me after all."

"Is that a yes to the coffee?"

He laughed. "Sure. I'd love some."

"Why don't you come on in? I'd hate for you to get a chill."

He followed her into the house. Ollie came up, sniffed him, and then trotted right behind.

"That's Ollie."

"Hey, boy." Ollie pushed his head under Alan's hand, forcing the pat and causing Alan to laugh.

"He likes you." Nikki handed him the coffee.

"He knows I love animals."

"Come in. Sit down."

They sat down in the family room and for a few seconds sipped their coffee silently. Surely Alan felt as tense as she did. Ollie broke the silence by laying his thick head in Alan's lap. Although Nikki had pretty much decided that Alan Sansi wasn't a murderer, that moment with her big silly dog trusting the man implicitly cemented it for her. Ollie had good instincts.

"I suppose you're wondering what I'm going to do about the workshop," Alan said.

Nikki set her cup down. "Kind of. I'm sure everyone is."

"I forgot how good coffee can be." He smiled. "I've been thinking about it all night and then out on my run and maybe this isn't the best time to conduct a workshop. Maybe everyone needs some space to digest what has happened and then we can regroup at a later time."

He looked sad. Really sad. Nikki thought about it for a moment. "Can I suggest something?"

"Of course."

"I found it kind of weird that when Iwao was killed, the group moved on so quickly, you know. We didn't change up the program. Nothing. I understand that you were trying to get people into a different frame of mind, but isn't there something to be said for talking about what occurred and how people might feel about it?"

"There is and it's also something that I was thinking about while on my run. I've tried so hard to get people to live in their spirit mode that I tend to forget we are also humans and we have to acknowledge that humanity in all of us. I tell people that we are spiritual beings being housed by a body and we are here for the human experience. I suppose that I have forgotten the latter part of that teaching—the idea that we are having a human experience, and if that's so, then we need to feel the feelings. It's possible I've mixed up feelings and ego a little too much and clouded everything when my intentions were to only make things clearer."

When he looked at her again, Nikki could see the lines framing his blue eyes. The passive smile he'd worn since being at the vineyard had faded, and he appeared drawn and even frightened some—he now seemed human. "Maybe, and maybe it's that recognition you acknowledged that makes you the great teacher you are. Instead of bailing on the workshop, can you change it so that the members work through whatever it is they need to around all of this? I would imagine that for some it could be sadness. I mean, you seem pretty sad about it, and for good reason. Iwao was a student of yours."

"Iwao was not so much a student in the way that, say, Simon and Marco are. They truly believe they are working on their souls."

"Aren't they?"

"Absolutely." He took a sip from his mug.

"Then what do you mean about Iwao?"

He closed his eyes, squeezed tight, and then opened them. "Iwao wanted to be a part of the movement of New Age philosophy. Directly in the sales of it. What he failed to understand is there is nothing New Age about anything that I, or many of my colleagues, teach. These teachings have been around since the days that Christ walked the earth and spread his message, or the Buddha, or Krishna. Many of the great teachers of the past have been preaching the same messages that I do. The difference now is that there is what I call a movement in which people who are not necessarily serious about their own personal growth, or that of others, are trying to capitalize on the teachings because they see dollar signs. Look at what the book *The Secret* did. Since then, and even somewhat before that book and movie, people all over were trying to get on the bandwagon to make a buck all in the name of enlightenment."

"How about you?" Nikki asked.

He shook a finger at her. "That's what I like about you. You don't hold back at all."

"No I don't. I've been accused of that and I'll plead guilty."

"Some might say that I am only out for the almighty dollar, but it's not true. I've been spreading my beliefs for over twenty-five years and I truly believe what I teach. The reason we have the money we do is because I don't believe in *lack*; therefore, I never live in a *lack of*."

"I'd say not. I know how much it is to become a member of this group."

"Yes. Did you also know that seventy-five percent of that membership fee goes directly to two charities I sponsor? One is for abused children, the other for abused animals. I believe abuse to be the downfall of our society. Abuse can and does wreck the soul. If you don't believe me about the charities, I will happily show you the books. The other twenty-five percent of the fee covers the expenses for these events. Much of which I subsidize."

Could she just go crawl under a rock right about now? Yikes. "I'm so sorry. I didn't mean to offend you."

"Not at all. You didn't. I don't go around advertising the fact, and the reason I do have people pay that large sum is because I want to know they're serious about it. There is a commitment level there. Even the superwealthy feel a hit at a hundred thousand dollars. It's not something you want to throw away."

"I would say so. But what about Iwao and his lack of sincerity? Why was he in the group? You're not the only one to tell me that he wasn't here for the real deal, by the way."

"I'm sure that I'm not. Iwao needed this group. It was my hope, as it is for everyone who joins, that even though their initial intention seems apparent and good, that they discover the real reason for their involvement. Take Simon and Marco. They think they're here because they want to lose all sense of ego by dropping the name brands and the fancy cars and all the expensive things they buy. But that's not why they're really here. They're here to figure themselves and each other out. They don't need to get rid of all that external stuff, although I always suggest it, especially at first. If you can be comfortable and happy with nothing, then you have it made. We come here with nothing and we leave with nothing. My guess is those two moments—the one of conception and the one at the point of death—may be the two happiest moments of our lives."

"I suppose."

"I know. I get off on tangents. Iwao joined us with the hopes of becoming my publisher and promoter in order to take what I'm doing to his country and make me what he called me the other day, 'a superstar.' That's not what I'm about. I'd hoped that through being with us, Iwao would discover there is real truth in what I say and what people discover through these workshops and that it isn't simply a dollars-and-cents game."

"I see. You have a loyalty to Inspiritus and Rich Higgins."

"I do. To Rich's mother actually. Rich is new at this and sometimes we don't see eye to eye. He can have a tendency to only think about the bottom line. But he is coming into my family, and because of that, I think I can guide him. My family and my daughter will be a part of his growth and experience."

"You really don't allow much to bother you."

"No. It's a waste of time. But what's happened with Iwao and Mizuki does bother me. I didn't know Mizuki at all.

This was the first time that I'd met her. I'd heard of her, although she'd never joined Iwao at a workshop event."

It was not the first time his daughter Sierra had met her, however. Nikki thought about revealing that photo to him and then decided against it.

"Do you have any idea who would want to kill them and why?"

He shook his head. "No. But as you already know, people are not always what they seem."

"That's the truth."

He stood. "I better get back and see what my girls and son are up to and start the day. I like your suggestion. I think what I'll do after breakfast is have the meditation be focused on feelings about these deaths and then we can have some discussion if people are open to it. You're a good teacher yourself. Will you be joining us at all?"

"Maybe for a bit, but I'm having some people over for dinner tonight. In fact, I'd love it if you and your family joined us around six."

"I think that would be wonderful. Thank you, and thank you for listening and teaching me."

Ollie licked his hand as he got up to leave. Nikki walked him to the door and, closing it behind him, leaned against it. Yes, people definitely aren't always who they seem to be. The question was, whose mask was the killer hiding behind?

Twenty-four

NIKKI showered, dressed, and then dropped off the applications with Hayden before heading out to do the grocery shopping for the evening affair.

"Did you find out anything?" Hayden asked.

"No. Everything looks kosher to me."

Hayden sighed. "Good. I'm glad I could help."

Nikki didn't want Hayden to know what she'd learned about Kurt. If Hayden wanted to, she could read the applications herself and make her own determinations, but there was no need to rile the woman up. She'd been decent enough to let Nikki have them.

She'd tried to call Derek on her way to the store but he didn't answer. Was he ignoring her? He wouldn't do that. She didn't like that in almost three days they'd hardly spoken. Was he angry with her? And what about this Sophia? Argh, Nikki was driving herself nuts with thoughts like that. It was totally ridiculous. Derek was simply busy making his deal with Vicente Salvatore and she knew that couldn't be easy. If it were her deal, she'd have given up on the old man a while ago.

After putting the groceries away, she made herself a sandwich, allowed Ollie to eat half of it, and then tried Derek again. This time the call went straight to voicemail. Huh! Okay, then. She knew she should go down and see what was going on with the S.E.E. group and touch base with the boys. Ollie whined at her.

"You're right. I've been ignoring you. Want to go for a run?"

Ollie stood up and made the sound he always did before they went on a run—it sounded kind of like a dying seal. She was never sure exactly what that meant. Either he dreaded getting up, but did it to please her. Or it was the sound of sheer joy at the prospect of stretching his long legs. It didn't matter. She'd been planning on running with him that morning and then she'd blown it off. Now they were heading out. She'd go check out the meditation program afterward for an hour, see if she could learn anything new, then get back home and start fixing the meal.

Once on the trail, hearing her feet pound the earth beneath her as she weaved in and out of rows of grapevines, making it a game for Ollie, Nikki let go of thoughts of murder, notions of beautiful Italian women trying to scam her lover, and philosophies from New Age, old age, or whenever. It was her, the ground, and the dog—all moving together.

At one point she sprinted up the hill on the shadiest section of the vineyard. That was the best place for Chardonnay grapes. In the newest vines taking hold, small buds illuminated the ends as the sun cast down a soft, light yellow, like a baby chick's new fuzz. As she went farther up the hill, Ollie at her feet still, the vines matured and twisted into fruitful plants with grapes filling with their sweet juices.

The ends of these plants now glowed a soft green that she was certain no artist had ever captured. This scene was God's painting.

When the pair reached the top of the hill, Nikki looked out over the Malveaux vineyards—awe-inspiring rolling hills of grapevines in all shades of greens and purples, intermixed with dark chocolate soil and almost an earthen red soil in other areas. Ollie sat down next to her, panting, also taking it in. She scratched his head. "What do you say we get some water?"

He wagged his tail and they were off again down the hill this time. As they rounded the back side of the hotel, the Dumpster that Housekeeping used glared at her. The sun beat down on the green metal. Nikki stopped in front of it. The note that Juan wrote to Iwao had never been found. It could be in the Dumpster. How hard could this be? She could just rummage around a bit. Right? Ooh, yuck! Ollie sat down and looked up at her.

"I'll just see what's at the top. You stay." She opened up the lid and luckily found that all the trash bags were tied up the way Housekeeping had been asked to do. It kept down on the flies in the area. She pulled out the bags and that was when things got messy.

There was something so wrong about going through others' trash—and so disgusting. Ollie sat there looking as grossed out as she was. She riffled through items that made her want to barf, but she kept on going. And into the fifth bag, she hit pay dirt. A crumpled-up, handwritten note on legal paper. She unfolded it. *Keep the party for yourself this time. I'm done dealing with you.* This had to be the note, didn't it? Juan was right. The note had not been signed, yet this had to be his just by the tone of it. Who else could have written it? Ruben? Maybe. Anyone else? Nikki didn't have a clue but knew she needed to get this to Robinson and she desperately needed to wash her hands. At least twice. With antibacterial soap.

She shoved the note into the waistband of her running pants and started off toward the café to get herself and Ollie some water and wash her hands. She'd take a shower as soon as she got home.

They kept a water bowl in the kitchen of the café for Ollie. When she got there, Nikki scrubbed her arms and hands a few times with soap and water and then got herself a bottle of water. Setting the bottle down, she spotted someone sitting alone in the corner of the café. The way the sun shone over the open-air café made it difficult to see the person's face. Honeysuckle and ivy cascaded throughout the café from overhead and up the side of the walls, casting shadows on the ground and in the corners.

The kitchen faced the café, like a trattoria—very wine country chic. Nikki squinted. Who was that?

Ollie followed her out of the kitchen and she walked over to the person. It was a woman. She looked up as Nikki and Ollie came toward her. It was Sierra Sansi. Her face was tearstained and she looked miserable.

"Sierra? You okay?"

"Sure, I am. I'm perfect, just like the rest of my family."

Now what was the comeback to that?

Twenty-five

THE only way to handle a loaded statement like the one Sierra had dumped on Nikki was to ask a loaded question. "Why aren't you perfect?"

Sierra's sad blue eyes, the same as her father's, looked at Nikki. "There are too many reasons."

Nikki was dealing with a victim. Or a psychopath...

"Oh, come on, Sierra. I realize I don't know you all that well, but you seem fine to me. You seem like a great young woman."

"Ha! My sister doesn't think so, my mother doesn't think so, and my brother definitely doesn't think so." She wrinkled up her nose. "Do you smell that? Something smells like trash."

"Hmmm. No. I don't." She wasn't about to tell Sierra about her Dumpster escapade. "What about your dad?" Nikki pulled up a chair opposite Sierra and took a seat. Ollie dutifully plopped down next to her. The Mexican pavered floor probably felt good against his skin.

"My dad thinks everyone is perfect. No one can do any wrong in his eyes."

Nikki cupped a hand under her chin and leaned her elbow on the table. "Have you ever thought, Sierra, and again, I don't know you very well, but I do know people tend to be their own harshest critic, so have you ever thought that maybe it's not about anyone else in your family or outside your family? Maybe it's *you* expecting yourself to be perfect. I understand you do martial arts. That type of discipline demands a certain level of perfection, doesn't it?"

"I don't do it anymore. You really don't smell anything rotten like?"

Nikki did her best to will the stench off her body. "Nope. I heard you were really good at martial arts. Why did you quit?"

"Who told you that I was good?"

"Actually, your sister did."

"Hayden said that?" There was a spark in Sierra's eyes.

"Yes, she did. She even mentioned that you had done some movie-related stuff, like stunts and choreography for a martial arts movie."

"That's true, but not now. It was kind of a passing phase. It wasn't for me." Sierra fidgeted with the ends of the white tablecloth.

"Oh, come on." Nikki coaxed. "There is far more to this than you're telling me. You said the other night on the wine train, before everything went south, that I seemed like I'd be a good best friend. Tell me your story."

Sierra looked at her, and a gaze that Nikki recognized crossed Sierra's face. She knew it because she'd had that same look in her own eyes many times—from that early distrusting age of about four. "Look, I'm only here to listen.

I like your dad. I think he's cool. I think he has some good philosophies and a nice energy about him. I've actually learned a few things from him in the last couple of days, including that sometimes the best soul to share your fears and doubts with is the soul of a stranger." Okay, so Alan had not said that to her, but it kind of sounded like something he would say.

"You buy into that crap?"

Ooops. Maybe Nikki was wrong. "Well, don't you?"

"I don't know. Sometimes. I straddle the fence, you know? When my life is good and on target, I think my dad is a genius. But when it all goes to hell, I think he's full of it."

Nikki sat back. "Let me guess... These days you think he's full of it?"

She nodded. "Basically. I do. But he believes it. My mother believes it, so does my sister even though she says she doesn't know. She's too *pragmatic* for such spiritual matters."

Nikki smiled at her. She was jaded but funny. She could relate to Sierra. "I like people and I think you seem like a nice woman, but if you don't want to share with me, it's fine. I need to check in with the meditation your dad is running. Thought I might give it a half hour or so, and then I have to get home and start fixing dinner for tonight. Your dad told you about it, right? You coming?"

She nodded.

"Good. If you ever need a friend, some people think I'm okay." Nikki knew it was evil. In all sincerity, she meant it, though, and wanted to hear the woman's woes and felt for her, but c'mon! There was no denying that she wanted to find the truth about Iwao and Mizuki. If in becoming Sierra's friend she learned something that could help, then whom had she wronged? She had to get this girl talking—especially about her connection to Iwao and his nephew. And that meant it was not beneath her to use reverse psychology.

Nikki stood. "See you tonight. Come on, boy." Ollie perked up. Well, his ears did anyway.

Sierra grabbed her hand. "No. Sit down, please. I need to talk to someone, and like I said, sometimes I think my dad is brilliant, and since he thinks a stranger's soul is better than that of someone you know, here goes nothing."

Nikki hoped she wasn't going to hell for that little lie. She looked upward for a second. The words "sorry" and "forgive me" flashed through her mind. Surely God would understand that she'd only stretched the truth in the name of justice. Wouldn't he?

"I was really into martial arts." Sierra looked at her. "And my dad had a connection, actually through Juan Gonzales here, and was able to get me on as a stunt choreographer for a movie and it was good. I enjoyed it." Her voice shook when she spoke.

"Sierra?"

"I met someone on the set and I fell in love with him. He was, um, well, he was Iwao Yamimoto's nephew," Sierra stammered.

"Really?" Of course, Nikki knew this, but Sierra telling her opened up a whole new group of possibilities to explore.

"Yes." Sierra closed her eyes, tears forming. "It was one of those things that you hear about or see in a movie—true love at first sight." She wiped her face. "I started martial arts when I was seventeen. I'd been getting into some trouble and my dad could see that I wasn't going to go with the flow, like Eli or Hayden. I needed another outlet. I got good at it and I liked it. It also got me away from the party scene. Then three years ago, after one of these workshops, my dad introduced me to Juan Gonzales. He'd recently joined the group."

"I don't mean to interrupt, but I was curious about how long a member can be a member before there is any turnover?" This was a question Nikki had forgotten to ask Hayden but had been curious about it.

"There's kind of an unofficial rule, because my dad doesn't like rules or really believe in them. He feels that a member should head out on their own when they're ready, but the unsaid rule is after five years, so I think that either this year or maybe next will be Juan's fade-out. But some people only come in for one year, or even just one event, and then they're finished with it. I think some don't want to pay the annual dues or they feel like they got what they needed, but others stay for a while. Mr. Gonzales is one of those and so is Mr. Pearlman."

Nikki figured there could be a clue within the length of time that the men had been members. One of those gut feelings. "So, your dad introduced you to Juan because he was involved with movies?"

Sierra nodded. "More than that. Juan had a girlfriend who'd written a screenplay, kind of like a romance version of *Kill Bill*."

"Not sure how that would work," Nikki quipped.

"It didn't exactly. But my dad told Juan that I was a black belt and that martial arts was my thing, and Juan asked my dad if I would come and do some choreography and stunt work for the movie."

"I take it that you did?"

"I did and that's where I met Jen. He was the star of the production, and from the minute I saw him, he took my breath away. Like I said, it was love at first sight."

Nikki could understand that. It hadn't necessarily been love at first sight for her, but it had at least been lust. Derek said he'd felt the same way. Too bad it had taken so long for them to get it right. "Did you meet Iwao Yamimoto while doing that movie?"

"Yes. He was one of the financiers on the film and he'd been behind Jen getting involved. I don't think Jen ever wanted to be any kind of star. In fact, I know he didn't, but Jen was like a son to Iwao in many ways. Iwao and his wife had never been able to have children and Jen's parents both died when he was pretty young. Iwao and his wife, who is really Jen's aunt, raised him. Jen was very close to his aunt. But then when he was a teenager, he said that she started having some emotional problems that escalated until she had to be institutionalized. I know it really affected him because she was like a mother to him. And his uncle was always *involved* in his life."

The way Sierra said the word "involved" sounded almost bitter. "Did you think he intruded too much in Jen's life?"

She sighed heavily. "I think Iwao Yamimoto was not someone who really knew how to love others, including his nephew. Control was how he worked. He saw Jen as a good way to make money. Jen is so good-looking and sweet and funny and I think Iwao always wanted to be the big man. I don't know how to explain it, but Iwao had these dreams and visions of being, like, a Japanese Donald Trump or something. He was really caught up into the glitz and glamour of the celebrity world and also the world of big business moguls here in America."

"You didn't like Iwao, did you?" Nikki reached down and gave Ollie a scratch on the head.

"I won't lie. No. I didn't. I thought he used Jen. I thought he used a lot of people and I'm not surprised that he's dead."

"What about Mizuki? Did you know her?"

Sierra looked down, her face darkening. "A little bit. I met her once when Jen and I went to Hawaii. His uncle and Mizuki were there. We couldn't really speak to each other. She was very submissive and didn't speak English, but she seemed like a nice person. I liked her from what I knew. It made me not like Iwao even more. I know that I shouldn't say that because he's dead."

"What happened with the movie?"

"It went nowhere. Juan Gonzales and Ruben Pearlman, who did the musical score and helped finance the movie, lost a ton of money. And I'm pretty sure that when Iwao put it all together, he inflated everything. Juan brought Ruben in, and the irony is, that's how Ruben got involved with the S.E.E. members. Then Iwao insisted I help him get in with my dad."

"I would bet there were some hard feelings between Ruben and Juan toward Iwao."

She shrugged. "I think so, but my dad is big on forgiveness and preaches it. He knew a little about what had gone on between the three men because I'd told him. My dad is hands-off, though. He doesn't like to get involved in other people's problems and he hates gossip. I think part of the reason he let Iwao join is because he wanted the three of them to figure out the *lesson* behind their *journey* together."

"And how about you? You didn't stay with Jen?"

"No." She became noticeably emotional again at the mention of this.

"When we were in Hawaii together, I thought Jen was going to propose to me. He wanted to tell his uncle about our plans for the future. We'd talked about marriage. Then I woke up on the last day and Jen was gone. Iwao told me that he'd gone back to Japan and gave me a letter Jen had written for me."

"What?"

"I know. It didn't make sense to me then and it still doesn't. All he wrote was that we weren't meant to be together and he wanted me to find someone else."

"That doesn't make sense. Did he ever contact you again?"

"No. I tried to find out where he was and had no luck. Iwao said that he was back home and had met someone else. He actually told me this when he came here on Thursday. I was shocked to see that he was here. I didn't think he and Juan and Ruben had ever dealt with their issues. Knowing I would be here after the breakup with Jen...it didn't make sense that he was here. The only thing I can think of is that he is completely motivated by money and that he desperately wanted to get my dad and Eli to publish their books with his company. He had some big plans to turn my dad into a celebrity motivational speaker. He told my dad that he was going to get him on television here and in Japan and together they would be rich."

"That's not your dad's motivation. The money."

"No. Not at all. Anyway, that's my saga...and I do feel better after talking to someone. It's hard in my family. Even though we're supposed to *be* who we are, it isn't always possible."

Nikki reached across the table and covered the woman's hand with her own. "I think who you are, Sierra, is a good person." She smiled. "And I'm sorry about the way things happened with you and Jen." Nikki couldn't imagine if Derek left her without any explanation. And then to find out he'd wound up with someone else? Unbelievable.

Sierra looked up, past Nikki, her lips quivering. Her face paled.

"Sierra, are you okay?"

"Jen," she replied.

Nikki turned around to see a handsome Japanese man—sculpted cheekbones, dark hair slicked back, brown eyes trained on Sierra's face. Jen Yamimoto stood between the arches of the café and the hotel lobby.

Twenty-six

NIKKI stood up and walked over to the man. She introduced herself. Sierra hadn't moved from the table.

"Hello. I'm Jen Yamimoto. I've come because I've been informed of my uncle's death." He looked past Nikki. "Sierra?"

She finally stood and came toward them. "Jen."

"I didn't know you would be here. I didn't know that my uncle had come for a workshop. The police told me when they called me, but oh, wow, it's so good to see you."

Sierra stared at him.

Jen looked at Nikki, his hands clasped in front of him. "I'm sorry. Could you excuse us?" Then he looked back at Sierra.

Nikki glanced at Sierra, who was beginning to cry again. She didn't know if she should leave her alone with a man who'd broken her heart. "Sierra, is that okay?"

"Yes," she replied in a whisper.

"If you need me, please call my cell phone. It's on the list that I gave everyone when they checked in," Nikki told her.

She nodded and Nikki called for Ollie, who jumped up.

Back into a run, she and Ollie headed down to the house. She had a big meal to put together and her time spent with Sierra didn't leave any room for her to head over to the meditation and yoga for the afternoon. Not to mention the fact that she smelled like garbage.

There were a lot of things Sierra had said that Nikki needed to process, and now with Jen Yamimoto showing up, there was an additional element racing through her mind. Jen might have had a motive to murder his uncle. Had he really just arrived in the Napa Valley?

Twenty-seven

NIKKI didn't have as much time to prepare as she'd hoped. She hadn't made a meal for this many people in a long time and she'd lost her knack for it. Ollie was underfoot the entire time she diced, chopped, and sliced, and she nearly tripped over his large frame more than once. She should have gotten takeout. Pizza would have been ideal.

She looked at the clock and could see she had less than an hour left. When she'd come home from her outing, she'd showered, towel-dried her hair, and donned a robe before preparing the meal. Now she needed to pull herself together quickly before the guests arrived, so she put the cornbread in the oven, stirred the chili, and headed into her bedroom. Once there, she sprayed on the perfume that Derek bought her, the one that smelled like cherry blossoms and something sweet, maybe vanilla. Oh, and did it remind her of the night he gave it to her. The night he suggested they live together.

She'd walked into his house that evening, amazed at how romantically Derek had set the mood. He'd gone all out. She couldn't remember ever seeing it look so beautiful. Acoustic guitar played on the surround sound, candles illuminated the room, and there was even a path of rose petals. Yes, it was straight out of a romance novel, but Nikki had reveled in all of it. What she hadn't known was what the big deal was all about. He'd told her that morning he planned to grab some steaks and they could barbeque and maybe watch a movie that night. Things had gotten serious between them, and for the past several months they'd typically spent most nights together. She even had a drawer and a portion of the closet in his room designated as her own, even though she was only up the hill at the hotel. So the minute Nikki nonchalantly opened the door to Derek's house was the minute she knew that night was not just about barbeque.

"Derek?" she'd called out.

"Follow the roses." His voice came from the bedroom. This was going to be good.

Following the rose path didn't lead her straight to the bedroom, though; it led to the bathroom, where he had the door closed. Outside the door on the floor were two champagne flutes and a bottle of Dom. He'd taped a note on the door. *Move in with me*, it read.

Nikki had reread that note ten times in a fraction of a second, her smile growing each time.

"Did you read it?" he'd asked.

She could hear him in a bath.

"Yes."

"I'm not good with rejection, you know, so if you're in, then bring the champagne and get in here with me. If you're not, go quickly so I can drown myself. But stick the champagne in here first, so it won't be as painful."

She'd opened the door and picked up the bottle of champagne, walking into the bathroom. Derek had sunk under water and rose with a big smile, tossing his wet blond hair. "Thank you for saving my life."

"You knew I'd say yes."

"I was hoping, because drowning is not how I want to go out of this world. You coming in?"

Nikki had undressed, popped the cork on the champagne, and poured them each a glass. Stepping into the warm bath, which was also topped with rose petals, she'd handed him his champagne and slid down into the water. They'd toasted and before long their glasses were empty and there was more water on the floor than in the tub.

He'd given her the cherry blossom perfume later after they'd made love—in the bed this time—and told her that he'd never been so happy. Neither had she.

Nikki missed him now, wondering why he hadn't called her all day. She knew why she hadn't called him; another murder would send him over the edge. She'd checked the weather report and knew he wasn't getting out of New York tonight.

After pulling on a cute pair of dark jeans and a mocha-colored silk blouse, she brushed her hair straight back and patted on enough makeup to keep her from looking like death warmed over. Then Nikki headed back into the kitchen for the finishing touches. She couldn't believe she'd actually pulled it together.

The food smelled incredible—cornbread, chili, and green salad. It wasn't gourmet by any means. Just good old-fashioned cooking at its finest. She set the large dining room table for ten. Petie would probably wind up sitting on his mother's lap. It would be an interesting evening, and Nikki wondered what everyone's reaction would be to having Robinson join them.

The first to show up were the Sansi family and crew. Nikki was surprised to see that Jen was with them. Sierra was all smiles.

"Thank you for inviting us into your home. I hope you don't mind that we brought an extra guest," Lulu Sansi said, wearing one of her flowing skirts, the daisy sandals, and again a poet blouse. Nikki hadn't gotten a chance to know Lulu or her and Alan's son, Eli, at all. They were at all of the events but stood back from the crowd and allowed Alan to take the spotlight.

"Not at all. I met Jen earlier this afternoon. Glad you could join us." Whatever had transpired in the last couple of hours between Sierra and Jen had obviously changed everything between them, because they looked very much together and it sent some red flags up in Nikki's mind. How juicy was this? Long-lost love that mysteriously disappeared years ago suddenly returns? Nikki was dying to get the lowdown on this one.

But instead she played hostess, serving up the drinks and some appetizers, as Simon and Marco joined the group, all designer duded out and announcing their future plans to become parents.

"But before we adopt"—Simon placed a hand on Alan's shoulder—"we would really like it if you could perform a partner celebration for us. A kind of marriage, well, duh, I mean a wedding, okay. It's so hard to know what others will think and say. But who am I kidding? It's you and me. I'm so wound up. Sorry."

Marco put an arm around him. "Breathe." He smiled at Alan and everyone laughed.

The laughter stopped when Robinson walked through the door.

"Oh, no," Hayden Sansi said. "What now?"

Nikki looked at Hayden, and Rich put a protective arm

around her. "Tell us there hasn't been another murder," he said.

"No, man. I'm only coming for dinner. I was invited." Poor Robinson probably felt like the angel of death; the sight of him sent people running in fear.

All eyes, including Robinson's, now turned to Nikki. "Yes, and we're waiting for one more guest. Oh, look, here she is now."

Saved by Alyssa and Petie. They came through the door and Alyssa gave Nikki a hug before glancing around. Seeing all of the strange faces looking at him, Petie started to cry. As much as Nikki hated to see a kid crying, she knew that if anything can break up an uncomfortable silence, it's the universal fuss that swirls around a kid's tears. Among the oohs and aahs and soothing words being spoken to the toddler, Nikki made her way back into the kitchen and, much to her own chagrin, slammed down a glass of wine. Wrong thing to do maybe, but she was going to have to handle the evening with finesse. She hadn't exactly planned it out— how everyone would react to one another's presence—but Hayden was clearly displeased that Robinson was joining them for dinner.

Robinson came into the kitchen a minute later. "What are you up to, Sands? I doubt you're hoping I'll convert and join this group."

"Of course not." She'd leave the matchmaking part out of it. "I thought maybe if people were in an intimate situation, you could learn more about them."

"Technically, I shouldn't be here. I'm the detective on a murder case where I've had to question all of these people and none of them is above suspicion yet. Where's the dog?"

"I put him in the bedroom. With all of these people, I hate to have him running around. Trust me, he prefers it that way."

"I'm not liking this, Sands."

"Lighten up. Have a drink." She handed him a glass of Merlot and spooned out bowls of chili. "Go set these in there for me, please. Oh, wait," she said. "Did you find a DVD in Mizuki's stuff?"

"Yes. Why?"

"Duh. I'm wondering if it's the DVD I told you about. The one Iwao was trying to hand to Alan the other day. I'm thinking there might be something on there to lead to the killer."

"There was nothing on it, except a Japanese soap opera. My guess is that the geisha brought it to keep herself entertained."

"Then that's not it." Nikki was disappointed, but the odds that Iwao and Alan shared a mutual interest in Japanese soaps was slim to none.

"Probably not, but we haven't found any other DVDs," he replied.

"You need to keep looking," she said.

"You always this bossy?"

She frowned at him and handed over a bowl. "Please. I know there's something on that DVD. Now take these bowls out." She took out the macaroni and cheese she'd put together for Petie and called everyone in for dinner.

Robinson started to sit down between her and Simon but she stopped him. "Nope. I sort of have an arrangement. Do you mind sitting over there? And then, Alyssa, how about you next to the detective? I mean Jonah. Right? We can call you Jonah since this is a social affair." So much for casually seating the guests in their assigned seats.

Simon leaned in and whispered, "Smooth."

She kicked him under the table.

Eventually everyone was seated exactly where Nikki wanted them.

"This is wonderful," Alan said, tasting the chili. "And the wine. I don't drink much wine, but I really like this." He held up his glass of Merlot.

"I'll tell Derek. We only produced a few cases of it. I think we have two left. It's one of our best wines and I thought it would be nice to serve it tonight."

"We appreciate it and we appreciate everything you've done for the group." Alan paused. "Nikki, I wanted to let you know that after the meditation practice we did today, I decided to wrap up the event tomorrow morning and allow everyone to go home. I've already informed the family and I'll let everyone else know in the morning. Many of the members aren't getting what they hoped out of this, for obvious reasons, and would prefer to leave. Is that all right with you, Detective?"

Nikki wasn't surprised to hear that Alan was ending the event early; he had done his best to plow through, but with the occurrence of two murders, he couldn't very well be expected to continue. Apparently enlightenment could take one only so far. Even Alan. Nikki had certainly done her best, though. And it seemed that she had done her best with Alyssa as well, since her friend was noticeably gazing at the handsome detective.

Jonah nodded his head toward Alan. "That should be fine. But I'd like to be here when everyone is getting ready to go. I need to be sure I have all the information I need. If anything changes by the morning, I'll let you know."

Alyssa glanced at Nikki and smiled and winked back. Nikki leaned into Simon. "I may not be smooth but I think I do a good job at matchmaking."

Petie started to get restless toward the end of the dinner and so everyone moved into the family room to let him run around while Nikki served strawberry tarts. Luckily for her, she had frozen a dozen of them the last time she made them, and therefore, she didn't have to prep them today like she had the rest of the meal. From the kitchen, she could see Robinson playing on the floor with Petie and Alyssa. Alan was over by the fireplace, talking to Rich and Hayden. Jen and Sierra were outside in the backyard, and Eli and Lulu were visiting with Simon and Marco.

Eli was different. Nikki had failed to get to know him this weekend. He never said much. Even over dinner, he almost seemed like wallpaper rather than a person sitting there. Marco was right—Eli appeared to be walking in his father's shadow but it overshadowed him so much that he really had no apparent identity of his own. But that didn't give him a motive to murder Iwao Yamimoto and Mizuki. Nikki mentally crossed him off her list.

She took a good look at the rest of the Sansi family. Lulu, like Eli, kind of hung back in the shadows, but she wasn't the wallflower her son was. She seemed to play the supporting role to her husband—the good and devoted wife and mother. Nikki could find no motive for her to want to murder anyone either.

What about Hayden? She was practical, in control of much of her father's business. But Nikki also could not figure Hayden into this murder business. Her arms were wrapped around Rich, who was another elusive one in this crowd of suspects. Had Rich Higgins been flying under the radar? Could he have wanted Iwao dead? Iwao had been trying to get Alan to change publishing houses. Would that make Rich angry enough to murder him? But then why kill Mizuki? No. He didn't seem to be a likely candidate either.

Then there were Sierra and Jen. Why had Jen left Sierra and why had he returned? Yes, because of his uncle's murder, but was there something even more sinister there? She didn't know. Nikki opened up the sliders to take Jen and Sierra their desserts.

"Oh, my gosh, this is wonderful. Thank you," Sierra said,

eyeing the strawberry treat. The light had come back into her cornflower blue eyes. She'd fixed herself up for the evening and was wearing a turquoise sweater and a long denim skirt.

"You're welcome."

"Thanks for having me," Jen said. "Your home is lovely and your food is delicious."

"I'm pleased you could come. How are you doing with everything? With your uncle's death and his . . ."

"Mistress?" Jen asked. Nikki didn't respond. "Of course Mizuki was his mistress. She had been for many years. I'm fine, I think. There are things, plans that I have to make. My auntie is incapable of that. She's been hospitalized for years."

"I'm sorry to hear that," Nikki replied.

"It has been hard. I love her very much. I go to visit her often."

"You're living in Japan then?"

"Yes."

"Not for long, though." Sierra held out her hand and showed off a beautiful antique-looking ring. There was an emerald diamond in the middle of the sterling setting, surrounded by small emeralds. "This had been his mother's ring." She looked up at Jen and smiled.

He put an arm around her, kissing her on the cheek. "We've missed so much time together," he said.

Nikki cleared her throat. "Not to pry . . ." Yeah, right. "But I'm curious. Sierra told me about your breakup while in Hawaii a couple of years ago. I know it's not my business, but why? What happened?"

Jen and Sierra looked at each other. "My uncle. That's why. He said if I married Sierra, he would no longer pay for my auntie's care. I couldn't afford it and I could not put that on Sierra's family. I left her and I've hated myself for it. But my uncle controlled everything in my life and in the lives of those around him. I'm sad he's gone, but now I won't be controlled by him any longer."

"Why would he do that? Want to keep you two apart?" Nikki asked.

"Control. And for this." He held out Sierra's hand. "The ring. It has been in my family for over two hundred years and my uncle is a traditionalist. Or he was, anyway. He did not want me to give this to a white woman. He had an arranged marriage already planned for me, and the woman I was supposed to marry already had the ring. When the police called and told me what had happened, I went to her and she gave it back. I think she may have been as relieved as I was. I know there's another man she's in love with and now she's free to be with him. And"—he beamed at Sierra— "I'm free to be with the woman I love."

Sounded like a decent motive right there. "Do they still have arranged marriages in Japan?" Nikki asked.

"Some. Old families. Old money. A lot of tradition," he replied.

"Sounds to me as if your uncle was a complicated man." Jen smiled. "To say the least."

"We are together now and that's what counts. I hope they find this killer and we can put everything behind us and move on with our lives," Sierra said.

"Me, too," Nikki replied. "I better get back inside and see if anyone else needs anything. Do you?"

They didn't. Nikki closed the sliders behind her, full of questions about Jen and Sierra.

Her mind was racing with these questions, along with questions about Kurt Kensington. His strange behavior and what she'd learned about him on his application still made him look like the number one suspect in her book. She wished she could get Robinson to see eye to eye with her on that. There was also this Gonzales-Pearlman angle, and she knew that Robinson felt the answers were snarled up in that web.

She shook her head. Wherever the answers lay as to who had committed the murders, they weren't going to be found tonight.

Dessert went over as well as dinner, and before long everyone was getting ready to leave. Everyone except for Alyssa and Robinson. Petie had fallen asleep with his head in his mother's lap on the couch.

Nikki said good night to the guests who were leaving. Marco kissed her on the cheeks as usual. "Beautiful, Bellissima. Lovely party. Thank you." She kissed him back.

Simon wrapped an arm around her and leaned a head on her shoulder. He glanced at Alyssa and Robinson. "You are good. I'm impressed, Snow White."

Nikki didn't bother the couple, who continued to talk while she did most of the dishes. It was after ten when they told her good night and Robinson carried Petie out to the car for her.

Alyssa walked ahead with Petie's bag. Robinson thanked her.

"Learn anything?" she asked.

"Not a damn thing about the investigation." He smiled. "But I did discover you sure can cook. I had a great time, Nikki."

She closed the door behind Robinson. She wanted to tell him what she'd discovered about Kensington, her thoughts on Jen and Sierra, and give him the note. But at that moment, after seeing him with Alyssa and Petie, she decided to wait until the morning. Maybe tonight she hadn't been able to tie this mystery together, but at least she was making people happy.

Partygoer Chili
with Hahn Estate Merlot

Nikki has herself in one spicy mess, but at least she's good at mixing things up. Way to go on the matchmaker front. If you have to put together a shindig for a group of your family and friends, or else enlightened dysfunctionals (who could also be family and friends), then fix a pot of chili and uncork this simple, soft Merlot by Hahn Estate, with fruit flavors of black cherry and raspberry that are the perfect pairing with this chili.

SPICE MIX A

1 tbsp onion powder
1 tbsp ground cumin
1 tsp garlic salt
3 tbsp chili powder
½ tsp salt
½ tsp pepper

SPICE MIX B

3 tbsp chili powder
1 tbsp ground cumin
1 tbsp brown sugar
½ tsp salt
½ tsp onion powder

CHILI

1 tbsp cooking oil
3 lbs London broil, cut into ¼" cubes
1 small onion, finely chopped
1 green pepper, chopped
8-oz can chopped green chilies
8-oz can tomato sauce
12-oz can beer
13-oz can beef broth
13-oz can chicken broth
3 tbsp chipotle hot sauce
½ tsp Tabasco sauce

In a large Dutch oven, heat cooking oil over medium heat and cook beef until brown on all sides. Add onions, peppers, tomato sauce, beer, beef broth, chicken broth, and spice mix A. Bring to a boil, lower heat, and simmer for about 1 ½ hours.

Stir in spice mix B, chipotle sauce, and Tabasco. Simmer ½ hour longer.

Twenty-eight

THE night had been interesting on so many fronts. Nikki was tired but she wanted to write it all down and sort through her thoughts. Ollie climbed up next to her. "You're getting spoiled," she said. "Wait until your master gets home." Thinking about Derek made her sad. She wished he'd call.

If there was anything at all to that "ask and you shall receive" verse, or the law of the universe stuff, then it must've been working because the phone rang and on the other end was Derek.

"It is so good to hear your voice. Why haven't you called?"

"You wouldn't believe me if I told you," he said, sounding exhausted.

"Of course I would. Is everything okay?"

"For the most part." Derek's voice sounded funny.

"Derek, what in the heck are you talking about?"

"I don't think this thing between us and the Salvatores is going to work out."

"Why? What gives?"

"Today, Vicente decides he wants to go to the Catskills. It's freezing-ass cold and he wants to drive to the *Catskills*. Let me remind you that the biggest snowstorm ever is going on here."

Uh-oh. He'd had a few drinks. Not like Derek to sound tipsy and even then some. He would often have a glass or two of wine in the evening, but never enough to make him slur. And he was definitely slurring tonight. "Uh-huh."

"Right. We all get in the limo, and don't ask me why I agreed to this. Right now I feel so stupid."

"Who is 'we all'?"

"Vicente, and get this, he has a bodyguard."

"Is he in the mob?"

"I wonder. Total ass, though."

"You're kind of scaring me." She scratched Ollie between his ears, reminding herself that there was nothing to be scared of with him right there.

"And his daughter was with us, too."

"Sophia, right?" She jumped up and went straight for the computer. She'd forgotten to Google "Sophia Salvatore." She kept the phone in the crook of her chin. Ollie did not follow her. Bad dog.

"Yeah, yeah. Her."

"Oh." Oh. Sophia Salvatore was listed on some site about Italian winery owners. The photo was small. She stood next to her father, but small or not, Nikki could tell she was gorgeous. Just as she'd thought. "What happened?"

"Okay, so we get halfway there, going as slow as can be, and even the bodyguard is trying to explain to Vicente that we should go back to the city, but you think that old fart is listening to anyone else? No. Claims he's on his death bed practically and may never get back here and something about his aunt who moved to the Catskills when he was a boy and he wanted to go back because he'd spent a summer with her before she died and it was the best time of his life. Talk about sentimental." Man, was Derek rambling tonight.

"Oh, Derek."

"It gets better. We get out and the driver gets lost, and the next thing I know, we start having car trouble and the driver has to pull over. He calls his dispatch service and they tell him it's gonna be at least two hours before anyone can get out there. So, we're sitting there with the heater on, and I'm still trying to make a deal with this guy, and all he wants to do is drink port and shove his daughter on me while telling me I need to marry her."

Nikki's hands folded into fists. "He what? That—"

"I know. Don't get yourself all worked up."

"Excuse me?"

"I love you and only you. Finally, after something like three hours or more...God, I don't know, I lost track of time...but finally some guy pulls over in an old pickup and offers help. About that time another limo pulls up for the Salvatores. I was three sheets to the wind by then, and I told Vicente to forget the deal. He was too difficult to work with and I didn't want to marry his daughter. I paid the guy who stopped to help us two hundred dollars to drive me back to Manhattan. I just got back here."

"Oh, no." Nikki tried not to laugh.

"How about you? How was your day? Tell me they caught whoever murdered Iwao. I'm hoping I can get out of here in the morning. They're saying there's a chance."

"No. They actually don't have a suspect yet."

"Hmmm."

She couldn't tell him now about Mizuki. Not after the day he had, and he sounded like he needed to go to bed. "Gosh, it must be two o' clock in the morning there."

"Don't I know it. I'm worried about you, and I miss you."

"I miss you, too, but you don't have to worry. I have Ollie at my side."

"Yeah. Good. How is the boy?"

Nikki removed herself from the desk and went back into the bedroom, sliding in between the covers. "He's good."

"You in bed?"

"Yes," she said.

"Nice. I wish I was there. What are you wearing?" he asked.

"Well, um. It's lacy and blue and very pretty." She was never good at this kind of thing, and lacy, blue, and pretty wasn't even close to what she had on.

"Liar."

"I know."

"I know what you're wearing. You're wearing one of my old T-shirts and a pair of flannel pajama bottoms."

"Nope. I have your boxers on."

He cracked up. "I can't wait to see you."

"You better get some sleep."

"You, too. I love you, Nikki."

"I love you, too."

A few minutes after they'd hung up, Nikki thought about getting back up and writing down her thoughts about the night. Instead she opted for falling asleep, knowing that there was a man a few thousand miles away, a man who really loved her, who was keeping her warm with his words.

Twenty-nine

EARLY the following morning, Nikki checked the news and found out that the airports were still closed on the East Coast. The snowstorm was causing major mayhem all over the country, and after talking to Derek last night, there was nothing she wanted more than for him to come home.

She grabbed the notebook she was going to use to write down her murder theories and notes, and then the phone rang. Maybe it was Derek and the news was wrong. Instead, it was Robinson.

"Hey, I was just calling to thank you for last night. I know it was kind of weird under the circumstances and I'm not sure everyone there was exactly pleased to see me. I got the feeling that I threw a few people off their game. But after the Sansis left, when it was just you and Alyssa, it was cool. I can't remember having such a good time in ages."

Nikki looked out the family room window and watched a few ducks fly in on the pond. She grabbed her sweater off the back end of one of the chairs and wrapped it around her. The early spring morning had a chill to it. She wondered where Robinson was sitting or what he was looking at. Was he already at work? "Did you like Alyssa?"

He laughed a little. "Don't think that I don't know what you're up to. I know you're playing Cupid, but I can't say that I'm unhappy about it. Your friend Alyssa is cool and, yeah, I like her. A lot."

"She's a good lady and she's been through some hard times." Nikki watched the ducks fly off and went back into the kitchen, where she started doing dishes from the night before. She'd had a few left over to clean and hated coming home at the end of the day to dirty dishes.

"I get the feeling you're now going to give me the don't-hurt-my-friend speech."

"Sounds like you've heard it before."

"What's all that noise you're making?"

"I'm doing the dishes and don't try to change the subject. Yes, I am playing Cupid, but I will still give you that warning. I don't know you all that well, Robinson, but you've got some dimensions about you that I think are really great. Still I'll wager there's a bad boy lurking in there somewhere."

"You and your theories. I'm a cop."

"You know what I mean by bad 'boy.'"

"I suppose so. But hey, I like your friend and I don't want to hurt anyone."

There was a softness in his voice that she'd never heard before. The sincerity rang true and she hoped that her matchmaking would pay off for all involved.

"You were good with her little boy, too." Nikki finished loading the dishwasher and walked over to the cupboard to get out Ollie's food. He heard her opening the can and moved at a rate much faster than his usual drag-along self.

"I like kids. Actually I love kids."

"Robinson?"

"Yeah, Sands?"

"You okay?" She dumped the food in the bowl, and tossed the can. Robinson didn't sound right.

"I'm fine. I…" He let out a long sigh. "I had a little boy once. His name was Neil. After Shaq. You know, Shaquille O'Neil? I'm a fan."

"Oh." Nikki didn't know what to say. She'd had no idea and she had a feeling Robinson was verging into territory she wasn't sure she wanted to enter with him.

"I lost him when he was about the same age that Petie is. I lost him and his mom. Five years ago. To a car accident."

"I'm so sorry. I don't know what to say."

"You don't need to say anything, Sands. I don't talk about it much, but after playing with Petie last night and meeting his mom, I don't know what happened, but like I said, I haven't felt that good in a long time. It reminded me of what living is really all about. All this other stuff don't mean so much without a real life. I guess I have my work, and I do a decent job, but that's about all I have now. And, you know, I'm starting to remember that isn't what really counts. It's family. And it's friends. You know it is. That's why you're who you are and why you do the things you do for people. You get that."

"Thanks. That means a lot." She'd never thought about it, but she supposed she did get that—sort of. She didn't have a close family, other than Aunt Cara. But she had her friends and they were as much a family as any could be. And of course, she had Derek.

"I guess that's it then. I wanted to say thanks and I'll be by sometime this morning. I want to speak with Juan Gonzales and Ruben Pearlman again before they leave about their dealings with Yamimoto. I'd also like to talk with the nephew some more."

"Okay. Good. I have something for you that I forgot to give you last night." She hated to shift gears on him after what he'd unloaded on her, but she knew he'd already shifted. He didn't want to talk about the tragedy in his past any further. She told him about the note she'd dug out of the garbage and her idea that maybe it was the one Iwao had thought Juan had sent to him. She also filled him in on what she'd learned about Kurt and Jen's possible motives.

"Nice work. I've already got a jump-start on Jen Yami-moto. I want to be sure he flew in from Japan. When I called the number for him there to tell him what had happened to his uncle, I got a voicemail message in Japanese. I left a message to have him call, but I didn't tell him about his uncle, so he must have heard it elsewhere. I'll come on by and get that note from you in a bit. I think Jen's probably clean, though. I'm looking deep into this Gonzales and Pearlman angle. Those dudes lost a lot of money with Yamimoto. Money can be a great motive to kill."

"Right. I don't know about Ruben Pearlman, but as you've reminded me before, that's why you're the real detective. I'm sitting down to write out some of my impressions and some of the things I've learned over the last few days."

"You're good, Sands. On all levels, you're good."

She hung up the phone with a different feeling about Robinson. She'd liked him and his quirkiness before learning of his wife and child, but now she thought she might just understand this guarded detective.

Thirty

NIKKI didn't know how this investigation would end. She was stumped, and from everything she could tell, so was Robinson, although he seemed convinced that Ruben and Juan were involved. Maybe Juan was, but she simply could not imagine Ruben having anything to do with the murders.

She called Derek's cell and got no answer so she turned on The Weather Channel. It sounded like things were going to be clearing up back East and planes might actually start flying. Her fingers were crossed that Derek was in the air and on his way back home to her.

"Ollie, want to go for a run?" Ollie didn't move off the couch. "Not interested today, huh?" That was fine. She should check in with Alan and see where everyone was and if he wanted to set up a time when he and Derek could talk further about their negotiations.

Nikki decided to take a run on her own first, this time without the revolting trash-hunting activity on the side.

Once out in the fresh air, she felt a real sadness—almost an emptiness. How had she failed to really help Robinson? The one time when she'd actually been *asked* to help solve a crime and she hadn't been able to put two and two together. Dammit. There were too many pieces and none of them fit.

Running down through the Chardonnay grapes, she heard footsteps behind her. She glanced back to see Kurt Kensington. She didn't like that one bit. She mentally scolded Ollie for preferring a nap over jogging. Perhaps she should have had the same mentality?

"Howdy," Kurt said, coming up next to her, breathing hard and sweating.

"Hi."

"Sansi told all of us that we could head out today. Guess he wants to do a lunch first. You know about that?"

"No. I planned to meet with him after my run. See if I could track him down. Did you enjoy the time you had here?" She didn't know what to ask him. The only real encounter she'd had with him was during the dream board session, when she'd determined that he was a no-good creep. His bizarre application only strengthened the possibility that he could very well have killed two people—brutally. She knew he was capable of killing.

"I did. I've learned a lot, believe it or not."

"Good." *Oh, Lord, get me out of here.* She kept trying to keep distance between them but he had no problem keeping up with her.

"I know you don't like me. I know you think I'm crazy. I'm not, though."

Sure, that was reassuring. "I did think your dream board was strange." What else was she going to say? The guy was crazy!

"Maybe so. I do have a dark sense of humor. I went through some bad stuff in Iraq."

She kept on running.

"I'm not a bad man, Nikki. I'm not. I'm who I say I am. I thought when I came here that I wanted to write the scary stuff. The violence and murder and horror, because that's all I've lived over the last few years."

What was he trying to tell her? Adrenaline pumped through her, not just from the run, but because she was trying to carry on a conversation with someone who was at best a lunatic and at worst a killer. Fear coursed through her. Kurt was a big, strong guy and she was out here alone with him.

"I know my poster was dumb. In bad taste. War warps your mind."

Great, now he was admitting that he was demented?

"I don't want that in my life any longer. These past few days, I've realized that I want to spread light, not darkness."

"That's good stuff." Why was this guy not running out of breath? She was.

He grabbed her arm and she jolted back.

"Hey!" she yelled.

"Sorry. I need to talk to someone."

Why her? "I thought that's what we were doing," Nikki said.

"We were talking, but I don't know if you're really listening and I want your attention."

This was not good. "I'm all ears. I promise."

"I read these graphic novels and many times they're violent," he said.

"Right." She edged away from him.

"I think I could write a book with the intensity of the graphic novels, but have it be all about good, forgiveness, and love and getting the things in life you want."

"Like a children's book?" Yes, he was looney tunes. Completely!

"I could do that."

"Yes, you could. I encourage you and wish you well on all your endeavors." Nikki started up the pace again. "I hope you don't mind, but I really do need to talk with Alan."

"No. I understand. I didn't want to leave here without talking to you and letting you know that I'm like everyone else—totally normal. Or at least I want to be."

"Thank you for sharing. Have a safe trip home if I don't see you." She ran faster than usual and looked back to see if he was going to keep running with her. He'd stopped and seemed to be watching her. Kurt seriously unnerved her. Maybe he hadn't murdered Iwao or Mizuki, or maybe he had. Either way, having him run alongside her had not been pleasant.

Up at the café, she took out her cell phone and saw she had voicemail. "Hello, Nikki. It's Hayden. My dad was wondering if he could get some of that wine you served last night to take home with us. If so, you can drop it by my room. Thanks."

She hung up the phone and went into the café to grab a water bottle. Nikki was pleased that Alan had liked the wine enough to ask to take some with him. She hated going into the warehouse, but she'd do it for Alan.

"Hello, Bellissima."

Nikki swung around to see Marco coming into the kitchen. "What's going on?"

"I'm preparing the lunch for everyone who is leaving today from the S.E.E. group."

"Where's Simon?"

"Did I hear someone call my name?" Simon came dancing through the archway into the kitchen. "Look what I have." Simon's bubbly, singsong voice made Nikki grin. He placed a handful of photos of babies up on the refrigerator. "I'm visualizing, and guess what? We have an appointment with a private adoption agency. Tomorrow!"

"This is wonderful." Marco gave him a hug.

"Group hug!" Simon demanded.

Nikki put her arms around the two of them and squeezed. "That's awesome, guys."

They talked for a few minutes about the agency and how Simon found them.

"Can I get one of you to help me get a box of wine down for Alan? He wants to take some of the Merlot home."

"Sure, hon. You keep chopping there, sweetie," he told Marco.

"Chop, chop."

They started walking out of the kitchen when Marco called Simon back. He held out Simon's cell phone. "The agency," Marco said.

Simon turned to Nikki. "Hang on a second. I'll be right there."

This thing about Marco and Simon adopting seemed to be the real deal. Nikki could see it now. They'd adopt a baby girl, name her Diamond or something else bizarre like celebrities did. Then they'd deck the poor child out in designer duds made by Prada, or whoever else had the marketing brilliance to sell onesies for the price of a Benjamin. They'd feed her organics only and stuff good energy and all that vibration nonsense into the kid's brain. Hmmm. Maybe they could adopt Nikki instead? It really didn't sound like too bad of a life.

She flipped on the lights inside the chilly warehouse. It smelled like aged oak and fruit. The blend itself was intoxicating and Nikki took in a big whiff of it as she always did when she came in here. She closed her eyes and took in several deep breaths. Breaths to slow down...good stuff. Oh, man, maybe Alan Sansi and all his preaching were getting to her. She supposed she could concede there was something to all of it, especially the relaxation parts. She could get into that.

Nikki found the row she needed. There it was. The

Merlot. Good stuff. She could see why Alan wanted to take some home. Looked like Alan wanted to do one of two things—either go out of this thing in style, or get totally shitfaced and forget any of this ever happened.

She'd need the ladder to get to the case she wanted. She walked to the end of the row and slid the ladder down. A light shone through a vent in the roof. There were birds flying around it. If she didn't come in here often, this place might kind of spook her. It was huge, quiet, and cold.

Nikki made her way up about five steps on the ladder and grabbed the edge of the box to pull it out. Good thing she'd been doing some of that Core Power stuff that was all the rage these days. Nikki had gone from one exercise program to the next. She had a bad habit of watching infomercials and then ordering whatever the latest craze might be. But the Core Power yoga started after going to a class with Simon one day. She'd liked it and it had made her pretty darn strong.

When she had the box in her arms, she started to work her way slowly down the rungs. What happened next was a blur, like watercolors swirled together. Not a pretty scene, but a rather dark blend of reds, browns, and black that made Nikki think of death, blood, and murder.

She found herself on the ground. Wine bottles crashing around her, glass shattering everywhere. A bottle hit her on the side of her cheek, too close to her eye. What the hell . . . ? How had this happened?

And then she saw him—a hooded figure all in black, standing over her, a rope pulled taut in his hand. Nikki tried to move but he'd kicked the ladder on top of her, right onto her stomach. It almost felt like something had punctured her in the gut and she knew she was about to meet her maker.

Her heart raced at a rate that would've given most people a heart attack. Her mouth went as dry as the air inside an empty oak cask. She hoped God above would let her through the gates of heaven. She hadn't exactly been a good girl much of the time.

Then she heard the voice of an angel—Simon.

"Oh, Snow White. Where are you?" Her friend's voice rang through the warehouse. "You were supposed to wait."

The man bent down to grab her and she squirmed enough and screamed enough so that he turned and ran.

"Lord, what was that? Marco!"

The boys came running around the corner just as the back door to the warehouse slammed. They bent over her. "Don't move. Oh, God! Oh, no! Nikki? Marco, call 911." Simon pulled the ladder off her. He knelt down and cradled her head in his lap. "No, no. You poor baby. Are you okay? Please tell me you're okay."

"I'm okay," she whispered, right before she passed out.

Thirty-one

NIKKI hated hospitals. Hated them. They smelled of Lysol and alcohol and there were sick people—lots of sick people. Not to mention people running around barking orders at you. How was it that anyone was expected to recuperate in one of these places? Weren't doctors and nurses always telling patients to get some rest? That was what Nikki had just been told by her unpleasant nurse in the emergency room.

Simon hovered over her and barked as many orders at the nurse as she'd asked questions of Nikki. "Can we please get some Diet Coke in here for her? She likes Diet Coke. Also, I think she's a little warm, so a cool cloth would be good. When will the doctor be here? This is ridiculous. It's been two hours or something totally insane. What kind of operation are you people running?"

The nurse, who looked as old as God and as happy as the devil, squinted her eyes. "Excuse me, Liberace, the last time

I checked, her name"—she pointed at Nikki—"wasn't Hillary Clinton or the likes of her. And in case you haven't taken note, this is an emergency room, not the Ritz-Carlton."

"Well, I never," Simon said, completely put out by this witch.

"Now you have," the nurse replied, imitating him.

"Si, please let the woman do her job," Nikki begged. "I'm fine. Really I am."

Marco stood at her head, stroking it. "I am so happy I came with Simon to get the wine for you. He would have had to leave you to call the emergency people. I was chopping and then he said he needed me to help him with the wine because I'm stronger than he is."

"You are," Simon said, rubbing Marco's arm.

"If we were only there a few minutes sooner, this wouldn't have happened to her." Marco leaned down and kissed her on the cheek. The thought crossed her mind that these two would actually make good parents. They had worry down to a science.

Another half hour, and another meltdown from Simon, and the doctor appeared.

"You're the doctor?" Simon asked.

"Yes." He showed him his badge. "Dr. Woodruff."

Dr. Woodruff looked fifteen with curly dark hair and dark eyes. He was slight and honestly he didn't look as though he'd ever shaved—baby skin like a baby's butt.

"Honey, I have Dolce and Gabbana T-shirts older than you."

Dr. Woodruff wasn't amused.

"Simon," Nikki warned.

Dr. Woodruff asked the same questions that the nurses and everyone before him had asked, and she was pretty sure that Robinson would be showing up sometime to ask the same questions again before she'd be able to leave. All she wanted was to go home.

The doctor examined her with the boys out of the room. "Anything hurt?"

"Everything," Nikki replied. "I feel like I've been pushed off a ladder, clobbered by a maniac, and then almost strung up to die."

"Ah." The doctor winced.

Nikki doubted he'd heard that story before. "My stomach really hurts where the guy pushed the ladder down on me. I'm not usually a baby, but it does hurt."

"Can you point to it?"

Nikki did so.

"It's not exactly your stomach, is it?"

"No." Now why did she feel embarrassed? The kid was a doctor.

"That's where your ovary is on that side. To be safe, we should have an ultrasound done. I may call in a gynecologist to do an exam on you."

"What? Why?" There was nothing Nikki could think of that might actually be worse at that moment—hoisting her legs up in a pair of stirrups so some teenager could take a peek at her parts. It was hard enough going to her private physician, a woman in her fifties.

"A precaution. We should be sure that your ovary didn't rupture. Looks to me like you were dealt some pretty hard blows." He touched the side of her face.

She winced.

"Good thing you don't need stitches, but that will bruise up. Not pretty."

"Thanks," Nikki replied.

Another hour or so passed, and Simon had finally calmed down when a tech rolled in an ultrasound machine. He ran the instruments over her, but gave no indication one way or another as to what might have happened, if anything. She could be badly bruised, but a ruptured ovary? That sounded horrible.

Finally Dr. Woodruff came back in. Simon and Marco had gone to see about getting a sandwich, which was fine with Nikki because she'd tired of Simon's mother henning about four hours earlier. "Sorry, but it's a busy night here and our on-call gynecologist is backed up. But I did show him the results of the ultrasound and he said that you do not have a ruptured ovary."

"Thank God."

"But."

Uh-oh. Nikki didn't like the sound of that.

"He said that you had a cyst in there that has ruptured. He suggested I go ahead and give you a basic exam."

"No."

"No?" he asked.

"No."

"Okay," Dr. Woodruff replied, realizing that she was serious.

Dr. Pipsqueak was not going in there.

"Can you just tell me what you and this other doctor could be thinking?" Nikki asked.

Dr. Woodruff pulled up a chair next to her bed and sat down.

"This is not my place since I'm not your gynecologist or your husband."

"I don't have a husband. You're scaring me."

"All right. My colleague thinks it is possible you could have some issues getting pregnant. Considering your age and that you had a cyst on your ovary, he suggested that you could have endometriosis. He believes your cyst could be caused by this. He suggests that you see your doctor as soon as you can if you want to have any children."

"Okay." She tried absorbing what he was telling her. "Are you saying that I won't be able to get pregnant?"

"Again, I'm the wrong doctor here. I really don't know. But it's likely that you could have a difficult time, and if you do want to conceive, you may want to speak to the man in your life, if there is one, and the two of you may want to get the ball rolling."

"I see. Can I go home now?"

He stood up and rubbed his hands together. "Yes. I have to sign off on the release papers, but you can go only if you sign saying that you refused a gynecological exam and that you will be seeing your regular doctor as soon as possible."

"Sure. Yeah. I can sign that." Nikki watched the doctor leave. Wow. The thought of never being able to have a baby had never crossed her mind. She figured when the time was right, they would have one. Yes, she knew it could be a little harder as she neared the middle age milestone, but all the same, she didn't expect this. What if she couldn't conceive? How would Derek feel? And if she could, they obviously needed to start sooner rather than later. How was he going to feel about that?

She didn't know the answers to questions she hated asking even herself.

Thirty-two

SIMON and Marco had insisted on staying the night with her. After a couple of Tylenol she felt okay physically. Mentally was another story. Neither of the boys wanted to leave her the next day, but she insisted they go to the adoption meeting they'd scheduled. Derek had been trying to get a flight home since last night, but with everyone else also trying to get home, he'd been delayed and ended up having to spend the night in the airport.

When she'd last spoken with him, it was close to two o'clock in the morning. She could hear the strain and concern in his voice. Simon had called and told him what had happened, and he'd decided that if planes were still delayed come morning, he was going to rent a car and drive to the closest city he could find that had an operational airport.

"Are you sure you're okay?" he asked over and over.

"I'm fine. I really am. Plus, I have the boys and Ollie here. I miss you. That's really the most pain that I'm in."

"I miss you, too, and I am on my way. I'll do whatever it takes to get home."

She couldn't wait to see him. But there was this pit in her gut about how to tell him what the doctor had said.

Although her body ached some, it was her mind that was filled with the most discomfort. She needed some fresh air. Robinson had asked both Ruben and Juan to come back to the station because neither of them had been able to confirm their whereabouts when Nikki had been attacked yesterday. Everyone else appeared to have alibis—even Kurt Kensington, who'd showed up at the spa for a sauna after running with her.

Robinson had also checked in on her in the morning and gone over the statement she gave in the hospital to the officer he'd sent over. He'd wanted to come himself, but he'd also wanted to make sure everything was done properly at the warehouse. More than ever, Robinson was determined to get this guy, and he seemed certain it was Ruben or Juan.

Nikki resigned herself to believing that Ruben or Juan, or both, had something to do with the murders and attacking her, but she still could not wrap her mind around Ruben being a killer. She'd heard that Rose Pearlman was down at the police station, wreaking havoc and making all sorts of threats about lawsuits and whatnot. Nikki didn't wish her on Robinson, or anyone for that matter.

What still bothered her was that the one clue she felt was missing in this whole thing was that stupid DVD she witnessed Iwao trying to give to Alan. Why this troubled her, she didn't know. But it did, and it got her to thinking about where that DVD had gone to.

And how about Jen and Sierra? He shows up at a convenient time, does not seem all that distraught over his uncle's death, and suddenly he and Sierra are madly in love again.

Was it all coincidence and were they telling her the truth? Or was there something more sinister? The alibi that each one of them had when Nikki was attacked was based on being with one another. Could they be behind the murders? If Iwao had threatened to stop supporting Jen's aunt's hospitalization if Jen married Sierra, could that have sent Jen over the edge? He had time to plan and execute a murder, didn't he? Had Robinson been able to find out yet whether or not he'd still been in Japan the night his uncle was murdered?

One idea came to mind. It was kind of a last straw, but why she hadn't thought to do so before, she didn't know. She needed to head up to the hotel and check some things out. Running was out of the question today, but taking a walk to kill some time with Ollie would be a good idea.

The boys had told her that when the Sansis had heard what happened to her, they'd decided to stay an extra night, partly because Robinson and his crew once again needed to interrogate everyone and partly because Alan Sansi was concerned for her welfare. She wanted to thank him and tell them good-bye.

She went into the garage and changed out a load of laundry, then grabbed Ollie's leash and called him. He climbed off the couch and obeyed. This time she wasn't taking no for an answer from him. Not after yesterday. The two of them headed slowly up the hill to the hotel, where Nikki wanted to check in with Alyssa.

Alyssa was behind the front desk with Petie, who was playing with some plastic cars. She came around the desk and hugged Nikki. "Oh, my God. Simon told me what happened. Are you okay? You poor thing. You look—"

"I know. I know. I hope I don't scare him." She pointed to Petie, who was totally absorbed with his toys." Nikki had seen herself in the mirror and it wasn't a pretty sight. There was a nice purple and black bruise under her eye on her right cheek and a small cut near her chin. She did look worse than she felt.

Ollie lay down at their feet, evidently exhausted after the five-minute walk.

"You won't. I'm sorry I had to bring Petie today. Kathy at the day care center is sick, and so is her helper. I'm hoping he doesn't catch it."

"Me, too. You don't have to be sorry that you brought him in. He's always welcome here. I can take him down to my place and watch him. I'm lying low today," Nikki said.

"I couldn't do that to you. You need to rest."

"I'm fine. It looks a lot worse than it is. Really. I'd love to have his company. Derek will be back tonight, and after yesterday, I want to catch up on some housework and take it easy. I know he loves *Thomas the Tank Engine*. I have all those DVDs for him at our house. I bought them to bribe you to let me have him for a few hours at a time." She laughed. "Come on. Let me take him. I'll make him some lunch. Oh, by the way, have you seen the Sansi family at all? I'd like to tell them good-bye."

"They went into Yountville, except for Rich Higgins. He asked me for directions into the city because he said that he had a meeting and would be back this afternoon to head out with Hayden and her family. It's good news about everything. I talked to Jonah, I mean Detective Robinson..." She blushed. "He said that he thinks he has the killers in custody. He's working on proving it now. That must make you feel better. Jonah is a good guy. He's worried about you, like we all are. He said something today about having security at your house."

"I have it. His name is Ollie and he weighs as much as I do. Trust me, with him around, I feel safe. But if you're nervous about me watching Petie after what happened..."

She glanced down at the dog. "Or you're worried about Ollie…"

"No. Not at all. I know Ollie is on it. He wouldn't let anyone through the door who shouldn't be there, and as far as Petie around the dog, I've seen how good Ollie is with him. I'm worried about you is all. I don't want you to overdo."

"I won't. Promise."

"Okay, then. If you're sure. He's all yours. But instead of walking back, why don't you let me drive you down to the house. The kid comes with practically an entire bedroom." She laughed.

"You don't mind him riding in the back, do you?" Nikki asked, pointing to Ollie.

"No." She waved a hand. "Not at all. Hey, you didn't just come up here to see if you could play babysitter. You didn't even know he was here with me," Alyssa said.

"True, but I'm happy about that. I actually did come up for another reason. I was thinking about something. When Mr. Yamimoto checked in the other day, you processed that, right?"

She nodded. "Yes."

"Did he have anything put in the safe? I'm actually helping out Robinson."

Alyssa's eyes grew wide.

"Yeah, I know, probably against my better judgment. And don't tell him that I told you, even though it sounds like he's been filling you in on some things, too."

"Sort of. I asked about the job and he was kind of telling me what he could, but he didn't mention you were helping him."

"I figured. But I've been wracking my brain all morning and I know I'm missing something. I don't think that Ruben Pearlman committed the murders. Maybe Juan Gonzales.

Maybe. Since you checked Yamimoto in, I thought I'd ask and see if he had any special requests that seemed strange. I don't know." Nikki tossed her hands up. "Or did he place anything in the safe?"

Alyssa shook her head. "No. It was a normal check-in process. I thought it kind of strange that his wife, well, his girlfriend or whoever she was, stood back and didn't speak. I thought it was a cultural thing. Maybe she was supposed to do that. Wait a minute. There is something about her, the girlfriend."

"What?"

"You know what? Edna said something about her to me."

"She did?"

"Yeah. She mentioned that the lady—in room twenty-three—brought down a large envelope and there was only one word printed on the front and it read SAFE, so Edna put it in the safe for her."

"Dammit."

"What?"

"Let's get it out. I asked Edna myself if she'd met the woman or seen her, and she said no. But she obviously had." Nikki shook her head. "I'm worried about Edna. Did you know that last week she locked herself out of her house, or thought she had? She didn't remember that she kept a key under a potted plant near the front door. She mentioned to me that it might be time for her to leave the job."

Alyssa scooped up Petie and they walked back to the safe. She glanced behind her. "I hope not, but I understand if she does." Alyssa passed Petie to Nikki as she twisted the combo on the safe. "That's so sad."

"I know, but I'm not sure what to do. I'll talk to Derek and see if we can figure something out. We should also talk to her family. She has to have some family close by."

Alyssa nodded and opened the safe. Petie tugged at the ends of Nikki's hair. "Hair," he kept repeating.

Alyssa pulled out the envelope and pried Petie's fingers from Nikki's hair. "Here, I'll hold him while you open it."

Nikki tore open the envelope as they walked back to the front desk. She dumped the contents onto the desk. There it was—the elusive DVD.

Thirty-three

"WHAT do you think is on that?" Alyssa asked as they drove the two minutes from the hotel back down to Nikki's place.

"I don't know. But whatever it is, it was important to Iwao or Mizuki. My guess is that it could have some answers that neither Robinson nor I have been able to find."

"You're really into helping him, huh?"

Did Nikki sense some jealousy? "No one wants Malveaux to be associated in any way with murder and I think he knows that I kind of keep tabs on things here. I'm always listening. You like him, don't you?" Nikki noticed her shift a little in her seat. Petie was in the back, patting Ollie on the head and laughing.

"I do. I think I could like this guy a lot. He's different, but not in a bad way, and he's been through a lot of stuff, which makes me think he can understand what I'm going through and what Petie is going through."

"Please be careful, though."

"Don't worry about that. I'm not going to jump into anything. You know that my first priority is my son and his health. But I have to say that Jonah is fine to look at, so if he wants to take me to dinner every so often, you know, to get to know me a little better, I don't think I'll protest." She smiled.

"And I would agree with that. All of it. You need to get out and he is a good guy." Nikki wondered if Robinson had told Alyssa about his wife and child yet. Maybe the perfect match had been made between them. Robinson could definitely understand heartache and pain. He would be good for Alyssa and she would be good for him.

They pulled up in front of Nikki's place. Alyssa carried a tired Petie inside for Nikki. Ollie followed them into the house.

"Hey, this is good timing. I can get some work done up at the hotel. I think he's going to go to sleep. Where should I put him?"

Nikki had his big bag. "Do you have blankets in here?"

"Yes."

"Okay, let's put him in the guest room. There's nothing he can get into in there if he wakes up. It's pretty sterile." Nikki pulled out Petie's blankies and put them down on the carpet. Alyssa laid him down and spread some more blankets on top of him. He started to protest, but Alyssa kept rubbing his back and shushing him.

A moment later, Nikki took over while Alyssa quietly slipped out. Rubbing the baby's back and watching him sleep were as close as Nikki had come to bliss in a long time. Petie's face looked so sweet and innocent—completely serene. She couldn't fathom what this child had already been through in his young life and what he had yet to face, or what his mother was facing with him. A sense of protection came over her, watching him, and she wished she could give him her own heart.

After what the doctor had told her last night, and being here with Petie, Nikki knew that, without a doubt, she wanted to be a mother. To live here in the ranch house, help grow grapes, make wine, and have children with Derek. There couldn't be a better life. Domestication at its finest.

Thinking about being a wife and mother, she remembered the laundry that needed folding out in the garage. She also had to watch that DVD. She reluctantly lifted herself up and headed out to the garage, where she thought she'd fold all the clothes while watching whatever was on the DVD. The clothes had sat in the dryer too long and had wrinkled up quite a bit. She decided to run them through the dryer for another few minutes and went back in the house, where she first peered in on a sleeping Petie, then grabbed a water and sat down to watch what Mizuki had found important enough to stow away in the safe.

What Nikki saw caught her off guard. She thought the DVD Iwao had tried to hand over to Alan had something to do with Sierra. But it didn't.

It did, however, have everything to do with his other daughter—Hayden. Nikki now understood why he kept insisting Alan watch it. If he had, she doubted that Hayden Sansi would be getting married anytime soon. Especially to Rich Higgins.

Thirty-four

WHY wasn't Robinson answering his phone? Nikki paced back and forth. He had the wrong men in his interrogation room. This was her third attempt to reach him in the last ten minutes, and she was getting desperate. Ollie stood and followed her, whining away. He knew she was troubled. Instead of letting the poor animal remain stressed out, she got him a doggie bone from the kitchen and then went out to the garage to call Robinson again. She didn't need Ollie waking up Petie. And this way she could kill two birds with one stone and take the clothes out of the dryer as she called.

She sighed with relief when she heard Robinson's voice. "Where have you been?"

"Nikki? You sound like my wife. If I had one. I was interviewing Gonzales again. I think he might crack. Why? What's up?"

"Neither Gonzales nor Pearlman did this. But I know who did and why."

"You do?"

"Yes. It's Rich Higgins."

"The publisher? Hayden Sansi's fiancé?"

"Yes. It is and I have evidence here." She went into her bedroom and took the note out of her nightstand drawer. She'd put it there after getting back from her run. It all made sense now. She reread it to herself while Robinson was on the other end of the phone. *Keep the party for yourself this time. I'm done dealing with you.*

"I'm walking to my car as we speak. Start filling me in."

"Okay. Remember how I brought up this DVD thing with you a few times? How the first day of the program, I saw Alan and Iwao arguing and that Iwao was trying to get him to take the DVD, and he refused?"

"Yes. I remember. The only DVD we ever found in any of Iwao or Mizuki's things was the soap opera she had."

"Right. There was another one. I knew there had to be. I have it, and on it are meetings between Iwao and Rich Higgins. On the outside of the DVD there are three dates written—the dates of the meetings. The first is right after his mother died. It's in Iwao Yamimoto's office, I think. It must be Japan, and I'm sure from the way the footage is shot that Higgins had no idea he was on camera."

"Keep it coming."

Nikki could hear his keys jangling.

"In it they're talking about Yamimoto buying out Inspiritus and making it a subsidiary of his publishing house, VisionScope, which is located in Canada."

"What does this have to do with the murders, Sands?"

"Just listen. I'm getting there. The first meeting goes nice and everything is kosher between them, kind of setting the stage for things to come. Then about three months later, Higgins is back in Yamimoto's office. In this one, Higgins is raising the bar on how much he wants Iwao to pay for the company, and Iwao is saying that he wants Higgins to convince Alan Sansi to do worldwide major events. And to promote VisionScope. Higgins tells him that Alan would never do that. He's not into commercialism at all. Mind you that Hayden and Higgins have been engaged at this point for a few months. I asked Hayden on the hike the other day how long they'd been engaged. She said almost a year. All of this took place last year. Higgins then tells Iwao he wants out. He says he can't sell because of pressure the family will put on him and the loyalty Alan felt toward his mother. He tells him that he's had second thoughts. So, Iwao ups the ante and offers him another three million dollars on top of the twenty million he'd already offered him."

Robinson let out a low whistle, his car engine running in the background.

"Right. It looked like the deal was back on. But then, in a third and final meeting only two weeks ago, Rich tells Iwao he can't go through with it. His new wife alone will be worth that kind of money and more, so he'll have no need to sell his publishing company. Iwao still tries to convince him and insists they go to his home for dinner. No hard feelings if he doesn't want to change his mind. Iwao even says those exact words on the tape, but apparently that wasn't the case. Because get this, there's not just a meeting on there. Iwao takes him to his home and there's a little party that goes on."

"Let me guess. It's Higgins and a private party with a girl."

"Not just any girl. A party with Mizuki and several friends. But Rich Higgins told me the other night that he'd never met Iwao until this weekend."

"I have to ask, how do you think Iwao got all of that on tape?" Robinson asked.

"He must have had cameras all over his offices and his home, and then transferred the footage onto DVD with hopes of showing Alan what a scumbag his future son-in-law is.

He figured that once Alan knew the truth about Higgins, he would jump ship and go with VisionScope. Why would he continue to do business with a man who was going to sell the publishing house he'd help grow right under his feet? Not to mention marry his daughter when he wasn't exactly showing how devoted and faithful he would be."

"Why didn't Iwao tell him what was on that DVD?"

"I asked myself the same thing and the only answer I can come up with is that Alan didn't want to hear it. When I saw them arguing the other day, Alan was adamant about not wanting to get involved with any situation surrounding his daughter."

"Where did you find the DVD?"

"It was in the safe this entire time. The hotel safe. You have to see it. I'm telling you that Higgins killed Iwao and Mizuki. He had to have known about the DVD somehow."

"I'll be there in fifteen."

Nikki flipped shut the phone. Rich Higgins. How stupid. Here he was about to marry a beautiful, sweet woman from a decent family, and running a productive publishing house. His mother had to be turning over in her grave. The man must have wanted more, just as Iwao Yamimoto wanted more. Iwao's desires dug him a grave, whereas Rich's would see him behind bars. But what about yesterday's alibi? Robinson told her that everyone but Ruben and Juan could prove their whereabouts during the attack. Did that mean Hayden had been covering for Rich? Why would she do that?

Higgins knew if he sold off Inspiritus to Iwao that his engagement to Hayden would be broken. The Sansi kids were loyal to their family, and Hayden would not marry someone deceitful like Higgins. And Rich Higgins had probably started thinking this thing through. The Sansi family was worth way more money as a family and a business than Inspiritus. In the long run, and after a kid or two,

Higgins would be entrenched in a family that had all the perks of the good life and a guaranteed inheritance. Who knew what Higgins had planned for the future? Nikki got the feeling this guy would kill again if he needed to—if he thought he would gain something from it. By murdering Iwao, Rich gained his silence. The DVD proved his initial attempt to sell off Inspiritus behind the Sansis' backs. He'd murdered Mizuki because he was afraid that if Iwao had told anyone about Rich Higgins, it would likely have been her.

But why had he attempted to kill Nikki? Because she had been asking questions. She'd tipped her hand by asking Hayden in front of him for those applications and saying that she occasionally helped out the police. How stupid she'd been!

Nikki couldn't wait for Robinson to arrive. She busied herself with folding the clothes and placing them in the basket. She started to head back through the garage door when she heard the click and felt what she knew to be the barrel of a gun in her back.

Thirty-five

"I'VE been waiting all morning, trying to figure out how to get you alone."

Nikki closed her eyes for a second and shook her head. It was Rich Higgins.

"But all morning you've been inside with that killer dog of yours and I couldn't take that chance. Plus, I know you have that kid in there."

Nikki shuddered at the reference to Petie. She could hear Ollie at the door, scratching and whining to get out. He had to smell her fear because his whining and agitation increased. She prayed Higgins wouldn't open the door and hurt her dog. Worse yet, if he got inside the house, would he harm Petie? Robinson better have the gas pedal to the floor.

"I need that DVD."

"What? I don't know what you're talking about. I'm sorry."

"Liar!" He spun her around so she faced him.

His face was contorted and filled with rage. He didn't look like the charmer and handsome man that she was sure Hayden Sansi loved. "I don't have it."

"Yes, you do. I saw you this morning with the girl at the front desk. You don't think that I haven't been watching you? I told you that already. You're a problem. A real problem. You ask way too many questions. I couldn't believe you when you asked for those applications. I knew I had a problem then. Too bad for me that your buddies showed up and saved you yesterday. And then this morning I've had to cover my butt with Hayden and her family to follow you and track you down. I've been trying to get ahold of that DVD ever since Yamimoto told me he had proof of my cheating on Hayden and being willing to sell out under Sansi's feet." He cringed. "I can't believe he taped all that, otherwise I never would have killed him. Ever! It would have been Yamimoto's word against mine." He started laughing.

The guy was insane.

"You don't think Alan would have believed him?" Buy time, buy time. Robinson was on the way. That fifteen minutes was down to ten. *Drive, Jonah, drive.*

"You're kidding, right? I'm practically family. Alan is hands-off. Remember, he believes that everyone needs to follow their own journey. His children's journeys are not his to live."

"Then why would he care if you had a party with some Japanese women that was a wee bit X-rated? Or that you wanted to sell a company he helped grow?"

"Sarcastic bitch, aren't you!"

Ollie scratched violently at the door. Nikki's side ached. She needed to set down the laundry basket and see what kind of leverage she could get on Higgins. Could she defend herself at all?

"What were you afraid of then, if Alan refused to see the DVD? What was the big deal?"

"The big deal was Lulu and the rest of the family might have seen it and they aren't exactly as philosophical and mellow as dear old Dad. Yamimoto told me that he would give me twenty-four hours to make a deal with him, this time for a lot less money *and* I had to convince Alan of the benefits of pimping himself to the world. Can you believe that? That little asshole wanted to blackmail me! I had no choice."

·"You wrote that note to Iwao about the party and the business dealings."

"Of course I did. I gave it to his whore, Mizuki. That's when he came to me and told me about the DVD and said that he wanted his way or I'd be out of the way. God, you're lippy. I need that DVD, and I know it's in your house."

"How do you know that?"

"I watched you and that other woman with the baby bring it down here."

"If that's so, why did you wait in the garage for me?"

"I'm not totally heartless. I would never hurt a baby, and your friend didn't stay long enough to watch it. I only take care of necessary problems and you've become one."

"So, Hayden isn't involved? How did you get her to give you an alibi yesterday? You had to have been the one to attack me."

"Shut up! That's what I mean. You're too mouthy. Hayden is easy to handle. I gave her a glass of wine, put something in it to make her fall asleep, and she thought we both took an afternoon nap together. Never knew I was gone."

Yep. Total psycho. Ollie's whine on the other side of the door turned into a low howl between long growls. She eyed the side door.

"Don't think about it." He had spotted where she'd been

looking. "I locked the door. You rely on that dog a little too much. And as far as he goes, he's becoming a real problem, too. But I need that DVD, and if I have to kill you and that dog to get it, I will. But I'd rather not kill the dog." He grinned maniacally.

C'mon, Robinson. I'm running out of time here... She prayed Petie wouldn't wake up.

"But if I have to, I will. So, here's the plan. I brought Fido—"

"His name is Ollie."

"Whatever. I brought the doggie a nice big bone with meat still on it, right here in my pocket. You will toss it in, in front of me, and then subdue the dog. If you don't subdue him, I will have no problem pulling the trigger. None."

She would not let him kill Ollie. But more importantly, she had to protect Petie. The little guy was inside sleeping. There was no telling what this madman was capable of.

"Do you understand me?" he growled, his face purple with rage.

She nodded, her stomach knotting into a mixture of fear and adrenaline. She tried to keep her hands steady and her knees locked because at some level she felt she could collapse, and there was no room for cowardice at a time like this. Think! And do it quickly! "Can I put the laundry basket down so that I can get the bone?"

He eyed her with an intensity that literally sent a shiver down her spine. "You want to put the basket down?"

"Yes. If I'm going to give the bone to my dog, we should probably start with me setting the basket down."

"Are you being smart with me?" he yelled. "You think you're so smart! You and your talk on wine! I could see how you think everyone is so beneath you! Now look at you. Bet you don't feel so high and mighty now!"

She didn't move.

"Okay, yeah, put the basket down."

Nikki turned back around to set the basket on the washer. She wasn't even thinking, knowing she had to act fast. This man was going to kill her.

"Just set the thing down, I said!"

With every ounce of strength, Nikki swung the basket around as hard as she could, which was enough to catch him off guard and cause the gun to come out of his grip and fly through the air, knocking it to the ground. It went sliding under the washing machine.

Nikki used a roundhouse kick on his knees. Higgins wobbled and then came up, lunging at her. He grabbed her arm and pulled her back toward him. His strength by far outweighed hers, but she had agility and speed on her side as she rounded her foot around his knee, causing him to fall off balance again. He let go of her arm and she darted for the back door. She reached for the handle as he grabbed her shirt and dragged her backward. She cocked her fist and, with every ounce of strength she could muster, pulled herself around and cold clocked him in the face. He brought a hand up to his eye. Now he was good and pissed off. "You bitch!" Not the first time she'd been called that before.

He charged her and pushed her hard. This time, Nikki was thrown off balance and into the back door. As Higgins started coming for her again, she turned the handle on the back door and Ollie rushed out and jumped Higgins, knocking the man straight to the ground.

"What the . . . !"

A glass window in the side of the garage crashed to the ground. Robinson stood outside the door yelling, "Nikki! Nikki, are you okay?"

Ollie had Higgins pinned. Nikki hit the open button on the garage remote and saw Robinson, gun pointed at Higgins, as the door rose up. Nikki sank to the floor. Ollie found the dog bone in Higgins's pocket, tore the pocket off, and with instructions from her, got off the man so that

Robinson could cuff him and cart him away. "Yeah. I'm okay," she replied.

Ollie came over, licked her face, and then went back to his bone. She wrapped her arms around him. Boy, did she love this dog.

Thirty-six

PETIE slept through the entire ordeal. Robinson had called in backup and transferred Higgins into the squad car to be taken to the jail and processed. It would be a long time, if ever, before Higgins saw the light of day.

Once Robinson took Nikki's statement, he turned personal. "I shouldn't have asked you to get involved in this." He put a friendly arm around her and gave her a noogy on the top of her head. "You get yourself in deep shit every time so there better not be a next time, Sands."

"I'm fine, and I'm glad that you did ask me to help out. I'm starting to believe that everything happens for a reason, like Alan Sansi says."

"Oh, yeah? What do you think the reason is behind all of this?" He shoved his hands into his jeans and rocked back onto his cowboy-booted heels.

She shrugged. "Well, for starters, you would never have met Alyssa if this hadn't happened. I mean I didn't think I'd see you again after what happened last year. You know, I figured that was just one of those things. Then you were back at your job and I was at mine."

"Which job would that be? Vineyard employee or amateur sleuth?"

"Funny. No, I do not plan to go into detecting full-time. I like managing the winery and I have plans for the future." She sighed.

"Sounds heavy."

"Kind of. But I'll fill you in if we're going to be seeing you more often around here, which from the look of it, is the case."

His cheeks reddened a little as he glanced down at his hands and nodded.

"Are you blushing, Robinson?"

"No. Hey, where's the kid?"

"Petie? He's still sleeping."

Nikki showed him to the back room, where Petie was just waking up. She picked him up and he said, "Mommy."

Oh, that twang in her heart!

"Want Mommy." He grew a little louder.

"I can take him up to her." Robinson reached out for Petie.

"You don't have to do that," she replied.

"I know. I want to. I want to ask her out to dinner." He smiled widely. "I think we could have some fun together."

She patted him on the shoulder and handed Petie, who didn't fuss, over to the detective. "I think so, too." Petie leaned his head on Robinson's shoulder. "Would you look at that? Guess you two bonded the other night."

"I think so." He stroked Petie's hair.

He looked like a dad, and a good one, too. It made Nikki think of Derek.

She walked Robinson out the door and helped him get

Petie in the car. Robinson went to the trunk and took out a car seat from the back.

"You always carry a car seat?" Nikki asked.

"Always."

"Oh." She had the feeling that the seat had belonged to his son, but she didn't ask.

"In my line of work you never know when it might come in handy."

"Right." She buckled Petie into his seat.

Robinson flashed another movie star smile at her and slipped his shades on. "You're real good, Sands. I've said it before, but I'll say it again—real good."

She watched Robinson drive up the hill to the hotel. She'd have to head up there herself, have a tall glass of cold water, and take a minute to *breathe.* Nikki wanted to be there when the Sansi family returned from their lunch so she could tell them what had happened. It was not something she looked forward to, but it was better they hear it from her.

The Sansi family took the news somewhat in stride. At least Alan remained his usual self and didn't get too excited or angry or anything. He just put an arm around his daughter and said, "I'm so sorry, honey."

Hayden didn't remain as calm as her father. She lost it. "You're kidding? How? What! This is impossible!" Tears rolled down her cheeks and in between sobs she continued to question everything that Nikki told them. She explained it all a few times before Hayden collapsed into her mother's arms, finally accepting this horrible news. Lulu stroked her hair. Alan wrapped his arms around his wife and daughter and spoke in hushed tones. Nikki knew that this was one of those blows that would take a long time to heal. Luckily the woman had a supportive, loving family to help her get through it.

Sierra hugged her sister, too.

After some time they pulled apart. Alan and Lulu escorted Hayden to the car.

Sierra and Jen came over to Nikki. Sierra shook her head. "My poor sister. She doesn't deserve this. I could kill that guy for doing this to her." She brought a hand to her mouth, realizing the faux pas she'd made. "I mean I could do him some serious damage." She frowned and stretched out her hand to Nikki. "Thank you for everything. You've been wonderful, and I'm sure this hasn't exactly been easy. I can't believe Rich would do such a thing. I thought he was a jerk, but a killer? I had no idea," Sierra said.

"It's good that you two are figuring things out after what you've been through, as well. You belong together."

They smiled. "We think so, too," Jen said.

Despite what had transpired, Sierra did look amazingly well. Only days earlier, Nikki had pegged her for a bit of a lush, or at least a lost soul. The benefits of true love had helped heal her. Now she was sobered up and had a glow coming from her.

Alan settled Lulu and Hayden in the car and came back to let Nikki know that he'd be in touch with Derek in the next week to take care of the negotiations about the licensing agreement with the spa products and wine. With Lulu caring for Hayden, Alan walked Nikki back down to her place.

"I'll call the other members personally and let them know what has happened."

"Thanks," Nikki said.

Alan gave her a hug. "Life is good, Nikki Sands. You will get all that you wish for. I can guarantee it. Good comes to those who do good."

She nodded. "Yeah. I think so, too."

She closed the door behind her, walked straight to her bed, and lay down for a long nap with Ollie alongside her.

Thirty-seven

DEREK made it home right before dinner and immediately smothered Nikki with care. He made a bubble bath, poured her a glass of wine, and cooked her a homemade meal of his famous chicken-fried steak, cheesy biscuits and gravy, and green beans drenched in butter.

"I do most of the cooking around here because if I eat like this very often, I'd have to either give in and grow large or run a lot more often, and frankly, I don't want to run more often."

"It's good, though, right?" He winked at her.

"Oh, my God. Do you have to ask?" She rolled her eyes and smiled. It was wonderful to have him home. "Do you see anything left on my plate?"

Over dinner they talked about what had happened while he was gone. She found out from him that the reason his notes on the meeting had included a mention of Iwao's

VisionScope was because Derek had been thinking about doing a book on his belief in organic farming and how they go about it at the winery. Alan had suggested talking to Iwao about it, knowing that Inspiritus didn't do any type of horticulture books.

As the evening wound down, Derek took her hand in his while they plopped down on the sofa together.

She leaned her head against his chest and let out a sigh worthy of the stress she'd endured over the week—now all gone. Almost. There was that thing—the baby thing that the doctor suggested she talk to Derek about.

"You know," he said, "you really have to stop putting yourself in danger the way you do." He kissed the top of her head. "If I'd been here, this wouldn't have happened. I could kill that guy for hurting you. To think I could have lost you. No more troublemaking." He squeezed her hand. Robinson had pretty much told her the same thing. "Because I'm never leaving you alone again."

"I don't go looking for trouble."

"I know. It somehow finds you."

They chuckled, knowing it was true.

"I'll try to avoid it from now on," she replied. "Really, I will."

"You will because, like I said, I'm going to be right here with you."

Ollie sidled up to the couch and nudged her hand. She scratched the top of his head. As soon as she'd stop, he'd nudge again. Now this was perfect.

"Speaking of trouble. I have something for you." Derek removed his arm from around her shoulders.

"You do?" She lifted her head and smiled. "And why would that remind you of trouble?"

"You'll see." He got up and went back into their bedroom and came back with a floral printed gift bag. "For you. I trekked through the cold and snow because a man can't come home empty-handed to the woman he loves, right?"

She sat up straight, taking the bag and moving the pink tissue aside to pull out an exquisite Tiffany blue negligee complete with panties. It wasn't lacy or racy, but simple, pretty, and definitely something she could wear to get the two of them into trouble. "It's beautiful."

"No. It's hot. You had me going the other night with visions of you in blue and lace. But I think we'll have to wait a few days before we can put it to good use."

She laughed. "Oh, I don't want to wait."

"You have no choice. Tonight, you put on those old pajamas of yours and let me hold you. Your body still has some healing to do."

"That does sound good," she admitted. She closed her eyes momentarily. Waiting to tell him what she needed to would be foolish and unfair. He should know. The sooner the better. Just in case... "I have to tell you something," she said. "It's about what the doctor told me."

He faced her looking worried and anxious. She relayed to him what the doctor had said. They sat in silence for a minute.

"Perfect timing. I think you missed something." Derek pointed to the gift bag.

"What? Didn't you hear what I said? Don't you have any thoughts? Or feelings about this? I mean, I may not be able to conceive, and if I can, we have to get started now. That is, if you want a baby with me. I don't how you feel about this. It's serious."

"In the bag," he replied.

"Derek! We need to talk about this."

He sighed. "You can be so petulant. Look in the damn bag."

What was he up to? Nikki peered back into the bag and

moved the tissue aside again. There it was—that little blue box. She gasped. It was a Tiffany box. Oh wow.

He took it from her, and got down on his knee. "I was going to wait and do this all romantic like, but after the last few days and then you being hurt, I don't want to wait. I want you. I love you and I want you to be my wife, and I want a family with you. I don't care how we have a family, and if we need to start now, great. I'm ready. Let's get you feeling better because it sounds like we might be busy here real soon. I mean, if you say yes." He winked at her. "I'm going to ask you again, because nothing can come between us. Nikki, will you please do me the honor of being my wife?"

She wiped the tears from her face. "Yes. Definitely. I will marry you."

Chicken-Fried Steak, Biscuits, and Gravy
with Luna Pinot Grigio

There is nothing like down-home cooking and a romantic evening—sort of. A five-star restaurant also sounds good, but at least Nikki didn't have to cook this time. It's doubtful she's complaining about this recipe of chicken-fried steak and that sweet added ingredient of a wedding proposal. No one ever said that Nikki and Derek were traditional. Fingers crossed, these two will make it to the altar. Never know what kind of trouble could be ahead for Nikki Sands. For now, though, this author is happy to see her ride off into the sunset with her dream man.

A beer typically goes down well with this meal, but for the wine lover's purpose, something in the light, white wine category would be fitting for this heavy meal like Napa Valley's

Luna Pinot Grigio. The Luna Pinot Grigio has a deliciously sensual nose of pear, peach, and apricot. With a swirl of the glass, the wine lover will experience an added bouquet of citrus and pine nut flavors. On the palate, there are flavors of apple, pineapple, and dates with a tinge of oak. The wine has a full body on the mid-palate and finishes out with notes of orange and thick honey.

EASY HOMEMADE BISCUITS

⅓ cup butter, softened and cubed (may substitute ⅓ cup shortening)
2 ¼ cups self-rising flour
1 cup buttermilk
3 tbsp melted butter

Cut softened butter into flour with a pastry blender or 2 forks just until butter cubes are coated with flour. Using your hands, gently combine until mixture resembles small peas. Stir in buttermilk with a fork just until blended. (Mixture will be wet.)

Turn dough out onto a generously floured surface, and pat to ½-inch thickness. Cut dough with a well-floured 2" round cutter (avoid twisting cutter—it will seal the edges and prevent proper rising). Place on lightly greased baking sheet.

Bake at 450° for 9–11 minutes or until lightly browned. Removed from oven and brush warm biscuits with melted butter. Serve immediately.

EASY CHEDDAR BISCUITS

Add 1 cup shredded sharp cheddar cheese to butter and flour mixture just before adding buttermilk. Drained, minced pickled jalapeño peppers may be added at this point as well. Proceed as directed.

Chicken-Fried Steak

salt, pepper, and garlic salt to taste
1 (6-ounce) round steak cutlet, tenderized
1 cup all-purpose flour (more if needed)
4 eggs
1 can flat beer
1 tbsp Adolph's Meat Tenderizer
cream gravy (see recipe below)

Sprinkle salt, pepper, and garlic salt on both sides of tenderized steak to taste. (To tenderize: place cutlet between wax paper sheets; pound steak with meat mallet till ¼-inch thick.)

Place steak into a tray of flour, then pound it with stiff fingers, working from the center out, until it reaches the size of a dinner plate or an old LP record. Flip several times and repeat pounding.

Mix eggs, beer, 1 tsp salt, and Adolph's Meat Tenderizer in a shallow bowl. Add enough flour to make a thin, watery batter. Beat till smooth.

Dip meat into batter, then back into the flour tray and cover with flour. Pound again with fingertips until moisture is absorbed.

Cook in a cast-iron skillet in deep fat at 350° until golden brown.

Cream Gravy

3–4 tbsp flour
1 cup heavy cream, half-and-half, or milk, more if needed
salt and pepper

Pour off most of fat from skillet, reserving 3–4 tbsp in skillet.

Add flour to skillet and stir till lightly browned, scraping up all bits of steak coating crumbs.

Remove skillet from heat, slowly add heavy cream, half-and-half, or milk, stirring constantly until mix begins to thicken.

Return skillet to medium heat, continue stirring till gravy is of desired consistency. Correct seasoning and serve.

RECIPE INDEX